RED
HOT

Also by Niobia Bryant

RED
HOT

NIOBIA
BRYANT

Kensington Publishing Corp.

http://www.kensingtonbooks.com

ISBN-13: 978-0-7582-6536-4
ISBN-10: 0-7582-6536-0

First Kensington mass market printing: September 2012

10 9 8 7 6 5 4 3 2 1

Printed in the United States of America

RED
HOT

PROLOGUE

Holtsville, South Carolina

Kael Strong looked up from reading the local newspaper to see Lisha, his silver-haired wife, of more than forty years, stepping out onto the wrap-around porch of their home. His heart still pumped double at the sight of her. Kael knew that even blindfolded he would be able to locate her among a crowd of women by nothing more than her scent or the pull of the fiery chemistry that never stopped blazing between them. He loved her and needed her. Period. Point-blank.

And he knew it was the love between him and his wife that played a big role in all of his sons following his lead and claiming the women they were meant to spend the rest of their lives with. Kade, his eldest married son, had been blessed with love a second time after the death of his first wife, Reema. Garcelle Santos had been just the woman to heal his heart and help him raise his daughter, Kadina, who was starting the school year as a freshman. Now they had a son, Karlos, who was the perfect addition to their family.

Kahron had completely forgotten his playboy ways when Bianca King had arrived in town to run her father's struggling horse farm—the business Kahron had been hoping to purchase in order to expand his own cattle ranch. The pretty vet now ran the ranch, her business, and her family—including Kael's grandson KJ.

Kaeden, who could very well have been the twin of Kahron, if they weren't born so many years apart, had found love with a woman who was his total opposite. Kaeden was the only one of his boys who had never taken to the outdoors—or womanizing—so Kael had been just as shocked as his boys when Kaeden proved to have won the heart of Jade Prince, a sexy outdoors guide. They were especially surprised, since Jade had her pick of men that came in contact with her.

And then there was Kaleb, the ultimate bachelor, who had a line of women willing to be his playthings, falling headfirst for Zaria Ali, a woman in her early forties who was more than fifteen years older than he was—even if she didn't look it. Their union blessed Kael with a third grandson, their recently born son, Kasi Dean, as well as Zaria's twin daughters, Meena and Neema. Of course everyone overlooked that Kaleb was just five or so years older than his stepdaughters!

That left just his baby, Kael's only daughter, Kaitlyn. She had him wrapped around her finger; and even though she was in her mid-twenties Kael found it hard to tell his daughter no. It would take a strong-willed—and very wealthy man—to tame her. Even now, she was off in Paris with her friends, and

Kael could only pray she didn't do too much damage during one of her infamous shopping sprees.

Yes, he was a lucky man with a good, strong, and loving family . . . and the woman before him played a huge role in that.

"Why are you looking at me like that, Kael Strong?" Lisha asked with amusement. She self-consciously raised her hand to smooth her hair as she moved to sit in the black rocking chair, which matched the one her husband sat in.

Kael smiled wolfishly as he reached out quickly to grab her wrist and then gently tugged her, until she was sitting in his lap. "I was just remembering how beautiful you looked on our wedding day," he whispered up to her before he kissed her cheek and snuggled his arm around her waist.

Lisha made a playful face. "That was a lot of years and a lot of pounds ago," she mused, lovingly patting the arm with which he held her securely.

"And everything has gotten better with age," Kael told her, using his free hand to slap her bottom. "And I mean *everything*!"

Lisha laughed at his roguish tone as he nuzzled her neck. "We are on the porch. Somebody might drive up," she weakly protested.

"Humph. That didn't stop us that rainy night back in 1992."

Lisha fanned herself at the memory. "Sure didn't," she purred, closing her eyes.

Brrrnnnggg.

"Damn," they swore fiercely in unison at the intrusion of the ringing phone.

Lisha reached into the front pocket of her apron for the cordless telephone.

"Man, forget that phone," Kael complained, reaching for it.

Lisha shook her head. "It might be an emergency with the kids," she said, slipping out of the role of lover to full mother mode as she answered the call. "Hello . . . yes, this is the Strong residence. I'm his wife."

Kael threw up his hands as Lisha rose to her feet and stepped away from him. "Go on back to sleep," he drawled, looking down at his crotch.

"What?" Lisha exclaimed. Her eyes were as round as her lips while her mouth formed a shocked circle.

Kael instantly rose to his feet. "What's going on, Lisha?" he asked; his protector instincts were kicking in.

Lisha pushed the cordless phone into his hand roughly. It was her turn to throw her hands up as she paced. "You get this phone call because you and the rest of the men of this family created this mess. I told you to stop spoiling her. I told you. Well, what you got to say now, Kael Strong? Wait to you hear *this* shit," she snapped, with eyes blazing.

Kaitlyn. And it had to be major. Lisha barely ever cursed.

Kael turned his back and pressed the phone to his ear. "This is Kael Strong," he said as Lisha continued to complain.

"I told you that y'all were not helping her with that mess!" his wife ranted.

"Mr. Strong, we were just explaining to your wife that major purchases of over thirty thousand dollars have been charged in Paris, France, to one of the cards on your accounts—"

Kael closed his eyes and hung his head to his chest as he leaned his hip against the railing of the porch.

"You better get your little chocolate version of Paris Hilton and Kim Kardashian or whoever the hell she *thinks* she is. Thirty thousand dollars! To buy what?"

"Mr. Strong, we wanted to make sure the card was not being used fraudulently."

"Yes, I thank you for the call, but I doubt very much that it is . . . although I would like to check with my daughter, who is in Paris, and make sure she hasn't lost the card," Kael said.

Lisha threw her hands up again even higher. "Enough is enough, Kael Strong. I'm calling a family meeting and I am putting a stop to this 'spoiling Kaitlyn' bull. I let y'all mess up my daughter for far too long. And I mean it. Enough is enough," Lisha said coldly. Then she entered the house in a flash, slamming the screen door loudly behind her.

Kael finished up the call, putting a daily spending limit on Kaitlyn's card. He knew that from out of the country his daughter had just sent his sex life into a cold freeze, and it wasn't going to thaw anytime that night.

CHAPTER 1

"Paris is my new favorite place!" Kaitlyn Strong sighed as she used her slender hand to push back the dark French silk curtains of the windows of her suite in the five-star Hotel de Vendome. The luxury hotel, situated in the center of Paris, had served as the perfect backdrop to her days spent in the middle of the shopping district, located just minutes from the historic museums. It was an enjoyable week of luxurious shopping, sightseeing, and partying for her and her two best friends, Tandy Ray and Anola Graham. It was their last big summer trip, and they had spent the last part of August, which slipped into the first of September, in beautiful Paris.

What more could three divas ask for?

She sighed, knowing that she was going to miss Paris. It was a long way from her small hometown of Holtsville, South Carolina. Not that she had a bad life in the small Southern town. *Far from it,* Kaitlyn thought, looking over her shoulder at the dozens of designer shopping bags from a hellified spree, where she denied herself not one blessed thing. *I deserve it.*

Plus my daddy wants me to have nothing but the best. . . . Why disappoint him?

Kaitlyn shrugged and turned to look back out the window, enjoying the Paris sun as it shone on the smooth and unmarred caramel complexion of her face. She thought about seeing her family, and that was the only thing that made leaving Paris (and her new *friend,* sexy Jean, the DJ) bearable. She reminisced about her father's kiss on her forehead, her mother's cooking, the teasing from her four older brothers, Kade, Kahron, Kaeden, and Kaleb. She thought about getting all of the family gossip from her sisters-in-law, Garcelle, Bianca, Jade, and Zaria; filling in her twin stepnieces, Meena and Neema, on Paris nightlife; surprising her teen niece, Kadina, with the rhinestone heart-shaped purse she bought for her, and pressing her glossy lips onto the cheeks of her nephews, Karlos, KJ, and baby Kasi.

They were a close-knit family and Kaitlyn loved them, but growing up as the only girl among such a manly bunch made it necessary to take these little girly getaways with her friends. Even with the addition of each of her brothers' wives, she still felt at odds with their settled-in lives of family and work.

Kaitlyn was all about having fun, and living well while doing it. She hardly had the time to waste brainpower on the daily comings and going of some man or the tedium of a job.

That mess is for the birds.

Her rancher father and brothers made sure that the princess of the family had nothing more to do on the ranch than ride her beloved horse, Snowflake. Not once had they inferred that she needed to hang around funky farm animals to make a living.

As if, she thought, looking down at her soft hands.

Bzzz . . . Bzzz . . . Bzzz . . .

Kaitlyn looked around the room at the sound of her cell phone vibrating. "Damn it," she swore softly as she searched through her discarded designer clothing, which littered the floor, and kicked off her shoes.

Bzzz . . . Bzzz . . . Bzzz . . .

She jumped onto the king-sized bed and pulled back the crisp cotton sheets and duvet, flinging pillows and lace panties over her head. And there it sat. Kaitlyn grabbed it as she fell back against the bed and checked the screen.

It was Jean—the sexy DJ with the smooth skin so dark that she was disappointed to find he really didn't taste like chocolate. "Uhm, uhm, uhm," she said aloud at the memory of his kisses and his touches.

But all of that was done, and she already had moved on. She and Jean had said their good-byes last night after walking through the Paris streets together. She had absolutely no plans to chitchat internationally with a dude from Paris and get all caught up in her emotions, particularly when she had no plans to visit Paris again, anytime soon. Kaitlyn had lots of male friends she could call in the States to dine, chat or party with. And since Kaitlyn was one party girl not giving up the panties easily there really was no reason to lead Jean on.

"Moving on," Kaitlyn said, sighing. She was already filing away the sexy Parisian as she let the call go to voice mail and dropped her cell phone back among the mess.

She rolled off the bed. She twisted her full lips as she looked at her empty Louis Vuitton luggage, her dirty clothes scattered over the suite, and the shopping bags filled with all of her fashionable finds. Right about now, it was all looking like a five-thousand-piece puzzle to her.

Packing is going to be a bitch.

She considered shoving it all in, wherever it fit, but then shook her head.

Knock, knock.

Kaitlyn shifted her slanted eyes to the door of her suite. She frowned a little at the thought of Jean standing on the other side.

I can't stand a clingy man, she thought as she made her way out of the bedroom and across the sitting room to open the door.

Kaitlyn's annoyed expression changed at the sight of one of the hotel's bellhops.

"Packages for you, *mademoiselle,*" he said with a heavy French accent.

Kaitlyn stepped back and opened the door wider for him. *"Merci,"* she said softly, her eyes dipping to take in his firm buttocks in his uniform pants as he entered the room and set the glossy shopping bags carrying the items she splurged on during her most recent shopping spree. He placed them on the gilded-gold antique French sofa.

She grabbed the sequined clutch she carried last night and pulled out a twenty-euro note to press into his hand as he nervously eyed her slightly exposed décolletage above her robe. Kaitlyn smiled at him teasingly as she used her fingertips to lift his chin and force his eyes to meet hers. *"Bonjour,"* she told him, with her eyes twinkling, as his face and neck immediately reddened as dark as tomatoes.

He backed away, turned, and then scurried for the elevator.

During their stay Kaitlyn and her friends learned

just how much white Parisian men loved them some black women. And the darker, the better.

Kaitlyn stepped back to close the door but then jerked it open and poked her head down the hall. "Hey, you. Come here," she called out as the elevator doors opened.

He turned and hurried back to her. "Can I be of service?" he asked.

Kaitlyn started to say something fresh to him, just for kicks, but decided against it. She glanced down at his name tag. "Listen, Gustave," she said sweetly. "Do you think my maid will pack my bags for me?"

"The maids are not allowed in the rooms with the guests," he said apologetically as he shook his head.

"I'll pay one hundred euro . . . but they only have, like, an hour. In and out."

The bellhop's eyes widened a bit. "I'll do it," he said, his accent making it sound like he said, "I'll do eet."

Kaitlyn bit her bottom lip flirtatiously as it was her turn to shake her head. "Oh no, Gustave. The only man who touches my undies is the one lucky enough to get them off."

He visibly swallowed as his neck and cheeks flamed again. "I'll ask my sister."

"*Merci* . . . and it'll be just between us," she whispered up to him, showing off her wide, playful, and innocent eyes.

Kaitlyn was a born flirt who knew when and how to turn it up. She could turn a grown man to mush without even breaking a sweat.

She laughed a little as he rushed back to the elevator as she grabbed her room key before walking down the hall to knock first on Tandy's door, and then she'd approach Anola's. During their many adventures they learned rooming together meant disaster . . . especially if one of her friends was in the mood to get it on for the night.

Kaitlyn was of the firm belief that even among good friends you never revealed *all* your business. Friends who became enemies had the ammo to destroy you. For Kaitlyn she wasn't even having it. There were plenty of things that no one knew but her and God. She liked it that way just fine.

Tandy's door opened. "Hey, girl," she said, her voice just as filled with sleep as her puffy hazel green eyes.

Kaitlyn pointed her thumb over her shoulder at Anola's door. "Anola still sleeping? Shit, even I been up for a few."

Tandy plopped down on the padded window seat and opened the sun-filled window as she lit a cigarette. "That's if she in there."

Kaitlyn moved over to press one knee onto the window seat as she opened the curtain. "Or if she in there alone," she drawled.

"Hello!" Tandy agreed as she ran her freckled fingers through her naturally curly reddish brown mop of hair.

Of the three Anola was more . . . *in touch* with her sexuality.

"Next time we come, we are definitely staying more than a week," Kaitlyn said, running her manicured ebony fingertips through her short-cropped pixie cut. Her hair color was such a deep jet black that it had to be dye. Like her brothers, she was prematurely gray. Unlike her brothers, though, Kaitlyn straight handled that with regular trips to her hairstylist.

Everyone in the family understood the dye; but when she suddenly decided to chop off her long, flowing, thick hair to the ultrashort pixie style, which framed her slender face, they acted as if she had slapped Baby Jesus.

"Definitely," Tandy agreed.

Kaitlyn pushed aside the thoughts of the Apocalypse that her haircut had caused. Instead, she looked down at the hotel's beautiful courtyard. A lot of the hotel's guests were already enjoying their breakfasts amid the Paris sun and the floral landscape.

"I'm hungry," she declared. "We don't need to be at the airport until five, so we have time to hit a few stores this afternoon. I have a maid coming to pack me up—"

Tandy nodded eagerly as she blew a stream of smoke out the window. "Ooh, good idea. She can do yours now and then mine while we have breakfast."

"Hundred," Kaitlyn called out over her shoulder.

"Cool."

She didn't have to look to know her friend shrugged without a care.

Tandy's father owned a huge trucking company; just like with Kaitlyn, money was never a problem. In fact, Anola, the daughter of a top cardiologist, was blessed as well.

Kaitlyn walked out the door and walked straight into Anola and a short, stout man kissing like one of them was about to leave this earth. Kaitlyn cleared her throat, and they still went at it as he turned her petite friend and pressed her body against her hotel room door.

Kaitlyn's eyes widened and her mouth opened as he grunted and raised the hem of Anola's short sequined skirt with his broad hand.

"I would tell y'all to get a room, but since he got you hemmed up against the damn door, obviously y'all ain't about *that* life," Kaitlyn quipped, flashing a comedic frown, before turning to head to her own room. She didn't do or watch soft porn on any DVD *or* in real life.

"*Au revoir,* Marques."

"*Jusqu'à ce que nous nous reverrons, Anola.*"

Kaitlyn paused at her door at the sound of their breathy good-byes. She had no clue what he said, but it was enough to make Anola push out a dramatic sigh as she pressed her fingers to her lips and blew him a kiss before he turned to walk to the elevator.

Kaitlyn rolled her eyes. "Anola, that was so *The Young and the Restless.* Like . . . really? Really?" she asked jokingly as her friend's boo-thang stepped into the elevator.

Anola fanned herself before raising her index fingers in the air to mark off well over eleven inches of length in front of her heart-shaped pretty face.

Kaitlyn arched a brow. "Ooh. Was it like *that*?"

"*Oui, oui,* on the wee-wee," Anola joked as she pulled her room key from her purse and unlocked her door.

Kaitlyn couldn't do a thing but laugh before they both entered their rooms.

"Ladies and gentlemen, welcome to Charleston International Airport. Local time is eleven twenty-five A.M., and the temperature is seventy-six degrees. . . ."

Kaitlyn allowed herself one final stretch before she removed her silk eye mask and looked out the window at the airport. *Home, sweet home,* she thought, feeling truly excited to see her family even as her five-ten frame ached and cried out from having been trapped in an airplane seat all night during their nine-hour flight from Paris.

First class or not, Kaitlyn decided, there was nothing better than sleeping in a bed.

"Glad that's over," Anola grumbled as they gathered their totes and prepared to deplane. "I'm going straight home and straight to my bed."

"Ditto," Tandy agreed.

Kaitlyn said nothing. *That reminds me, I gotta talk to Daddy,* she thought, remembering the eviction notice she received just before she left for Paris. Her landlord wanted her out of her place because of the three months of rent she was behind.

She knew admitting to her father that she used her rent money for her beautiful two-bedroom town house on other things wasn't going to sit well with him, but she had no doubt he would catch it up, like always. She would go on enjoying the upscale lifestyle of the James Island Village in Charleston.

There was nothing better than sitting on her private balcony and sipping wine as she watched the sun set over the lakes surrounding the island town. It was the only moment of serenity and calmness that she allowed herself . . . and she wasn't about to give it up. Not that, or the ten-foot ceilings and walk-in closets.

Yes, Daddy will straighten it out. No worries.

Kaitlyn slid on her aviator shades and reached for a stick of gum from her crocodile tote. She was regretting her decision to leave her convertible Volvo parked at the airport, instead of asking someone to pick her up. As soon as they entered the terminal, retrieved their luggage, and made their good-byes before climbing into their cars, Kaitlyn grabbed her iPhone.

She pouted as she tapped her iPhone against her thigh as she steered her vehicle along the empty road with her free hand. As soon as she pulled to a red light, she dialed her parents' landline number.

"Circle S Ranch."

The coolness of her mother's voice made Kaitlyn pause . . . for a second.

"Guess who's back? Hey, hey, hey," she sang into the phone, setting it into the cradle and making the call hands free.

"Welcome back. Your father wants to see you ASAP," Lisha Strong said.

Kaitlyn paused again and frowned a little bit. "Is something wrong, Ma?" she asked, checking the rear-view mirror before she eased down on the brakes and pulled off the highway. "You sound really weird."

"Just come straight to the ranch, Kaitlyn."

"Where's the joy for seeing your baby girl back home?" Kaitlyn asked, feeling offended.

"Oh, trust me, Kaitlyn Marie Strong, I want nothing more than to see you."

Kaitlyn sat up straight behind the wheel as she furrowed her brows at the use of her full name. "Uhm . . . okay, Ma. I . . . uh . . . should be there in, like, twenty minutes."

"Drive safe," Lisha said.

Click.

"Well, if that ain't 'bout a hot-ass mess," Kaitlyn said softly in surprise as her mother ended the call.

Still parked with her foot on the brake, Kaitlyn snatched up her phone and called her oldest brother, Kade. His phone rang endlessly before going to voice mail. Same with her calls to Kahron, Kaleb, and Kaeden. She didn't even bother with her sisters-in-law.

Something was up.

Kaitlyn sat there, tapping her fingertips against the steering wheel, mulling over her mother's coolness and her brothers not answering her call. One of them? Cool. Two of them? Iffy. All four? Impossible.

She wouldn't be surprised that as much as her sisters-in-law adored her, it had to irk them that her brothers always answered her call, no matter the time of day. Anytime. Always.

"A surprise party," she said, suddenly feeling clever as she started to dance in the driver's seat and snapped her fingers. "It has to be a surprise party."

Nothing else made sense.

Kaitlyn turned up her satellite radio and accelerated off the side of the road. The screech of tires and the blaring of a horn made her look over her shoulder just as a car skidded off the road to avoid hitting her.

Oh shit!

"Sorry," she hollered out the window, with a pained expression, before she accelerated forward, leaving the near calamity—and all thoughts of it—behind her.

She was anxious to get to her celebration. "Should I change first?" she wondered out loud.

The short-sleeved linen jumpsuit she wore was perfect for the end of summer travel, but to be the spotlight of a party? *Hmmm . . .*

Kaitlyn continued to mull it over as she sped like a race car through the Charleston traffic toward Summerville and then into Holtsville. When she thought she spotted a police car coming toward her in the distance, she slowed down, not wanting to risk yet another speeding ticket. Her father and brothers had said something about it raising the rates of her insurance.

Kaitlyn shrugged. She had family to see and a party to spotlight. She pressed her foot to the gas.

In no time she was crossing the bridge from Dorchester County into Colleton County and whizzing past a small and faded sign that read:

WELCOME TO HOLTSVILLE, SOUTH CAROLINA.

It was *the* picture of small-town America—small-town *down South* America. The number of people inhabiting the small town kept things real interesting. . . . And depending on which way the wind blew, that could be a good or a bad thing. Always a friendly smile and a wave? Good. People leeching onto everyone else's business for amusement and entertainment? Bad. Real bad.

As much as Kaitlyn had enjoyed growing up in the country, she had yearned to see and do and explore beyond the charm of the small Main Street area. She craved more than the star-filled skies and creatures serenading the night.

Still, it was nice to come home to South Carolina. And although she hightailed it to Charleston when she looked for her first place to live, it was nice coming home to Holtsville—especially with her family waiting there to be blessed with her smile.

Kaitlyn turned off the main highway and onto the asphalt-paved road that led to her parents' home and ranch. She stopped midway and put it in park before jumping out of the car to open the trunk and open her garment bag. She picked the least wrinkled item—a peach, ivory, and khaki color-blocked bandage pencil skirt and an ivory Lycra tank top.

Looking up and down the road for any on-coming vehicles , she quickly raced around the side of the car and changed clothes, hoping no one happened upon her in her sheer bra and panties.

Embarrassing!

She felt relieved when she finally slam-dunked her old outfit into the trunk. Back in the car she dug out her compact to check her reflection as she freshened up her makeup and finger-combed her pixie cut.

"I will pose for my big surprise and then beg off to run upstairs and get fresh," she told herself as she snapped her compact closed. Her old bedroom at her parents' was exactly as she had left it, and she had clothes there for the nights she didn't feel like making the nearly hour-long drive home.

Putting the car back in drive, Kaitlyn finished easing her car down the long and curving road. Soon the sizeable brick two-story structure came into view in front of her. As a little girl she would pretend it was a castle built for an ebony princess. And the home suited her fantasies with its countless windows and shutters. The landscaping of manicured lawns with topiaries, bushes, and flowers galore made her think of the homes of the wealthy that she saw on television.

Kaitlyn's memories faded as she parked her car in between her brother Kade's Tahoe and Kaeden's BMW. She did frown a bit at only seeing the vehicles of close family.

Maybe they all parked in the back or down by the farm to throw me off, she thought, climbing from the car and easily jogging up the stairs in her six-inch heels that brought her height to over six feet.

"'We like to party.'" Kaitlyn sang the Beyoncé hook as she slid her key into the lock.

It didn't turn.

Pouting, she tried it again.

Nothing but resistance.

"Well, what is the devil up to *now*?" Kaitlyn asked, stomping her foot.

Suddenly the door opened and she tilted her head up. Her eyes became confused at the empty foyer, since she was expecting to see a room filled with people.

Still frowning, Kaitlyn walked into the house and closed the door behind her just as she heard tiny feet pounding the hardwood floors as someone ran away from the door. And the steps echoed because the house was quiet.

Not surprise party quiet. . . . More like there ain't no surprise party or any other kind of party quiet!

Kaitlyn dropped her keychain onto the half table by the door before she headed in the direction where she heard the little feet. And then she heard voices.

"Are you sure about this?" a female voice asked.

"It's for her own good," her mother stressed.

Kaitlyn's steps paused before she forged ahead and stepped into the doorway of the family room. And there was the Strong clan assembled: her parents, Kael and Lisha; her eldest brother, Kade, with his wife, Garcelle, sitting beside him on the leather love seat, feeding animal crackers to little Karlos; Kahron, with his forever-present aviator shades pushed up onto his head, and his wife, Bianca, who was taking their four-year-old son, KJ, from his lap.

Her other brother Kaeden was sitting at the table in the connected dining room, with folders spread out before him. With the contacts he now wore, she barely knew the difference between him and Kahron. His wife, Jade, was sitting at the table with him, but she looked away when Kaitlyn rested her eyes on her.

"Did somebody die?" Kaitlyn asked, shifting her

eyes to her brother Kaleb, who was tapping the remote of the television against his thigh as his wife, Zaria, rose to her feet with their one-year-old son, Kasi, in her arms.

Kade's daughter from his first marriage, Kadina, came running up to her, reminding Kaitlyn of herself when she was in her early teens.

"Hey, Auntie Kat," Kadina said, hugging her close.

Kaitlyn hugged her back as she continued to eye the adults of the family over her niece's head. She looked down to find KJ patting her against her leg with one of his pudgy hands.

Releasing her niece, she squatted down. "Hey, handsome. You miss Auntie?" she asked as he leaned in to grab her cheeks with his hands before he kissed her on the lips. "I think you two are the *only ones* happy to see me," Kaitlyn said, perturbed, as she rose to her full height.

She looked at her father and was completely and physically taken aback when he released a heavy breath and looked away from her.

"What the hell is this . . . a wack intervention?" Kaitlyn snapped, feeling all her patience run out the door—the door that she now wished she had never walked through.

"Kadina, let's take the kids upstairs," Zaria offered, in jean leggings, heels, and fitted T-shirt looking nowhere near being in her early forties with twin daughters in their early twenties.

"Okay, Aunt Zee," Kadina agreed, scooping KJ up onto her hip. He instantly tugged at her sleek ponytail.

"Actually, I'm going to join y'all," Garcelle said, her Spanish accent just as strong as ever.

Kaitlyn frowned as she watched her brother Kade

reach out for Garcelle's wrist, and her sister-in-law
deftly avoided him to follow the other women out of
the room. Jade and Bianca also rose and scurried out,
behaving like the shit was about to hit the fan.

"Have a seat, Kaitlyn," her father, Kael, said, looking and sounding older than his sixty-odd years.

That touched her. "What's wrong, Daddy?" she
asked, her face filling with worry.

He covered his mouth with his hand.

"What are your plans for the future, Kaitlyn?"

She shifted an eye to her mother. "Huh?" Kaitlyn answered.

"What are your plans?" Lisha asked, settling back
in her chair and crossing her legs in the navy cotton
dress she wore. "Do you have more in store for your
life than shopping away your future ?"

That made Kaitlyn's back stiffen as she looked
around at her brothers and then back to her parents.
"What is this all about? Because it's really feeling
like an intervention."

"Kaitlyn, we're just worried that we've spoiled
you so much that you're not at all prepared to handle
the real world if you were on your own," Kahron
inserted calmly into the silence.

"Spoiled?" she said with attitude as her heart
hammered in her chest.

"Privileged," Kaeden stressed, rising from the
dining-room table to walk into the family room with
his hands pushed into the pockets of his tailored
slacks.

"Kaitlyn, why would you spend over forty thousand dollars in Paris while we're back here busting
our ass to make sure you can enjoy all your little trips
and shopping sprees?" Kade suddenly snapped, his
square jaw tight.

Kaitlyn's eyes widened in surprise as she leaned back and pressed her hand to her chest. "All of *that,* Kade. *Really?*"

"Yes, all of that," he shot back.

"Kade," her father said in stern reprimand.

"Excuse me for thinking that was my card to buy what I please," Kaitlyn stressed. The anger that flashed in her eyes hid the hurt that she felt at her eldest brother talking to her in such a harsh tone. It was his first time doing that . . . *ever.*

"Kat, it's your card that Mama and Daddy pay the bill on," Kaeden added.

"You have to know that was just crazy irresponsible," Kaleb said, shaking his head as he looked at her with serious eyes—eyes that were usually filled with laughter.

"I was in Hermès in *Paris* . . . not the Dollar Store in town!" she exclaimed with a shrug. "And I wasn't aware of a budget."

Lisha threw up her hands. "See what y'all have done?"

Kaitlyn's face filled with surprise and confusion. "What?"

Lisha fanned herself. "Kaitlyn, you have got to grow up. Your father and I aren't getting any younger, and you have no clue, little girl, of how to do anything but shop and travel."

Little girl? she fumed internally.

"Well, *this* ain't the surprise I was looking for," Kaitlyn then muttered under her breath as she finally plopped down onto one of the club chairs.

Kaleb reached over and patted her knee. "Kat, you have to understand that spending that amount of money in one whop when Pops pays for all your living expenses is crazy."

Was it? Kaitlyn wondered, shifting her eyes over to her father.

"That money is your living expenses for the year, Kat," Kaeden said. "You just took a trip to France and blew forty grand on shopping, and now you need a check for two grand to cover your rent."

He would know. After all, he cut her checks to pay her bills.

Kaitlyn bit the tip of her nail and made her eyes wide. "Actually, I need six grand . . . because I'm a little behind in my rent . . . and I got an eviction notice," she admitted, giving them all her most brilliant smile.

The brothers all groaned in unison and her mother swore.

That was seconds before the room erupted and everyone started chastising her . . . at once.

Kaeden: "You spent forty grand and you knew you were behind in your rent?"

And Kade: "That's the ranch's profits for two months."

And Kaleb: "Are you crazy?"

And Kahron: "It might be time for your first ass cutting, Kaitlyn."

And her mother: "What do you have to say now, Kael Strong? Huh?"

Kaitlyn's face filled with mock horror. "The Devil is a lie about y'all ganging up on me!" she snapped.

"Enough!"

The room instantly quieted at that one spoken word from Kael Strong, their father and the undisputed leader of their clan.

Kaitlyn turned in her chair to face him. "My goodness, Daddy, are you going broke and y'all not telling me?" she asked.

Everyone muttered beneath his or her breath at that.

"I thought by giving you everything you wanted that I was doing right by you," Kael began, his eyes locked on Kaitlyn's face. "But I was wrong."

Kaitlyn frowned.

"And so things have to change, Kat, for your own good," Kael said solemnly.

Kaitlyn's frown deepened.

"Yes, Kat, yes," her mother agreed.

She looked at each of her brothers and their faces were superserious. "What things? What changes? What—what are y'all talking about?" she asked.

All eyes shifted to their father.

As he began to speak, laying out the new rules of Kaitlyn's life, she felt like her world was moving in slow motion. Soon the buzz in her ears was so loud that she saw her father's lips move, but her mind was locked on *certain* words and phrases.

"Get a job. . . . Pay your own bills. . . . Move to a cheaper place. . . ."

Kaitlyn rushed to her feet in protest, just before she felt light-headed and collapsed to the floor. *This cannot be life,* she thought as she passed out.

CHAPTER 2

Quinton "Quint" Wells stepped back with the router tool in his hand as he eyed the detailed edge he had just placed on the armoire built of maple. All he had left to do was light sanding and then the application of a clear stain to protect it before he would surprise his daughter, Lei, with it. It was the perfect piece for the empty corner in her room—the space where her dollhouse had sat.

Quint smiled as he shook his head and stepped back up to trace her name carved on the doors in elaborate scroll. *My little girl is growing up,* he thought.

Lei turned twelve and declared she was too old for dolls *and* a huge six-foot dollhouse that he had built for her when she was three years old. Quint respected her wishes and moved the dollhouse into his work shed, but it had been so hard not to try and convince her otherwise.

For the past two years, he was a man raising a daughter alone, and he spent many a moment trying to relate to the many differences between them. The many, many differences.

Glancing at his watch, he tossed the router onto

the workbench and wiped his hands on his jeans before leaving the brightly lit work shed, which was just big enough for his tools and whatever project he was working on.

Hitting the switch, Quint left the shed and locked up before crossing the paved parking lot to walk to the rear entrance of the twenty-unit apartment building, where he worked as the manager and occasional handyman. Basically, he made sure everyone paid their rent on time and kept everything in working order—either by doing it himself or contracting someone else to do it.

It was the only apartment complex in the small town of Holtsville and was set so far back off the main road of the downtown area that most people outside of the town limits did not know about it. It offered plenty of privacy for what it lacked in luxury. It was an afterthought of a wealthy hometown boy who moved on to bigger and better business ventures and paid Quint to give a damn about the business he didn't. It was such an afterthought for the owner that he never even named the complex.

There were ten units on each level of the brick structure, with black wrought-iron stairs at both ends of the building. The stairs ran up to the balcony and led up to wrap around it, running across the front doors of the top ten units. The paved parking lot, landscaping, and shutters gave the small complex a charming, homey feel. It didn't look that much out of place next to the single-family and modular homes on the road.

Ever since he accepted the position, Quint made it his business to make sure common-sense rules were set and abided by. He learned early that it just saved everybody involved a bunch of headaches. So far, he'd only evicted one family because the teenage son was selling weed out of the apartment.

Thankfully, the tenants spread the word early and fast that he didn't tolerate foolishness. He simply wasn't going to have someone's badass teen or live-in lovers drawing the wrong element into the complex and making his residents—including his daughter—feel unsafe.

The job fulfilled no great passion of his, but it paid him well while being able to be home more for his adolescent daughter and find the time to work on his cabinetmaking. *Those* were his two great passions . . . and in that order.

Quint changed his mind and walked around to the front of the brick building. The sun was just setting and only a few residents were outside enjoying the final days of summer. He smiled and waved to them before making a mental note to call a painting contractor to come in and paint the apartment above his, since it was finally vacated by a young man who hadn't paid rent in two months.

But that's for tomorrow. Right now, I'm starving. He gave the front of the two-story building another quick look before pulling out his key to unlock the front door of the first-floor apartment.

"Quint . . . Quint."

He turned and looked over his broad shoulder as one of the tenants climbed from her small bright pink compact car. Quint bit back a smile and shook his head slightly as he watched Mrs. Harper walk around the small car and open the passenger door to pull her Yorkie terrier from the dog seat. She tucked the dog under her arm as he walked across the paved parking lot to meet her. Mrs. Harper was a petite and plump elderly woman, and her silvery blue hair surprisingly fit her ageless, dark chocolate complexion.

"Good evening, Mrs. Harper," Quint said, squinting his deep-set, hooded eyes as he watched her pop the trunk.

"You really are a good-looking man," she said in wonder.

As if she never saw me before, and said that before . . . and next she'll say . . .

"You really need to find a woman to soak up all that handsome before old age dries it up like prunes, baby."

Quint nodded his smoothly shaven bald head. "Yes ma'am," he said as if he agreed.

And that was a lie. That last thing Quint wanted in his life was a relationship. His casual relationship with female friends fulfilled the only thing he desired from a woman—and that he would allow a woman to desire from him. Anything else would open his daughter up to possibly being hurt, and he wasn't taking a chance with her heart while on a quest for his own.

Not after what Vita did to her. Not ever *after what Vita did to her. . . .*

"Quint, grab my packages for me," she said in her soft voice. "It's hard to manage them and hold my Fifi."

Quint literally shook himself and flexed his broad shoulders to come out of the pain of the past. He moved to grab the grocery bags from the trunk and fought the urge to remind her that she could just toss Fifi in one of the bags . . . since the dog had died last year and was stuffed like a teddy bear via a taxidermist. He just smiled a little and shook his head as he followed her to her first-floor apartment, directly next to his.

"We're home, Fifi," Mrs. Harper said as she stepped up on the curb and unlocked her front door.

Quint no longer found it odd that the woman found comfort in pretending the pooch wasn't dead and had no ability to answer her—but at least in life, it could've barked in response.

As long as she ain't asking me to talk with or hold or walk Fifi . . .

His elderly neighbor crossed the room to set Fifi on an embroidered dog bed, which sat at the foot of her pale pink recliner in front of the dated floor model television. He ignored the various shades of pink décor as he rushed his tall and broad figure down the short hall to her kitchen to set the bags on the round kitchen table.

"You going for a run tonight?" she asked, coming into the kitchen to begin removing her packages.

Quint got a rush just thinking about tossing on some sweats and doing his usual five-mile run across the length of Holtsville, but he shook his head. "No, not tonight. Lei has a movie she wants me to watch with her," he answered, admitting to himself the little bit of dread he felt because he knew it would be an hour and a half to two hours of something either emotional or centered around fashion or dancing. Girly things.

But he would do it. If he had to sit and watch some little knuckleheaded teen star doing some bad acting, then he would suffer through it for his kid.

Quint turned to leave and his shoulder brushed against one of her many picture frames on the wall. Like with all of the one-bedroom apartments, there wasn't much living space. Quint felt as if the walls were caving in on his six-foot-two, two-hundred-pound frame. This was especially true, since Mrs. Harper had packed into the small space the majority of the furniture and knickknacks from the home she had sold after her husband of fifty years had passed two years ago.

"Night, Mrs. Harper," he said over his shoulder, quickly taking two large steps toward the front door.

"Hold on!" she called out.

Quint kept going, right on through the door, before she had a chance to press a dollar into his hand like he was a twelve-year-old boy. He knew she meant well, but he was definitely too grown a man to be tipped for doing an elderly woman a favor.

He closed her door securely and made his way down the concrete walkway to his own front door. As soon as he entered the two-bedroom apartment, he spotted Lei already sitting on the leather couch, waiting for him with the TV and DVD remotes next to her. Paper plates and a bottle of strawberry soda sat next to the box of pizza and buffalo wings.

She looked up at him and smiled, her cheeks mirroring his dimples—the only feature they shared. Everything else about his daughter was an exact replica of her mother and his ex-wife, Vita: the round face and full features, her short height and thicker frame, which was developing far faster than her twelve years. She was Vita's Mini-Me.

So why did she leave her behind?

Quint's gut tightened at his now-familiar anger about his ex-wife packing up and deciding to move to Hawaii with her new boyfriend when he secured a position on a semipro football team—leaving her daughter behind to move in with him.

The difficulty hadn't been his becoming a full-time father. He had been in the home with his wife and daughter until the prior year, when he had caught Vita cheating and then ended the marriage. The difficulty came in helping his daughter heal from being hurt and feeling abandoned. That had taken a long time, and Quint would never forgive Vita for that.

Selfish bitch.

"So what we got tonight?" he asked, dropping down on the sofa beside her as he reached over to pull her ponytail playfully.

"An oldie but goodie," Lei said, picking up the remote to turn on the DVD player.

Quint leaned back against the plush sofa in surprise when the opening scenes of *Beverly Hills Cop* filled the forty-two-inch television screen.

"Hey, this my favorite movie. I thought it was your pick?" he asked.

Lei shook her head. "Daddy, *puh-leeze.* Anything I wanted to see and you woulda been asleep thirty minutes in," she teased him, sitting forward on the couch to open the pizza box.

Quint made a fist to offer her a dap, but then he paused and reached for the remote to place the movie on pause. A girl's relationship with her father affected how she dealt with her relationships. "Uhm, Lei . . . listen. I really appreciate you looking out for your pops and all, but I just want you to know that I promised you it was your movie pick . . . and—and you didn't have to give up *what you want* to make me happy," he said, accepting the plate she handed him, which was piled high with pizza slices and wings.

"Daddy, it's not even that serious," Lei drawled as she shrugged. "It's just a movie."

"But I want you to remember that what you want is important," Quint stressed, motioning with his hand as he tried to stay true to what he hoped was a classic *Cosby Show* moment.

Lei side-eyed him. "Is this about boys?" she asked, sounding bored before taking a bite of the pizza.

Quint nodded. "Hell yeah," he stressed, his face dead serious. "For the first eighteen years of my thirty years on this earth, I was one of those same horny boys who played all kind of games in a girl's mind to get what I wanted . . . and I don't want you falling for that shit."

Lei wiped her lips with a napkin. "So after those eighteen years, did you stop the mind games, or did you just become a horny man playing mind games?" she asked, her full eyes twinkling.

Quint held up his hands as he chewed on pizza. "In those two years before me and your moms . . . got . . . married," he finished weakly as he saw the light dim in her eyes a bit at the mention of her mother.

Vita barely found the time to call their daughter. She hadn't once asked her to come for a visit or made the time to travel back to South Carolina to see her.

"I got *Beverly Hills Cop,* one and two, Daddy," she said, picking up the remote again to start the movie—and change the subject.

Quint let it drop. He didn't know what to say to erase the truth of Vita's actions. "One and two—"

"But not the third one," she assured him.

"It sucked," they said in unison and then laughed.

Later that night after their movie marathon, Quint did change out of his jeans and T-shirt into oversized basketball shorts, a hoodie, and his favorite running sneakers. Grabbing his iPod, cell phone, and his keys, he slid them deep into the pockets of his shorts as he put on his stereo headphones. Leaving his bed-room at the rear of the apartment, he knocked on Lei's door.

He made sure to pause, not wanting to make the same mistake of knocking and opening like he had done when she first moved in. Her high-pitched squeal and mad dash onto the floor had scared the hell out of him. He learned then that his little girl was growing up, and the rules had changed.

"Come in."

Quint opened the door. Lei was lying across her bed with her thumbs flying across the keyboard of her cell phone.

"I'm going for a run," he said, pulling his hood up over his head and earphones.

"'Kay."

She didn't even glance in his direction.

Maybe I shoulda just texted her.

Quint closed the door and made his way out of the apartment, being sure to lock the door behind him. Since it was late, he decided to do only a mile or two instead of five. Mainly, he didn't want to leave Lei home alone for too long. He wasn't worried about his safety at all. Boxing was another of the physical activities he enjoyed to stay fit, and he would straight knock a fool out for trying him.

He filled his ears with Rick Ross as he jumped up and down, flexed his shoulders, and rolled his head to warm up his body. A few knee hugs and lunges and he started off. He headed out of the parking lot at a brisk walk, before upping it to a jog, and then he burst into a full-on run on the sidewalks of Holtsville's small Main Street area. Since darkness had fallen, there wasn't much traffic. However, Quint ran against the flow of traffic because the town served as a major thoroughfare from the much larger cities of Summerville and then Charleston to Walterboro, the next biggest city on the other side of Holtsville.

He made the left turn by Donnie's Diner, a Holtsville landmark, and soon continued on past Holtsville Elementary School. His cell phone vibrated in his pocket and he started to ignore it. "Might be Lei," he said aloud, stopping to run in place to maintain his heart rate as he pulled the phone from his pocket.

It was a text. He opened it: U BUSY?

Joni.

He curved his lips into a smile as he continued running in place. Joni was fine, sexy . . . and uncomplicated. No phone calls throughout the days. No desire to be wined and dined. No misconceptions of "it" being any more than what it was. Two adults fulfilling each other's desires . . . no strings attached.

Joni never contacted him unless she had some work for him to do for a couple of hours. He stopped running as he thought about taking her up on her offer. *She's hell with that tongue. . . .*

He looked back from the direction he had come. He could run and be to Joni's house on Frontland Circle in less than five minutes . . . but there was no way in hell he would have the stamina to run back afterward. *No way in hell.*

But . . .

Quint texted her back: Be there in ten minutes.

I'll run home and get my truck, instead.

Bzzz.

Quint opened the text: HURRY.

He headed back the way he came, and soon he was turning through the short brick columns flanking the entrance to the apartment complex. He pulled up short when he spotted Mr. Hanson from Apartment 12 coming out of the apartment of Mrs. Kilton. He wondered what Mrs. Hanson and Sergeant Kilton would think about it. Mrs. Hanson worked at night, and Sergeant Kilton was on a tour. *While the cats are away* . . .

Quint wasn't one to judge, and he understood the childish urges of most men. However, having been on the receiving end of unknowingly sharing his wife's goodies, he didn't respect cheating. An adult walked away from a relationship that wasn't fulfilling, emotionally or sexually. They didn't find a side piece to supposedly do the job.

But that was their problem. Not mine.

"Hey, Quint," Mr. Hanson said, walking past him to head for the stairs. "Damn good night, ain't it?"

Quint said nothing and just nodded as he pulled out his keys as he moved to the door of his apartment.

"Uh . . . Quint."

He turned to find the tall and thin older man coming back down the few steps he climbed to walk over to him.

"Yeah?" Quint asked.

"I was just dropping off their mail that was put in our box by mistake," Mr. Hanson said before laughing nervously.

"Huh?" Quint said, playing crazy.

The man looked surprised. "Uhm . . . nothing . . . n-never mind," he stammered before turning to jog up the stairs.

Quint just shook his head as he entered the apartment. "Leave me out of that shit," he muttered as he headed for Lei's room.

Man, save them lies for your wife.

He raised his hand to knock on his daughter's door, but he turned his head at the sound of the toilet flushing to look at the bathroom door across the hall. He continued down the hall to his master bedroom, which was decorated in various shades of charcoal with black leatherlike accents. He felt sweaty from the run and decided on a quick shower before he headed to Joni's.

Jerking off the earphones, he tossed his keys, wallet, and cell phone on the bed before rushing out of his running clothes and boxers. Naked, he strode across the slightly disheveled room to his en suite. It was relatively small for his height and athletic build, but he didn't complain. He was a simple man; and for him a bathroom was a place to wash and relieve himself. It didn't take a minimansion-sized room for that.

Quint turned the showerhead on full blast and didn't step behind the black curtain until steam began to coat the mirror over the sink and fill the small space. Beneath the sprayer he enjoyed the feel of the water pelting against the muscles of his shoulders, back, and buttocks before turning to let it flatten the soft hairs on his chest and the thick, curly bush surrounding his long dick. He closed his eyes and leaned forward to let the water coat his bald scalp.

He thought of Joni leaving her front door open for him, and he would enter her house to find her naked and waiting. Sometimes she wasn't one for needing or wanting foreplay. She *stayed* ready.

And that stirred his dick to life as he grabbed a thick washcloth and bar of soap to lather his body, giving a tug to his semihardness as he dragged the sudsy rag across it. Saving his face and head for last, Quint rinsed off the dark contours of his body before turning off the shower and pulling back the curtain to dry off while the steam of the shower beat away any chance of a chill racing across his nude form.

After a quick brush of the teeth, he headed back into his bedroom to throw on another pair of running pants and T-shirt—not even bothering with boxers. *For what?*

He sprayed on his most subtle cologne before he gathered the items he had tossed on the bed earlier. He noticed another text from Joni.

Knock, knock.

Looking up from his phone, he called out, "Come in, Lei."

The door opened and Quint's slashing brows dipped in concern at the flushed look of his daughter's usually bright and sweet caramel face.

"I think I ate too much. I don' feel good *at all,*" she said, leaning in the doorway as she rubbed her stomach and pouted.

Quint crossed the room and pressed his palm against her forehead and cheeks. "You feel warm, kid," he said.

Seconds later she turned and rushed back into the bathroom, slamming the door shut.

Quint followed behind her and tried to open the door. It was locked. He frowned. "Lei, I can take seeing you throwing up."

"It's not coming up anymore. Ugh!"

Not coming up?

And then his face filled with understanding. He stepped back from the door. "Either you caught a bug or it was something you ate."

"Uhm, Daddy, can this talk wait a sec?"

Quint smiled at her dry tone. He strolled into the kitchen and checked the fridge. Deciding on the bottle of cranberry juice, he poured a big glass and carried it to Lei's room to set it on her wooden nightstand.

Rubbing his hand over his eyes, he left the apartment and sat on the bottom of the steps.

Looking back down at his phone, he texted Joni back: Raincheck??

He couldn't go lay up or do a sex drive-by while his kid was sick. This was not going to happen. Joni could wait. Joni *would* wait.

Lei came first in his priorities, and Quint was not willing to compromise on that.

Quint worked at a metal-fabricating plant since his early twenties; but when Lei moved in with him two years ago, he requested a switch from third shift and was denied. He didn't quit, but he immediately started looking for another job. At the time Lei was just ten and there was no way he was happy about leaving her alone at night. Next-door neighbors at his house in Walterboro helped out, but he knew he couldn't impose on them forever. And it never once crossed his mind to send his daughter to live with his mother. Not once.

In the end it all worked out. He eventually found the job at the complex. There was a dip in salary, but it came with a rent-free apartment. He rented out the house, since the once-easy mortgage payment would be a strain. This way he still owned the three-bedroom brick duplex, and the rent covered the mortgage. He now lived rent free and could be home for his daughter. Win-win, win-win—even if the smaller living space was a bit of a loss.

Bzzz . . .

He looked down at his phone. Joni. NO PROBLEM. TILL NEXT TIME.

Seconds later a picture of her pressing her fingertips against her clit populated the screen. Quint couldn't lie. It looked good. Damn good.

"Shit," he swore, rising to his feet to walk back into the apartment to check on Lei.

She was deep under the bright colorful covers on her full-sized bed, with nothing but the tip of her head peeking out. He came around the bed to stand over her. "Feel bad?"

Lei looked up at him and nodded. "Thanks for my juice," she said.

"Well, I'm right here if you need. Just call out. Okay?"

She nodded and closed her eyes. "Thanks, Daddy."

He tipped the sides of his mouth up in a half smile. He had made the right decision. In that moment hearing his daughter say, "Thanks, Daddy" was worth more than a million pleasure-filled "Yes, God" sighs from Joni during the throes of passion.

CHAPTER 3

One month later

"Come on, Specs, you have to talk to Daddy for me," Kaitlyn urged as she paced the length of her brother's office in the renovated townhome, which housed his accounting business.

Kaeden dropped his pen. "Don't you think it's time you come up with a new nickname for me?" he drawled dryly.

Kaitlyn swung around to eye him incredulously. "That is so unimportant right now. Don't you think?" she snapped.

Shrugging, Kaeden sat back in his leather executive chair. "Kaitlyn, you've had a month to get yourself together. You only have another month before your allowance drops substantially, and just six months after that before you're on your own."

Kaitlyn came around one of the chairs before his desk to drop down into it. "I'm calling his bluff," she said, tilting up her chin.

"I wouldn't if I were you . . . and you know *I* know."

Kaitlyn bit her bottom lip as she looked at the serious expression on her brother's square and handsome face. Of course he knew. He was the accountant/business manager for her father's horse farm, which her eldest brother, Kade, was now running. Kaeden served in that financial role for all her brothers and their businesses: Kahron's own cattle ranch, which also housed his wife's veterinary practice, and Kaleb's dairy farm, with its new addition of a storefront.

Oh, he was deep in everybody's business. So he knew.

And they had not paid her back rent. She had to be out of her apartment in two weeks and counting.

She pressed her hands to her face and then ran her fingers up through the short ends of her pixie cut. "I'll just move in with one of y'all," she said flippantly, crossing her legs in the dark blue strapless jumpsuit she wore, along with a pair of cork-wedge heels.

Kaeden shook his head. "No, you will find a cheaper apartment that your allowance can afford and then find a job, Kaitlyn," he said gently.

Her back stiffened as she let her tote bag drop to the floor. "So you would let your own baby sister roam the streets and eat garbage to survive," she asked accusingly, locking slanted eyes on him.

Kaeden coughed and shuffled papers. "You are hardly about to sleep on subway grates and rummage through trash," he said.

Kaitlyn jumped to her feet. "I am stressed over this mess," she roared. "My hair is falling out."

She attempted to pull out the ends of her hair, but nary a strand floated down to the papers before him.

Kaeden chuckled.

Kaitlyn fought not to choke him, before she

dropped back down into her chair. She had already made the rounds through her entire family. Even the sisters-in-law weren't messing with it.

No one was going against her father's word.

No one was backing down from the so-called mission of getting her to grow up.

How exactly you could re-raise an already-grown woman in her middle twenties was beyond reason to her.

Especially when there isn't a blessed thing wrong with me!

"I handle the books for this guy who owns a small apartment complex right in Holtsville—"

Kaitlyn's eyes bulged. "You want me to move back to Holtsville?"

Kaeden leaned forward to press his elbows onto the top of his desk. "Oh, you're too good for Holtsville?" he asked.

She leaned back and eyed him intently. "You and Jade don't live in Holtsville," she tossed back, sounding very tit-for-tat.

He shrugged and smiled. "*We* can afford to live wherever *we* want."

Kaitlyn childishly flipped him the bird.

Kaeden laughed.

Kaitlyn forced a smile, but her eyes were sad. She hadn't seen her parents since the big powwow when she returned from Paris.

"They miss you too, Kaitlyn," Kaeden said, his tone serious.

She snorted in disbelief as she shifted her eyes past her brother's head to gaze out one of the large wood-framed trio of windows behind his desk.

"You can't punish them forever," he added.

Kaitlyn felt betrayed by her parents—by her father,

most of all. To her it was like all of a sudden he didn't care, and she wasn't his baby girl anymore.

"Yes, I can," she added softly.

"And if you honestly feel that way, then you haven't learned a damn thing yet, Kat."

She said nothing. There was nothing for her to say. Nobody else knew how it felt to walk in her Jimmy Choos.

Quint hated the smell of fresh paint and he left the door to the apartment wide open before moving quickly to open the four windows of the living room. He walked every square inch of the two-bedroom apartment to inspect the paint crew's work before he signed off on the invoice he would send to the owner for payment.

He honestly thought he had all the apartments locked in for at least a year and wouldn't have to deal with the drama of taking applications and dealing with a new tenant. It was always a toss-up on just how good or bad a tenant you got.

Quint was hoping for the best.

When he left the apartment, he locked the front door, but he left the windows open. Everything he put on his to-do list for the day was done. Lei was squared away at the kitchen table doing homework. She was finishing up her assignments, and she was not happy at all, since school just started a few days ago.

He crossed the parking lot and entered the small brick building that housed the office he hardly ever used. It sat at the front of the property, near the entrance. He used his key to unlock the door and plopped down behind the wooden desk, which he had made. He turned to open the small black file cabinet sitting next to it.

Quint fingered through the files until he pulled out the one containing his copies of rental applications. He went through each one and picked the top five to call their references first thing in the morning. Leaning back in the chair, he swiveled as he tilted his head back and looked up to the ceiling.

He felt tension across his broad shoulders—tension that not even a run or a pickup basketball game at the rec in Walterboro could help. Not even a few hours at Joni's. Nothing but the peace he received from woodworking would do it.

Quint was born in New York and lived there until he turned thirteen and started giving his single mother all kinds of stress by hanging out with the wrong crowd. A juvie arrest for joyriding in a stolen Benz led to her shipping him to live with her father in Holtsville. She was scared that Quint would turn out like his father—a convicted criminal with a long rap sheet, an even longer history of drug addiction. And not enough balls to make sure his kid had him or his last name. Quint couldn't point his father out in a lineup.

To Quint, his grandfather had stepped in and taught him everything that his mother had tried to. Everything he knew about being a man—a real man—was because of Denson Wells. His Pops.

The older man also taught him the skill and the joy of woodworking.

Quint took a deep breath as he felt his grandfather's loss to a heart attack several years ago. It was his grandfather's tools that he lovingly used and cleaned and cherished. It was the memories of his grandfather that were evoked every time he made a new piece of furniture.

But as much as he wanted to get lost in his work shed, he promised himself he would cook dinner. No more takeout or fast food for the week. Both he and Lei could stand a healthy meal with plenty of vegetables.

Pushing back in his chair, he rose to his full height and gladly left behind the claustrophobia-causing office, which was almost as small as his bedroom.

Quint turned from locking the door to find a tall and curvy woman, with short jet-black hair and shades that hid most of her face, standing in the parking lot. She was looking up at the apartment building. He paused when she looked to be talking to herself. Sliding his hands into the pockets of his jeans, he let his eyes take her in from head to toe.

The shades. Glossy lips. The flashy jewelry. The oversized name-brand bag swinging from the bend in her arm. Skintight jeans. And heels that had to be every bit of five inches or more. Surrounded by the trees towering over the property, the woman looked *completely* out of place.

Everything about her screamed money.
What the hell could she want?

"This *can't* be life," Kaitlyn said as she looked through her shades at the small brick apartment complex in front of her.

She eyed the cars parked in front of the buildings. Her cherry red convertible looked completely out of place surrounded by cars no older than 2005. Some were rusted. Some were dented. Some were wrecked. One was as pink as Pepto-Bismol, and almost as small as the actual bottle. Everything was *completely* American.

Kaitlyn looked back up at the building. It, in no way, compared to where she lived now. No way in hell.

It probably has roaches and shit.

"I can't. There is no way in hell this can be my life," Kaitlyn said, fighting the urge to stomp her foot in frustration. Tears welled up, but she swallowed them back and notched her chin a bit higher.

Why are they doing this to me?

The front door of the first-floor apartment opened and Kaitlyn's eyes shifted to see a short and curvy pre-teen looking out at her. She had a round face and slanted eyes, with her dark hair pulled back into a ponytail with a rubber headband. She wore khakis and a sky blue uniform shirt with sneakers.

"Hi," Kaitlyn said, raising her hand to wave.

The girl waved back before she closed the door and walked across the parking lot to a man standing outside a small brick building. No doubt, the man was handsome. Fine like "Stare at me, I'm a model." Bald head. Strong features. Eyes set so deeply that everything below his eyebrows appeared dark. He was tall. Real tall and built. She could see that, even with his jeans and bulky navy hoodie on.

Kaitlyn eyed them as he smiled at the teenage girl and then tugged her ponytail. She frowned. He had to be in his late twenties or early thirties. Way too young to be the father of a fifteen- or sixteen-year-old girl, right?

Is he one of those dudes who only messes with young girls?

They walked over toward her and Kaitlyn turned on her heels. She kept watching them. There was nothing about their demeanor toward each other that was at all sexual. Still . . .

As he came to stand before her, the girl waved again as she walked back inside the apartment.

"How you doing? Can I help you?" he asked, looking down at her.

Kaitlyn tilted her head back, thinking the man had to be as tall as her brother Kade. In her heels she was every bit of six feet, but he still looked down at her.

"Are you related to her?" she asked.

The man frowned. "To who?" he asked.

Kaitlyn pointed a slender finger at the closed front door of the apartment the young girl had disappeared into.

"The teenage girl," she said.

His frown deepened after his eyes followed where she was pointing.

"Are you from social services or something?" he asked, looking down at her once more.

"I'm always curious when I see a grown man sniffing around young girls—"

Quinton stiffened and his height rose an inch. "'Sniffin'? That's my *daughter*," he barked.

Kaitlyn's face shaped with surprise. "Oh . . . started early, huh?"

He crossed his arms over his chest. "She's twelve."

Kaitlyn's face became shocked. "Wow . . . she's . . . *developed*."

"Listen, why are you here—besides falsely accusing someone you don't know?" he asked, his aggravation with her barely contained.

Kaitlyn arched a thick, shaped eyebrow. "I'm here about renting an apartment."

He made a face and shook his head slowly. "This

doesn't look on your level," he said, sounding slightly disparaging.

Folding her arms across her chest, she continued to look up at him. "And you are?" she asked.

"Quinton Wells, the building manager," he answered. "And I already have a stack of candidates for the apartment."

Kaitlyn leaned back from the rudeness of his tone. She stiffened her back, not at all liking how he was trying to dismiss her. Kaitlyn Strong was never to be dismissed.

"Well, can I see the apartment *since* I made the trip—"

"Without an appointment," he inserted.

Kaitlyn snapped her mouth shut in surprise.

"Look, Miss—"

"Strong. Kaitlyn Strong," she supplied, snatching back her composure. And then she instantly hated how she sounded like a James Bond wannabe. The man was rubbing her the wrong way, but this apartment just might be her last resort.

One thing she learned in life was that money talked and bullshit walked.

"I don't think it would take up too much time from your day to show me the apartment . . . *please,*" she forced out as an afterthought.

Usually, she could wrap any man around her finger with just the right look, but she wasn't even willing to try with this tall and brooding man. It would be a waste of time.

He turned and walked through the break in the cars as he reached for a set of keys in his pocket.

Kaitlyn stayed rooted in her spot and posed with her hand on her hip like a mannequin.

He jogged up the stairs and stopped midway

before looking down at her. "I thought you wanted to see the apartment?"

"And we're mentally linked, so I should've read your mind that you changed your mind?" she snapped.

He shook his head like a parent seeing a child do or say something odd. "You want to see it or not? That's *if* you can see anything in those shades," he muttered under his breath.

Kaitlyn hitched her tote higher up on her arm and followed him up onto the sidewalk and up the stairs.

"Excuse me?" she asked, even though she had heard him clearly. "I'm sure your wife would love Gucci, baby."

He paused on the step and looked over his shoulder at her. "You're right, she would've . . . and that's why she's my ex-wife."

"Ooh, not a backhanded insult . . . that I couldn't care less about," she said flippantly, with a comedic twist of her glossy lips.

She was surprised when he just chuckled as he jogged up the stairs. Holding on to the wrought-iron stairwell, and careful not to twist an ankle as she followed him up the stairs, she was keeping it cute. Real cute.

"Those pretty shoes would catch all kinds of hell if a dog was nipping at your heels."

Kaitlyn looked up to see him on the second landing, leaning on the railing and looking down at her. She continued up the stairs at her same pace.

"I'm here to see the apartment and not for your impression of Joan Rivers on *Fashion Police.*"

Another chuckle.

She rolled her eyes as she finally reached the top.

* * *

Quinton had remained leaning on the railing as he turned his smooth, bald head and eyed her, squinting as the final rays of sun shone in his eyes. Everything about her spelled high maintenance and trouble, with a capital *T.* He couldn't do anything but shake his head.

She suddenly stopped and posed once more. "Want to take a picture?"

"No," he answered with emphasis.

"I can't tell," she shot back.

Quint rose to his full height and turned to unlock the door of the apartment, which was directly above his own. He pushed the door open and then stepped back to wave her through. He didn't even know why he bothered to show it to her.

She passed him and her arm brushed his stomach. It clenched involuntarily just as the soft, flowery scent of her perfume reached him.

Quint fought the instinct to jump back from her. And that physical reaction to her surprised him, because her slender build wasn't the thick and curvy shape he preferred on women.

He eyed the small tattoo on her neck's nape. It was partially covered by the soft tendril of her hair; he squinted to make it out.

She turned suddenly.

Quint shifted his eyes away from her.

"It's really small," she said. "My closet now is the size of this living room."

With her flashy car and even flashier wardrobe, Quint thought that nothing about the apartment or the complex seemed to suit her. He entered the apartment, leaving the door wide open.

"It's a two-bedroom unit, with a kitchen and two full baths. The master bedroom has an en suite. There is a small washroom in the back, which has the rear entrance leading to a balcony and stairwell, just like the front."

"No pool or tennis court or spa . . . huh?"

"No, definitely not."

He watched her move about the apartment. Her heels were clicking against the new laminate flooring like a senior citizen's false teeth. The little part of her face that was visible showed a grimace. Quinton felt himself bristle from her obvious judgment. He opened his mouth to tell her the tour was over.

She reached in her big bag and whipped out a cell phone. "Call Kaeden," she instructed as she breezed past him to walk down the hall to enter the guest bedroom.

Quint scrunched up his face. The woman moved throughout the world as if cameras were rolling on her and she was the star of her own show. A sitcom. Everything about her was a joke to him.

"I'm here now, Specs," he heard her say, her voice echoing within the empty apartment.

"It's . . . all right, I guess," she said. "I'm have to put a lot of my stuff in storage and just pray it doesn't have roaches . . . like I hope this place don't either. I am not looking for any kind of roommates. Ya know?"

Quint stood up straight from where he was leaning against the wall. *This rude bit . . .* He wiped his hand over his mouth and forced himself not to finish the thought as she left the bedroom and crossed the hall to the bathroom.

"Lord Jesus." She sighed and walked back out, giving Quint a withering look before her feet carried her down the hall to the kitchen.

Quint said a silent prayer for the dude she was on the phone with. His ex-wife, Vita, had been just as spoiled and self-absorbed. He knew she had been a handful for him. Foolishly, he thought his love and his forty-hours-a-week job would be enough for her.

He had been beyond wrong.

Quint had been looking off into the distance, staring out the window, but he shifted his eyes at the sound of her heels getting louder. She stepped into the hall. Her phone call was ended. She pushed her shades up atop her face.

Quint's eyes opened a bit in surprise as he took in her full face as she strutted up to him. Her face was that sweetheart shape with defined cheekbones and a little pug nose, with perfectly shaped lips. Her eyes were almond shaped and almost black in color, beneath thick, shaped eyebrows and the longest and fullest lashes he'd ever seen. Her short haircut framed her face and put even more emphasis on the defined features of her face.

She was a really pretty girl, but what surprised him the most was that her face wasn't heavily packed with makeup.

"I can be back in the morning with a check to pay for three months of rent in advance," Kaitlyn said with a look that dared him to deny her.

Quint said nothing at first as he eyed her.

She arched a brow. "Will that clear up that waiting list problem?" she asked.

She had spunk and fire—maybe too much of it. Did he really want this diva living above him? But three months' rent in advance! Did he really want to pass up *not* having to chase people for their rent or listen to sob stories (with actual sobs) about why they didn't have it?

"You have kids?" Quint asked.

She looked offended before stressing, *"No."*

"Criminal convictions?"

"Only if being this fine is a crime." Kaitlyn waved her hand up and down in front of herself. *"Heyy!"*

"Married?"

"And about to move into here? No, that wouldn't even be my life as wife. Trust."

"So it's just you moving into the apartment?" he asked, sounding doubtful as he remembered her phone call to Kaeden. Maybe he was just her lover/sponsor. She looked the type.

"I can hardly believe it myself," she told him.

"Kaitlyn Strong you said?" Quint asked.

She smiled, showing him a smile that was made all the more endearing because she had a slight overbite, which knocked a chink in her perfect armor. "You come on a bit strong too, huh?" he asked.

"Only for things I really want," she told him smoothly as she dropped her shades back down on her face and strutted past him, out of the apartment. She paused and looked over her shoulder at him. "So *you* don't have to worry. *Trust.*"

Quint walked out onto the balcony as she walked away and then down the stairs.

"First thing in the morning," he advised, hardly believing he was introducing this very complicated woman into his uncomplicated life. "And you'll have to do an application and credit check."

Kaitlyn pulled out the keys to her convertible and overdid deactivating the alarm and starting the engine with her remote. "Not a problem," she called up to him before climbing into the vehicle and reversing out of the spot.

* * *

Kaitlyn took a deep sip of her glass of red Moscato wine. She stood in the door frame of the double doors leading off her bedroom and out onto the balcony, overlooking the water surrounding James Island. She had two weeks to enjoy the view, and the space, and the high ceilings, and the gourmet kitchen. . . .

Kaitlyn sighed. *If I knew that splurge at Hermès would pop off all this drama . . .*

Her cell phone rang from its spot on her nightstand. Wearing her silk robe, she turned to pad barefoot back into her bedroom to pick it up. She checked the caller ID. It was her brother Kaleb. Out of all the siblings, she was closest to Kaleb and Kaeden because they were nearest in age. There was a pretty decent age gap among Kade and Kahron and then the three of them.

Still, she didn't answer him. She didn't feel like talking. She wanted to enjoy her beautiful apartment as long as she could, before she moved to the Holtsville Arms—her nickname for the apartment complex, which was a play on the Sanford Arms from those DVDs of *Sanford and Son,* which her daddy was always watching.

She thought about that rude manager. Quan? Quince? Quint. Yes, Quint. Fine? Yes. Rude? Most definitely.

Kaitlyn turned up her nose. She had enjoyed going toe-to-toe with him verbally, but too much of that mess would irk her nerves. She planned to stay clear of him. No matter how fine. And he was fine. Way too fine to be a dang-on apartment manager in little ole Holtsville, South Carolina. She'd seen male runway models who couldn't lick his boots.

A waste. She sighed, waving her hand dismissively as she shifted her thoughts to her new miniature apartment.

She could fit the whole thing in a third of her apartment now.

Kaitlyn had already decided to turn the second bedroom into a closet. However, a lot of furniture was too large for the apartment, so it was going in storage. Another bill.

Having never kept a job longer than a week, and accustomed to a lifestyle of shopping until she dropped and sending Daddy the bills, Kaitlyn couldn't believe the road her life was suddenly traveling.

Forgetting her rule about never lying on her comforters or coverlets, Kaitlyn set her wineglass on the table and fell face-first onto her bed.

Less apartment. Less allowance. Less shopping. A lesser life.

Why live it?

For a maniacal moment she considered letting the plushness of the silk comforter smother her to death. *Then they'll be sorry,* she thought childishly. *I'll sit high up on a cloud in heaven and look down at them crying for pushing me not to want to live.*

With an internal sigh she flopped over onto her back.

Bzzzz.

A voice mail. Probably from Kaleb.

She rolled off the bed to pick up her phone and access her in-box.

"Hey, sis. Kaeden told me about the apartment. Just let me know when you officially move in and I'll be there to help you pack up and move into the new place. You know we all love you."

She bit her bare bottom lip as he fell silent.

"Call Pops, man. He misses you," her brother finished.

Beeeeeep.

Truthfully, she missed her father too, but this all was so unfair. She couldn't pretend to chuckle it up, when she felt they were mean to cut her off. She was moving back to Holtsville, for God's sake, in an apartment that was just a few steps from a damn low-income complex.

Her phone rang in her hand and she looked down. Her heart pounded. It was Anola. Kaitlyn's shoulders dropped.

She didn't want to talk to her friends. And tell them what . . .

I can't afford to go shopping once a week.
I can't do lunch at the club.
I can't vacay.
I CAN'T DO SHIT!

If she told them, she could just see them looking at her sadly, right before they hauled ass to continue their fabulous trust fund lives.

Taking a deep breath, she finally answered the call.

"Hey, diva!" Kaitlyn said, sounding overly cheerful and fake as hell to her own ears.

"Hey, girl. I got Tandy on the line," Anola said.

"Whaddup, whaddup, whaddup," Tandy piped in.

"What y'all up to?" Kaitlyn asked, rising from her bed to leave her spacious suite and cross the floor to her kitchen. She paused in the hall to look out at the tall height of her gorgeous living room. She sighed on the inside. Deeply.

"We haven't heard from you and thought we could

all meet up tomorrow and hit King Street," one of them said.

Kaitlyn grabbed a bottle of water from her fridge. She loved shopping on King Street in downtown Charleston. Loved it. The best Charleston had to offer.

Kaitlyn made a wounded face and melodramatically clutched her chest as if she had been stabbed.

"I can't," she said.

"You can't?" they both said in unison.

She closed her eyes and sank down onto one of the bar stools around her granite island. "Uhm . . . my parents . . . uhm . . . uh . . . surprised me with a trip to—to Italy. Yes, a trip to Italy!"

"Ooh, I wanna go to Italy," Anola said.

"For school," Kaitlyn added in panic. "Yeah, for school."

Liar, liar.

Kaitlyn dropped her head in her hand. She had to get this mess all straightened out and get back to living her life, because with every passing day she was losing more and more of herself, the things, and the people she loved.

And that scared her.

CHAPTER 4

Two weeks later

"Daddy?"

Quint looked up from checking the oil under the hood of his Ford F-250 pickup. He spotted a tall, silver-haired man climbing out of his Tahoe and striding over to the office building. He shook his head and smiled, cutting his eyes over at Lei, who was leaning against his truck, watching him.

"Not another one," he mused.

Lei smiled as she nodded. "Yup. Another one."

Quint wiped his large hands clean on the rag hanging from the back pocket of his uniform pants before he closed the hood and headed over to his office. His eyes were on the man. He watched him knock; then the visitor tried the handle and then turned around to look.

Another of Kaitlyn's brothers. In the two weeks since she was officially approved for the apartment, he had been visited by two so far. All tall. All broad.

All prematurely gray. All overprotective of their sister.

Shit, how many more are they? Quint wondered.

"Excuse me, I'm looking for Quinton Wells," the man said.

"That's me," Quint said, extending his hand to the man, who was as tall as he was—if not taller. "And you're here to see your sister's apartment. Right, Mr. Strong?"

"Kade," he supplied, looking slightly taken aback as he took the hand offered to him. "Kade Strong."

Quint turned and headed across the paved parking lot. "Right this way," he said over his broad shoulder, heading over to jog up the stairs in his favorite well-worn Timberland boots. "You roll a little earlier than the other ones."

"Who else has snuck over to see the apartment?" Kade asked as they reached the top landing.

"Your brothers Kaeden and Kaleb," Quint answered, amused by it all. "Kaeden last week, and Kaleb on Monday."

Kade rolled his broad shoulders and shrugged in the tan Dickies uniform shirt and pants he wore. "That's our baby sister" was all he said as he entered the apartment.

Quint left him alone with it, and just remained outside, looking up at the last of the sun filling the sky as the kids in the complex left their apartments to walk to the entrance, where the school bus picked them up. He looked down and saw Lei still leaning against his truck, listening to her iPod—a recent gift from her mother. She received more of those than she did phone calls. And Vita hadn't been back in the state of South Carolina to visit her child or even to request Lei to come out to see her.

He shifted his eyes downward as loud bass-filled music suddenly echoed in the air. Several young men in an old Chevy Impala, which was decked out with rims and a colorful yellow-and-red paint job, rolled into the complex's parking lot. Quint frowned in distaste at the car, especially at the huge pictures of the Mr. Goodbar candy bar on the doors and the hood. The car slowed down as it rolled by Lei.

The one in the passenger seat leaned over to turn the music off as all four of the men leaned out the windows. Lei didn't even bother to remove her pink Beats by Dr. Dre headphones as she pointed up to where Quint stood.

The fellas all swung around to look out the passenger-side windows. They all looked seventeen or better, probably seniors in high school.

Nada. Quint made a motion with his hands for them to keep it moving. "She's only twelve," he said in a hard tone. "Keep it moving."

The car instantly rolled away.

Lei gave him a thumbs-up as she was already crossing the parking lot to head to the bus stop.

That made him chuckle.

"I got a teenage girl too."

Quint looked over to find Kade walking up to stand beside him.

"And knuckleheaded little boys are enemy number one," Quint remarked.

Kade smiled. "Exactly," he agreed, then turned to head down the stairs. "Oh, and—"

Quint held up his hand. "Don't tell Kaitlyn you came to check out the apartment."

"There it is," Kade told him, and then continued down the steps.

Soon he was climbing into his Tahoe and rolling out of the complex.

I should ask how many more brothers there are. That's three and counting. Damn!

Quint locked the apartment and headed downstairs. The Mr. Goodbar car was backing out of the complex and he spotted Mrs. Ruiz's son, Hector, now squeezed in the backseat with his friends. Quint went on his way. It wasn't his job to police the complex and be a tyrant. Plus he refused to assume that anytime he saw a bunch of young black or Hispanic men in a car that they were up to no good.

Quint was headed back to his work shed, anxious to spend a little time on the custom picture frame he was carving from one large piece of green wood for a widow out of Summerville. She had seen a buffet table he did for a neighbor of hers and had contacted him. He was already planning to save the extra income to get Lei a computer tablet for her birthday next month.

The office didn't officially open until nine, and that gave him two hours of free time before his workday. When he moved from the home he owned into the apartment, the only thing of major concern to him was paying a hauler to move his shed with him. Quint felt like he needed to put his hands to wood every single day. It was more than a hobby, and it was well worth the thousand-dollar fee to haul it from Walterboro to Holtsville in order to have it with him.

And he did get lost in the art of carving. It was a lot like making love to a woman: her body as soft and pliable as the green wood.

Stroking every curve and line, he approached her—and the wood—with his *tool,* filled with patience and skill. Stroke after stroke. In both making love and in carving, every single stroke mattered. And he was skilled and deft with his tools—all of his tools.

Quint stepped back from the wood to check his handiwork. The widow wanted the frame to have carved images that spoke to her relationship with her deceased husband. He didn't dare disrespect his skill by using an instruction booklet with patterns and guides. He did it all from pure instinct.

Just like sex.

Glancing up at the clock, he wasn't surprised to see nearly two hours had passed with ease. He cleaned his sharp tools carefully and put them away before leaving the shed to change into the khakis and button-up shirt he preferred to wear when he was officially "on duty."

"Good morning, Quantum."

He paused on the steps that brought him from around the rear of the building. He found Kaitlyn standing next to her car, with her convertible top down. She was dressed in a bright orange silk shirt with long sleeves, which looked like bells, lots of gold and colorful accessories, and high heels. Her jeans clung to her body like skin—completely emphasizing that although she was a little on the slender side, her hips and thighs were bigger. Fuller. Thicker. For a moment he wondered what the view looked like from behind.

"It's Quinton . . . and you better hope a bird doesn't use your car as a toilet," he teased, even as his heart hammered in his chest.

Kaitlyn looked up to the towering trees and frowned as she used the remote in her hand to lift the roof.

Quinton breezed past her.

"Uhm, excuse me?"

He stopped on his path to his front door and turned to eye her.

"My luggage," she said, waving her hand at the trunk.

"What about it?" he balked.

"They can't walk themselves upstairs," she said as simply as if she asked for the time of day.

Is she for real? Quinton rocked back on the heels of his boots as he eyed her. "And your point is . . . because I'm lost," he told her, feeling his ire rise.

Kaitlyn sighed in obvious annoyance. "I want you to help with my luggage—"

Quint flung his head back and laughed. "Oh, I'm not lost. *You're* lost."

"The movers are at my old apartment loading up, and it takes an hour to get here," she said, still looking at him expectantly.

Quint literally wanted to shake some sense into her. "On whatever planet you're from, I'm sure that make sense. Now translate it for earthlings," he said, his voice tight with rising annoyance.

"I can't wait for them to get here to get the luggage."

Quint bit his bottom lip as he eyed her. She was serious. "I'll help you with your luggage, like a gentleman would . . . if you ask me politely like a lady."

Kaitlyn sighed and walked over to stand close to Quint.

His eyes dropped to her eyes and her mouth. He forced his vision back up to her eyes.

64   *Niobia Bryant*

"Oh, kind sir, would you please be so kind as to help a poor little helpless lady with her luggage?" she asked in a docile tone, faking a Southern belle accent.

She was mocking him. Quint nodded slowly in understanding. "Frankly, my dear, I don't give a damn," he told her, in his best imitation of Rhett Butler from *Gone with the Wind*.

"Why are you so *mean*?" Kaitlyn asked.

"Why are you so *spoiled*?" Quint shot back.

A chuckle broke the tension that brewed around them as they stood there glaring at each other. They both swung their heads to the side and then tilted their heads down to find Mrs. Harper, still in her housecoat, with Fifi tucked under her arm, standing there looking up at them with a twinkle in her eyes.

"Is this your girlfriend?" Mrs. Harper asked.

"No!" they both barked out in unison.

Mrs. Harper leaned back a bit from the velocity of the denial.

"Mrs. Harper, this is Kaitlyn Strong," Quint said, leveling his tone. "She's moving into Apartment eleven."

"Oh, nice to meet you, Kaitlyn. Aren't you a pretty, tall thing," Mrs. Harper said.

Quint looked on as Kaitlyn extended her hand. Her dozens of jeweled bracelets flashed in the September sun.

"Nice to meet you," she said, smiling politely.

"And this is my precious Fifi."

Here we go, Quint thought, covering his mouth with his hand as Kaitlyn bent down to stroke her index finger against Fifi's chin.

"Hi, Fifi . . . aren't you . . ." Kaitlyn's words trailed

off, and she looked over her shoulder at Quint with an odd expression.

He motioned for her to let it go, and to his surprise she did. However, she did look a little weak on her feet as she snatched her hand away.

"I won't take up your time while you're busy getting settled in, but please come down and chitchat with me soon."

"Yes, ma'am," Kaitlyn said, although her face said different.

Mrs. Harper walked away and entered her apartment.

"Oh, hell to the no," Kaitlyn said, rummaging in a bright gold tote. "Was I just stroking a dead-ass dog? Like really, who does that?"

Quint looked on as she squeezed half of a tiny bottle of hand sanitizer into her palm.

"She's harmless," he said, moving past her to start taking the designer luggage from the small trunk. "Could you unlock your apartment door?"

"So I won?" Kaitlyn asked, looking smug.

Quint paused and then started loading the luggage back into the trunk.

"Okay . . . okayokayokayokay . . . I'm sorry," she screeched, turning to head up the stairs. "No elevator, huh?"

Quint ignored her—except for a quick glance to see that her bottom was full and round and shapely, like the base of a pear.

All those good looks wasted on a spoiled, self-indulgent airhead with more ass than manners.

He took the stairs two at a time, not even flinching under the weight of the bags.

"This room will be my closet, so could you put the

bags in here?" she asked, pointing to the guest room. "The rest of my clothes are coming with the movers."

The rest? Quint did as she asked, not even shocked that she needed an entire bedroom to hold all her clothes. His ex had all her clothes scattered throughout every possible closet in their house— including his and Lei's. And to his way of thinking, his ex and this woman standing before him were one and the same.

"I have to get to work," Quint said, ready to get out of her presence.

"Okay," she said, pressing a folded bill into his hand.

Before she could turn away, he held her hand with the money sandwiched in between their palms. "I'm not a bellhop," Quint told her, his voice hard and his eyes locked on hers.

Kaitlyn wiggled her hand free. "I didn't mean to offend you," she said softly. "I was appreciative of your help."

Quint pushed the money into her hand. "Then just say 'thank you,' Kaitlyn."

"Okay. Thank you."

Quint turned and left the apartment, closing the door securely behind him.

Kaitlyn hurried over to the window and peeked through the slats of the wooden blinds. She eyed him before his body disappeared as he descended the stairs. The man hated her. Absolutely detested her. Why?

She shrugged. All that fineness wasted on a rude asshole.

She turned from the window and placed her hands on her hips as she circled the living room. When she moved into her old apartment, she'd hired an interior decorator to buy her furniture and accessories and set up the whole apartment—even her closet. By the time she slid her key into the lock, all she carried was her purse, and she was home, sweet home.

Now?

Kaitlyn sighed. The $10,000 cost for an interior decorator was so completely out of her budget. The cost for the moving company to pack up her old apartment, load the truck, and then unpack everything was high enough; and that had come from her little stash of emergency cash.

That was back when my emergency was a trunk sale.

Her cell phone rang and she raced over to where her bag sat on the windowsill. Her foot gave out from under her and twisted, sending her tumbling to the floor. She kicked off her heels in frustration and jumped up to her feet just as the phone stopped ringing.

When she finally pulled the iPhone from the inside pocket, she saw it was her father's cell phone number. She turned and pressed her ass against the windowsill as she looked down at the phone. She raised her thumb to call him back, but then she decided against it.

She really missed her parents, but she had to make them regret their decision. Kaitlyn knew if she stuck to her guns, then guilt would send them running back and dying to keep her in the lifestyle to which she was accustomed.

Right?

But again she raised her thumb above the touch-screen keypad. It would be so easy to call him. *So easy.*

Kaitlyn did swipe her thumb across the screen, but it was to pull up her photo gallery. She smiled at the picture of her parents on their front porch, laughing together. They loved each other. Anyone could see that. And they made sure their kids always felt loved and wanted.

"Until now," Kaitlyn muttered, closing the photo.

She went back to the guest bedroom and began unpacking those items she had carried with her. She hung them in the small closet, waiting until the moving truck arrived with the dozen waist-high rolling racks she had bought to line the walls of the room, turning it into a huge walk-in closet.

Kaitlyn was pairing up her shoes, when she heard the metallic rumble of a truck. Barefoot, she padded out of her room and to the window to see her moving truck pulling into one of the empty parking spots. She dashed back into the guest room to slide her feet into a pair of flats before leaving the apartment. The door swung closed behind her.

"Shit," Kaitlyn swore, trying the knob and finding it locked. For a moment she let her forehead lightly drop against the door before she went down the stairs.

"I'll be right with you, fellas," she told the burly movers as they raised the tailgate of the truck.

Kaitlyn knocked on Quint's door and then knocked again. The door suddenly opened and he was standing there in low-slung khakis as he pulled on a crisp white shirt. Her eyes dipped to take in the athletic definition of his upper body.

The broad shoulders.

The ripped chest.

His narrow waist and eight-pack.

His chocolate skin was like a thin covering over pure muscle. And not bulky, oversized, steroid-fueled muscles. Just the body of a man who was physical and active and built for action.

Is the lower half as good as the upper half? . . .

"Kaitlyn," Quint said, closing his shirt and buttoning it up.

She shifted her eyes up to him. "So you work out?" she asked, feeling her pulse race.

Quint looked at her impatiently. "Is there something I can help you with?"

That cooled her ardor.

Good looks. Check.

Great body. Double check.

Attitude? Negative.

"I locked myself out," she said.

Quint patted his pockets. "Let me get my keys and I'll be right up."

"Thank you," she said stiffly. "Because my movers are here."

He looked past her to the large truck and all of the contents inside it. "Uh . . . that would be hard to miss."

"Smart-ass," Kaitlyn muttered under her breath. Then she turned to face the movers. "Right this way, fellas."

She headed back up the stairs and leaned against the railing as she watched the men begin to unload her furniture. She checked her manicure and looked up, just in time to spot Kaeden's wife Jade's yellow Jeep Wrangler roll into the parking lot. The bright color was hard to miss.

Kaitlyn straightened up in surprise as Jade, Garcelle, Bianca, and Zaria all climbed out of the Jeep. Each of them was dressed in yoga-type clothing and carrying plastic bags. She looked back to the car to see if her mother was with them. She felt both disappointment and relief when she wasn't.

"Here we go," Quint said, walking up to the door to unlock it.

Kaitlyn turned to lean against the railing and take in the view of his strong back and tight buttocks covered in his shirt and pants.

Quint turned and she quickly looked up.

He visibly paused as he eyed her, keeping one strong hand holding the door open.

Kaitlyn looked innocent. "Thank you," she said, while her sisters-in-law noisily made their way up the stairs.

"Kaeden said it's number eleven," she heard Garcelle say. Her accent sounded as heavy as Sofia Vergara's from *Modern Family.*

Kaitlyn strolled up to meet them. "Hello, family," she said, smiling begrudgingly as each one hugged her and kissed her cheek.

"You didn't think we were going to let you move into your new place by yourself," Bianca said.

Her brothers and sisters-in-law had all called and offered help, but she had refused them. They weren't willing to give the help she wanted, so she had refused to accept the help they chose to offer.

But now that they had appeared, she was glad to see them and grateful. She blinked away a sudden rush of tears.

"Thanks, y'all," Kaitlyn said softly, sounding more like the little girl who had grown up on a horse ranch in South Carolina than she had in a long time.

"Your mama is watching the babies," Jade added, reaching out to pinch Kaitlyn's wrist lightly. "She wouldn't come without knowing if you wanted her, but she's watching the kids and gave us all kinds of cleaning supplies. She misses you, Kat."

Kaitlyn's heart tugged, but she shrugged in fake nonchalance.

"Excuse me."

All of the women looked past Kaitlyn at Quint.

"Oh my," Zaria said, as she eyed the man.

"Yes . . . oh my," Bianca and Jade chimed in.

"Good morning, ladies." Quint smiled a little bashfully. His dimples deepened in his cheeks and softened the hard contours of his handsome face.

"Sweet Baby Jesus *and* a pair of dimples," Jade added.

Over her shoulder Kaitlyn eyed him with annoyance before she turned and stepped into her apartment. "Okay, thank you. Bye," she said with a curl of her lip. *Mean self.*

"So who are you again?" Bianca asked.

"Nobody," Kaitlyn snapped, fighting the urge to press her foot to his ass and nudge him on his way. "He was just going about his business."

He turned his broad back on her and extended his hand to the women, who had all come to block his exit. "I'm Quint Wells, the apartment manager. It's nice to meet you all."

Kaitlyn's mouth dropped open as he smiled and put on the charm for *them*. He made her feel like a fly that just landed on his food.

"Did you ever play sports?" Garcelle asked, poking his arm with a finger.

Quint preened under the attention.

Kaitlyn wanted to slap the twinkle from his eyes.

"Not professionally, but I run and lift weights and play sports for fun."

"Yes, yes. It shows," Jade added.

"Okay, then. Thank you. Bye," Kaitlyn said so quickly that it sounded more like "okaythenthank youbye."

Everyone eyed her. What could she say? The truth? *Never.*

"The movers are trying to bring in my furniture," she said weakly.

"I have a lot to do. You ladies have a great day," Quint said as they broke ranks to let him through.

They all looked over their shoulders as he walked away. Kaitlyn just rolled her eyes and turned away from them with a wave of her hand. She wasn't concerned about any of them actually wanting anything more than a little harmless flirting. They wouldn't give up their relationships with her fine brothers.

"Kaitlyn, you two would make beautiful *bambinos*," Garcelle said as the ladies finally entered the apartment and moved out of the way of the more-than-patient movers bringing in her oversized, over-stuffed living-room furniture.

"He's married." Kaitlyn lied to squash all conversation of a Quint-and-Kaitlyn hookup.

There was a better chance of heaven and hell merging than *that* mess happening.

It was after dark when the ladies took their leave and Kaitlyn was finally able to drop from exhaustion onto her sofa and take a deep sip of wine. She let her head fall back on the couch as she closed her eyes. She had *never* worked so hard in her life. She broke a nail and stained her favorite shirt before she finally changed into a unitard and comfortable shoes.

After the movers came and placed some of the larger furniture items where she wanted them, that left Kaitlyn and her sisters-in-law to hang pictures, put up curtains, hang her clothes on the many rolling racks in the guest bedroom, clean and decorate both bathrooms, make her bed, and hook up her television.

Kaitlyn sighed as she thought about it all, and she groaned from imagining how much worse it would have been without their help.

Knock, knock.

Kaitlyn sat up straight and wiped the bit of drool from her mouth, not even realizing she had fallen asleep until she was jarred awake.

Knock, knock.

Stretching as she rose to her slippered feet, she made her way to the front door. She opened it to find Quint's daughter standing there, still in her school uniform of khakis and a polo shirt. She was holding an aluminum foil–covered bowl.

"Hi, I'm Lei," she said, looking past Kaitlyn, into the apartment.

Kaitlyn eyed her. "Hi, Lei. I'm Kaitlyn."

"I know," she said simply, breaking into a smile. The dimples she had inherited from her father deepened in her cheeks.

"Can I help you with something?"

"I thought since you was busy moving all day that you didn't have a chance to eat yet," Lei said, extending her arms to hand the bowl to Kaitlyn. "So I'm sharing the jambalaya my daddy made for dinner tonight. It's real good."

Kaitlyn eyed the bowl before she took it. "Can your daddy cook?" she asked.

Lei shrugged. "A few things. Jambalaya is one of them. Can I come in?"

That caught Kaitlyn off guard. "Uhm . . . yes . . . I guess so," she said, stepping back to let her in. "Does your father know you're up here?"

Lei walked into the apartment and looked around as she shook her head. "No, he went running, but he wouldn't mind, and I left a note," she said as she stood before the huge black-and-white photo of Kaitlyn hanging on the wall over a buffet table and centerpiece.

Kaitlyn closed the door and took the foil from the bowl. It looked good. Damn good. Plenty of shrimp and sausage, just the way she liked it. Her stomach grumbled.

"Why'd you cut all your hair off?" Lei asked, turning away from the photo.

"I wanted to try something different."

"Was your moms mad at you?"

Kaitlyn headed toward the kitchen, and Lei followed close behind. "No, she wasn't mad. It's just hair," she said, scooping the rice onto a plate and grabbing a fork.

Lei sat on one of the high stools with a back that surrounded the tall wooden dining-room table in a deep mahogany stain. "My moms woulda freaked out."

Kaitlyn grabbed two bottles of fruit juice from the fridge, setting one in front of Lei, before she sat across from her at the table. She eyed the girl as she slid a shrimp into her mouth. "Uhm, so you live with your dad?" she asked, thinking of him and then pushing all thoughts of him away.

Lei nodded as she sipped the juice. "My mom

moved to Hawaii with her new friend and I moved in with my dad two years ago."

"At least you get to visit Hawaii," Kaitlyn said, all enthusiastic.

Lei made a face. "I ain't never seen Hawaii," she drawled dryly. "But it's cool. I got my dad, and my mom sends me all kinds of gifts. So I'm good."

Kaitlyn bit her bottom lip to keep from asking her why she hadn't seen her mother in two years. Instinctively, she knew the girl would much rather have her mother than the gifts, but she was putting on a brave front. That made her heart ache.

"Want to see my closet?" Kaitlyn asked, wanting to change the subject.

She figured all little girls were like her niece, Kadina, who loved Kaitlyn's clothes.

"Your closet?" Lei asked, looking skeptical.

Kaitlyn left her food behind and grabbed Lei's hand to guide her to her guest room. She opened the door and stepped back.

"Wow!" Lei sighed.

Kaitlyn used the bookcases she had in her old living space to place on either side of the window and then line them with her shoes. She used a dark bamboo blind on the window and then placed her oversized framed mirror in front of it. On opposing walls were the clothing racks. In the center of the room, her favorite Persian area rug warmed the room beneath the oversized round ottoman. On the wall opposite the shoes was a dresser holding her pricey lingerie; it was topped with her perfume bottles and jewelry cases. It was a miniature department store.

Kaitlyn actually loved the room, and she could see from Lei's eyes that she loved it too.

"Here, try on these," she said, crossing the room to grab a pair of gold-glittered flats.

Lei sat on the ottoman to kick off her Jordans and yank off her colorful sock so she could slide her now-bare foot into the shoe.

"They're so cute . . . and they fit," Lei said, rushing to yank off the other sneaker and sock to slide her foot into the other shoe, which Kaitlyn handed her.

"They are way cuter on your feet than they are on mine," Kaitlyn assured her, enjoying the girl's excitement. "You can have them."

"Oh, my God . . . thank *you*!" Lei hugged Kaitlyn and then eased past her to look at the reflection of her feet in the mirror.

In that moment Kaitlyn was surprised to find that playing the role of the Fairy Godmother instead of always being Cinderella at the ball wasn't bad at all.

CHAPTER 5

Quint was jogging back from the Summerville and Charleston split, with Jay-Z music coming through his earphones on low. He kept his eyes focused on the traffic as he made sure to stay on the side of the road. He knew running at night was risky, but all his running clothes had some accent on it that was reflective, and he was always careful to stay aware at all times.

As he neared the Holtsville town limit, he picked up the pace and finished the last few miles at a full-on sprint, which left him breathing deeply for air. He headed to the store and walked in to purchase a bottle of water. He grabbed Lei's favorite candy and headed for the register.

As she scanned his purchases, the cashier smiled and stared up at him.

"How you doin'?" Quint asked, trying to break the awkward silence . . . or at least break her staring.

"Good . . . and you?" she asked, stroking his hand as she took the money he offered for his purchase.

"I'm straight," Quint said. "Thanks."

He grabbed his stuff and headed out of the store. "Keep the change," he called over his shoulder.

Young girls were so forward, and that never turned him on—especially to fill the role of his woman, and not just a late-night, drive-by jump-off. Some dudes would take a woman like her, who came off all thirsty for love and attention, and just straight run through her.

That was his MO before he got married, but he was older now. The cashier made him feel like if she got to touch his hand again, she would suck his finger or some mess.

Quint walked the short distance down the street to the complex and guzzled nearly half the bottle of water, enjoying the coldness of it going into his mouth and down his throat. He waved to Mrs. Hanson driving by in her Dodge Durango truck, heading to work at a gas station in Walterboro. Before he could get across the parking lot, Quint spotted her husband coming around from the rear of the building and easing down to knock on Mrs. Kilton's door. Moments later it opened and all Quint spotted was a flash of brown skin before he slid inside the apartment.

Must be damn good, because he was working his neighbor's wife just as hard as his wife worked her night shift. As good as it must be, the question was "Was it worth it?" Quint just hoped he wasn't around if either husband or wife just backtracked or came home early on them.

Quint neared his door and spotted the folded notebook paper wedged between the door and the jamb. He opened it. A note from Lei. She was upstairs at Kaitlyn's.

That news made him frown as he turned and climbed up the stairs. Plenty of questions ran through his head as he stood before the door.

Knock, knock.

For some reason he could only envision Kaitlyn having his daughter running and fetching things for her from around the apartment as she sat on her high horse and gave out tips like the queen of England.

The door opened.

Kaitlyn eyed him from head to toe. He was aware that he stood at her door in his running clothes. His earphones were still wrapped around his neck, and the front of his shirt was soaked with sweat and clinging to him.

"Lei here?" Quint asked, trying to ignore the fact Kaitlyn wore a unitard that might as well be second skin, since it was clinging to her so hard.

Kaitlyn glared at him. "Well, hello to you too," she said dryly; then she turned to call Lei's name.

His betraying eyes dipped, but he forced himself to look past her into her apartment. He had to admit she had really transformed the place with her furnishings.

"Daddy, look what Kaitlyn gave me," Lei said, pointing her toe out to him like a ballerina as she held her Jordans in her hands.

"Miss Kaitlyn," he asserted, staring down at his little girl, who was wearing shoes that glittered more than a 1980s disco ball. Would it start at the shoes and travel up her body until his baby girl was a baby version of Kaitlyn . . . or worse yet—her mother.

"Sorry," she said. "*Miss* Kaitlyn."

"Uhm . . . thank you, Kaitlyn, but she can't take those," Quint said firmly.

"Why not?" Kaitlyn asked.

"Yeah . . . why not?" Lei parroted.

"Because . . . I said so," he said even more firmly,

knowing he sounded so cliché. "Now give them back and go downstairs."

Lei eyed him with her usual sad face, but Quinton didn't cave. So she kicked off the shoes and put her Jordans back on. Then she picked up the glittery flats to hand to Kaitlyn with obvious regret.

"Thanks, anyway, Miss Kaitlyn," she said softly. Then she brushed past her father and ran down the stairs.

He turned to follow.

"You really are an asshole, Quinton," she said from behind him.

He turned to face her again. "My daughter doesn't need anything from you . . . including your influence. We've already had one woman like you in our lives, and that was enough."

Kaitlyn's mouth opened in surprise. She stepped back and began to close the door, right before telling him, "Fuck you."

Kaitlyn paced every square inch of her apartment as Quinton's words played over and over in her head. It had been almost two hours since he hurled an insult and she hurled back an expletive—a word choice that she meant with *the* utmost seriousness.

She was *highly* offended.

"Humph, I would never leave my child behind! So oops, you wrong, *Quinton,*" she said sarcastically, slashing her hand through the air like he was there in front of her. "Even a dog raises its puppies."

She moved to sit on the sofa and crossed her legs. "Humph. I'm sorry your ex-wife was in such a rush to get away from your mean ass that she ain't take time to pack up *her* child. Not my fault. Hello, and hello again. *Boom!*"

Kaitlyn jumped up off the couch and headed for the kitchen. The bowl of jambalaya still sat on the table. She snatched it up and opened the back door to throw it in the covered garbage can outside the door. "I'ma put your jambalaya where I put your opinion of me. In the trash. *Boom!*"

She opened the lid, but she changed her mind. *I'm hungry.*

Kaitlyn looked down at the light on in the shed, at the rear of the property. She squinted her eyes in curiosity as Quint came out of the shed and locked the door. Her stomach burned at the very sight of him, and she knew she had to get some things off her chest. She flew down the back stairwell in her bare feet—usually a big no-no for her.

Kaitlyn boldly stepped in his path. "You owe me an apology," she told him.

Quint looked up in surprise and then looked down at the bowl in her hands. "Is that my bowl?"

"So now you gonna accuse me of breaking into your house and stealing a bowl of jambalaya," she snapped, her animosity and dislike of him brimming inside her. "See, unlike you, your daughter has manners—thank God—and offered me dinner, while you have given me nothing but rudeness, attitude, and—now tonight—insults."

Quint opened his mouth.

"No!" Kaitlyn snapped, holding up her hand. "Even though I don't have children, don't ever question the type of mother I would be."

"I—"

"I'm sorry your ex-wife was in such a rush to get away from your mean ass that she ain't take time to pack up *her* child. Not my fault," she said, pulling from her earlier thoughts about him. "Even a dog raises its puppies!"

Quinton's eyes hardened. "Don't talk about something you know nothing about," he said in a cold voice, which probably would have chilled Kaitlyn if she wasn't so heated in anger.

"No, don't you talk about something you don't know," she shot right back. "I only offered her the shoes because she had just gotten done telling me how she hadn't seen her mother since she moved to Hawaii."

Quint's face softened a bit.

"I was trying to take her mind off it, so I showed her my closet," Kaitlyn told him, flailing her hand and causing some of the rice to fly over the side of the bowl. "She liked the shoes. I never wear them, so I gave them to her. Big deal."

Quint wiped his face with his hand.

"So that shit you said to me earlier was completely uncalled for, and I didn't appreciate it," Kaitlyn told him forcefully, her anger making her eyes glisten. She turned from him, tired.

Quinton wrapped his hand around her wrist. "Kaitlyn—"

She whirled back around with her chest still heaving from her tirade and her emotions.

His eyes dropped down to take that in before his gaze shifted up to meet her eyes again.

Kaitlyn's heart raced at that, and then she noticed the heat of his hand against her flesh as he held her wrist. "The apology you owe me certainly ain't in there," she said, arching her brow.

Quint bit his bottom lip and looked away from her briefly. Then he turned his head back to look at her.

"Daddy . . . telephone," Lei called from the front of the building.

Kaitlyn's heart was pounding like crazy and she felt slightly breathless as his thumb pressed against her pulse point.

"Can she have the shoes? I'll take that as an apology," she said to him softly. She was a lot shorter without her heels.

"I apologize, Kaitlyn," he said, looking down into her face as he finally released her.

She felt the loss of his warm touch, but she still licked her lips because they suddenly felt parched from the heat she felt rising in her.

I must be horny.

Kaitlyn turned and headed back up the stairs. At the landing she looked down to find he was standing there under the circle of light caused by the light pole. He was still watching her.

"Can Lei have the shoes?" she asked, nudging her chin forward in a small act of defiance.

He just shook his head with a little laugh and walked away.

In Kaitlyn's world not saying "no" was just as good as saying "yes." She entered the apartment, dropped off the bowl in the kitchen, and then grabbed the shoes from where she had placed them back on the shelf. She slid them into one of her shoe bags. Just to be a pain in his ass, she added the black sequined version of the pair that she had as well.

She slipped on her shoes and headed out of the apartment to take the stairs. She paused, seeing Quinton sitting at the bottom of the steps, talking on a cordless phone.

"Your daughter needs to see you, and you promised to come for her birthday next month, Vita," he said.

Kaitlyn paused, grimaced, and then turned to creep back up the stairs.

"I'll pay for her plane ticket to come see you this summer, then," he said.

Kaitlyn rushed into her apartment. He probably would swear she was ear hustling on purpose. She set the bag on the table under her photo.

I'll give them to her tomorrow.

Kaitlyn walked into the kitchen and warmed up her jambalaya. She was leaning against the kitchen counter, tearing it up. She thought she would try her best tonight to enjoy a hot aromatherapy bath in her little tub before dropping into bed, naked, and letting sleep win that round.

She ate every last bite and set the bowl in the sink.

Knock, knock.

"Now what?" she wondered out loud as she paused to look at her front door.

Even with a family as large as hers, she never had *this* much company in one night. She paused on the way to the door when the thought crossed her mind that it could be her parents coming to tell her that the nightmare was over.

Kaitlyn snatched the door open. She couldn't help the disappointment she felt at Lei standing there. She set aside her disenchantment and smiled at the girl, hating that her father had to beg her mother to make a way to see her.

"Does your father know you're here?" she asked, just as she did earlier.

"Yes, ma'am. He said I could have the shoes if I wanted them, and to make sure I thanked you and called you *Miss* Kaitlyn," Lei said.

Kaitlyn turned to grab the shoe bag. "I had a black pair that I wanted to give you too, if that's okay."

"Oh, thank you, Miss Kaitlyn," she said.

She couldn't believe Lei was younger than Kadina, who was straight up and down, with barely a hint of boobs and no sign of hips.

"You're welcome."

Lei turned to leave with a wave.

Kaitlyn stepped out onto the balcony and leaned against the railing as she looked out at her new home. It was quiet enough. She mainly just missed her view of the lake.

She spotted Quinton coming out of his office with his cordless phone in his hand. Kaitlyn figured that when Lei came outdoors, he went in there to finish the conversation with her mother in privacy. She watched as Lei met him halfway and showed him the bag with two pairs of sparkly, girlie, supercute shoes.

Quint happened to look up and spotted her on the balcony. He waved, but his smile was faker than a hundred-dollar Louis Vuitton bag.

Kaitlyn's smile in return was full and toothy and completely genuine. She wiggled her fingers at him until he and his daughter disappeared from her sight.

Yet another man who has learned that Kaitlyn Strong always *gets her way.*

CHAPTER 6

Lisha Strong looked over the rim of her glasses as her husband stood on the balcony of their bedroom and looked out into the darkness. She bit her bottom lip as she closed the book she was reading and climbed from the bed to join him. She pressed her side to his, and he immediately brought his arm up to surround her shoulders. Since long before she could remember, this man was her lover, her friend, and her backbone.

His highs were hers.

His lows were hers.

And ever since they put their daughter on financial restrictions, there had been more lows than highs.

"She's okay, Kael," she assured him, looking out at the shadowed outlines of the trees as the full moon lit the sky.

He said nothing and just nodded his head.

"We're doing what's right. She has to learn to fend for herself. We'll always be her safety net, but first she has to learn to fly," Lisha told him softly. She looked up at his profile and felt her heart swell with the same love as it had when they were in their twenties.

"I miss my daughter."

Lisha raised her hand beneath his T-shirt to rub his back. "And she misses you too."

He grunted before he notched his chin higher—a trait he passed on to their daughter. The thought of that made her smile.

"She's having a tantrum. That's all. No different than that time she locked herself in her room and refused to eat for all of eight hours when we didn't let her get her nose pierced at twelve. Remember?" she asked him in amusement.

Kael chuckled and shook his silver-covered head. "Or the time she ran away to Kade's, when we wouldn't let her drive the four-wheeler alone at six," he said.

"Without a helmet," Lisha added.

They laughed together.

"And just as we ignored her little fits and tantrums before, and she would come right around . . . she will this time too."

Kael looked down at his wife and smiled before he pressed a warm and lingering kiss to her lips. "We'll see."

"Trust me, *husband*. Have I ever steered you wrong?" she asked, leaning back to gaze up at him as the moonlight reflected against the silvery glints in his hair.

"I have something you can *steer*, wife," he said with a suggestive wink of his brows before soundly slapping her buttocks.

Lisha broke free of him and walked back into their bedroom. Moments later her nightgown came flying through the doors and across the air. It soared like a ghost before landing on his head.

"That's what I'm talking about," Kael said, rushing into their bedroom and closing the double doors behind him.

* * *

Garcelle eased their normally rambunctious son from her chest. She rose from the rocker to place Karlos upon his new toddler bed, which was built like a miniature horse stable, complete with linens that had horses on them. Knowing his routine, she pushed his favorite plush horse toy close within his reach and then covered him with a light blanket. She gave it a ten count and then dimmed the lights before leaving the room and closing the door.

And her eighteen-month-old was good for the night.

She crossed the hall and knocked before opening her stepdaughter's door. Kadina was sitting in the middle of her bed, dressed for sleep but playing with her iPad. She looked up at Garcelle and smiled.

"I know. I know. Not too late," she said.

"Sí," Garcelle responded.

"I texted Aunt Kat and she wants me to spend the weekend with her," Kadina said.

"Good. You will love how she turned a whole bed-room into a closet," Garcelle said, winking.

"That sounds like my auntie," Kadina bragged, twirling the end of her fishtail braid around her finger.

"Yes," Garcelle agreed.

"I'm gonna ask her to bring me to Grandpa's around dinnertime, and see if she'll stay for dinner."

Garcelle sighed as she came farther into the room. "We all want her back in the fold, but she's a *little* angry, and sometimes it's best not to meddle and press things. It can make it worse," she said gently. Her Spanish accent made "little" sound more like "leetle."

Kadina looked distressed and shook her head. "I don't want to make it worse."

"Talk to your dad before the weekend and see what he thinks," Garcelle advised, turning to head for the door. "*Dulces sueños,* Kadina."

"*Dulces sueños,* Garcelle," she answered, wishing Garcelle sweet dreams as well.

Garcelle closed her bedroom door behind her and walked down the hall to her bedroom suite. She crossed the room and entered the en suite, pausing to pull her sports bra and T-shirt over her head. She pushed her bikini panties and wide-leg yoga pants over her hips to the floor as she eyed her husband lounging in their oversized tub. His head was tilted back against the rim of the tub. The steam from the water had the entire bathroom warm and made his full silvery curls flatten against his head.

He opened his eyes just as Garcelle stepped into the tub with him. He instantly spread his legs wider so that she could kneel between them. His eyes eased over her nude body as he savored every moment.

With a devilish smile Garcelle pressed her body against her husband's and pressed her lips to his as they both got lost in the steam . . . and created quite a bit more.

Kahron rolled off the couch when car lights flashed through the windows of his living room and onto the opposite wall. He padded in his socks and boxers to open the front door, where he watched his wife, Bianca, climb from her car like she carried the weight and worries of the world on her shoulders.

As soon as she had gotten in from helping Kaitlyn move, she had received an emergency call for her vet services. He had picked their four-year-old son, KJ, up from his parents when he was done working his horse ranch for the evening. He prepared a quick stew and rice for their dinner.

"Tired?" he asked, coming down the stairs to press a kiss to her neck, then surprising her by scooping her up into his arms. "I got you."

Bianca dropped her curly-topped head onto his shoulder. "Thank you, baby." She sighed contentedly.

He took the stairs with ease. Being a ranch owner who wrangled with horses and cattle for a living didn't call for a weak man.

"I know y'all trying to prove a point with Kaitlyn, but we coulda used the help today," she said. "I didn't even know there was an apartment complex down that road. Did you?"

Kahron nodded as he carried her through the house, into their bedroom. "Yeah, it's only been there for a couple of years. Don't worry. Kade checked it out and filled me in."

Bianca raised her head from his shoulder as they passed KJ's room and she spotted their four-year-old in bed, sleeping.

"I thought he was still at your parents'."

"I went and got him," he told her, his deep voice rumbling in his chest.

"We're a good team?" she joked, sleep filling her voice even as she chuckled at their inside joke.

"Damn right," Kahron said.

He loved that he had been the kind of husband over the years where she knew she could trust and allow him to be her strength when she had to give in to a moment of weakness.

* * *

"I'll tell you what," Jade said as she lifted the pan from the stove and used a spatula to lift a piece of grilled tilapia onto her husband's plate.

Kaeden looked up at her as he poured them both a glass of wine for the late dinner. "What?"

"If Kaitlyn's apartment manager, landlord, whatever, wasn't married, he would be perfect for her," Jade said, setting a bowl of salad and a bottle of fat-free salad dressing on the center of their kitchen table. "He. Is. Gorgeous. Oh, my God!"

Kaeden frowned as he took a bite of fish. "I've seen him, and I'm sure Gucci is not looking for him for their next photo shoot," he said mockingly.

Jade paused in placing salad on their plates. She eyed him. "When did you see him?"

Kaeden shrugged and made the move to push up the spectacles he hadn't worn in a year. A nervous gesture he had never overcome, once he got the LASIK procedure.

"I—I—I went by to see the place and check it out. Surveying the scene—"

"With your gangster lean," Jade teased, chuckling. "I'm just saying the man was nice-looking."

"Well, he's married, and off the market for my sister . . . and for my wife," he added in a dry tone.

Jade eyed him and then rose from her seat to come around the table and slide onto his lap as she wrapped her strong, toned arms around his neck. She began to plant kisses along his square jawline. "I was thinking that maybe it's time I took a little break from being an adventure guide," she said, feeling his dick harden against her buttocks like steel.

"Oh yeah?" he said, tilting his chin back so that she had clear access to his throat. "I thought you loved all that outdoors stuff."

Jade planted kisses from one side of his neck to the other. "Yes, but I want to make babies," she said softly, leaning up to look down into his eyes.

Kaeden's eyes widened.

"You want to make beautiful babies with me?" she asked.

Kaeden smiled so hard that Jade could count every white tooth in his head.

"Yeah. Hell yeah," he answered. His voice was filled with emotions as he reached up to rake his strong fingers through her ear-length auburn hair. He brought her head down to capture her full mouth for a deep kiss, which soon led to their meal being swept to the floor as he made fierce love to his wife atop their dinner table.

Kaleb stripped off his towel as he strode into their bed. "If Kaitlyn doesn't at least bring her ass to Sunday dinner, I'm going to that little sardine can she calls a home and drag her behind to Strong Ranch," he said, sitting down on the side of the bed.

Zaria got on her knees behind him and began to massage the tension from his strong neck and back. "That would be one helluva cat—*or Kat*—fight," she said.

"I just don't see how giving Mama and Daddy her ass to kiss makes any sense," Kaleb said, thrusting his hand into the air as he spoke.

Zaria kneaded his shoulders. "True . . . but I think you-all are not respecting the fact that your parents created this monster—"

"Monster?" he snapped, looking over his shoulder at her.

Zaria held up her hands as she dropped to her

buttocks in her black sheer teddy next to him. "I'm just saying that she's had over twenty-five years of them spoiling her, and just snatching it all away might feel to her like they don't care anymore. And so even though you don't agree, you have to understand her emotions right now. Everyone's position, understanding, and experience in the same family can be different. So take it easy on her. That's all I'm saying," she finished lightly.

Kaleb stared at her for a long time. "So wisdom is one of the pluses of marrying an older woman who is still sexier than most women half her age?" he asked.

"Most?" Zaria asked as she climbed off the bed and stood before him as she did a full circle.

"All," he assured her, looking pointedly down at his dick hardening between his muscled thighs.

Zaria straddled his hips and pushed his upper body down onto the bed.

"The baby—"

"Shush, he's not here. The twins are babysitting at their house," she said, speaking of her twenty-one-year-old twin daughters, Meena and Neema.

Kaleb raised his strong arms over his head and let something way better than Calgon take him away.

CHAPTER 7

Quint sat up straight in bed. His heart pounded and a fine sheen of sweat coated his muscular frame. He looked around in the darkness as he struggled to bring his pulse rate down.

It wasn't an easy task.

He dreamt that his daughter had run away to try to live with her mother and she never made it to Hawaii. She had gone missing.

His heart still pounded, as it had in his dream, as he thought of all the scenarios, all the possible causes of her disappearance.

Throwing back the thin sheet covering his nude frame, Quint sat up on the edge of the bed and rested his elbows on his knees as he ran his hands over his bald head.

"Damn," he swore aloud.

Quint rose in the darkness and walked across the room into his bathroom. He flipped the switch to bask the small room with light as he positioned himself before the commode. As he relieved himself, he looked up; his eyes locked with those in his reflection in the mirror. He didn't like what he saw. The truth was always hard to accept, and the emotions were clear in the lines etching his handsome face.

It wasn't fear but guilt.

Quint bent down to flush the toilet, deliberately not looking back in the mirror as he turned off the light. He slid on a pair of boxers and left his bedroom to walk down the short hall to ease Lei's door open and peek his head in. She was lying flat on her back, arm and leg hanging off the bed. Mouth wide open. She was completely asleep and unaware of her father's worries.

Easing the door shut, he made his way back to his bedroom. The clock on his nightstand read 2:28 A.M. as he climbed back into bed and pulled the sheets back up to his waist. He lay back and crossed his muscled arms behind his head as he stared up at the ceiling.

Life had a funny way of going by so quickly that a person never saw the wrong turns, never acknowledged taking the wrong road at the fork. Not until it was too late.

He hadn't been the best husband—thus his divorce. He could accept that because his ex, Vita, hadn't been the perfect wife either. But to admit that he hadn't been the best father to his daughter was a difficult pill to swallow. Very difficult.

In the last two weeks since Hurricane Kaitlyn landed at the complex, her influence and presence in his daughter's life was unmistakable. Nearly every day Lei rushed to finish her homework and chores to beat a fast trail upstairs to Kaitlyn's apartment, aka the fun zone. When she discovered Kaitlyn wasn't at home, she would be visibly disappointed and steadily looking out the window until she saw that obnoxious-ass red car of hers parked in its spot.

His relationship with his daughter had always seemed to be a good one; and although he knew as a father that talking about fashion and make-up or playing with dolls would never be at the top of his chosen to-do list, he hadn't realized just how much Lei missed all of those girlie things and more since she came to live with him.

Now Quint felt selfish, like he had put his life ahead of his daughter's; and that's not what being a good parent is about. He just pushed his head in the sand and assumed he was doing his part because he was there—unlike her mother. It should have been obvious that Lei needed a female presence in her life.

He was there for his daughter every day. He took her shopping or to the movies or they just chilled at home. He talked to her. He questioned her. He loved her and admonished her. He thought it was enough.

Now he knew that it wasn't. It couldn't be. Not when she was stuck to Kaitlyn like paper to glue.

Now, just two weeks after the new tenant had moved in, and Miss Kaitlyn was Lei's favorite person:

"Miss Kaitlyn is so smart."

"Miss Kaitlyn is so funny."

"Miss Kaitlyn is so pretty."

Miss Kaitlyn said this.

Miss Kaitlyn said that.

The last thing he wanted was for his daughter to be influenced by the person he believed Kaitlyn to be:

Vain.

Irresponsible.

Lacking direction in life.

Spoiled.

Like Vita.

His ex-wife's selfishness led her to no longer want to be or participate in her daughter's life because a man with a bigger bank account offered her a life of leisure on an island usually reserved for vacations. And Vita was so lost that when he reminded her that her daughter needed her, she was completely oblivious to the logic in that.

"Even a dog raises its puppies."

Kaitlyn's words flung at him in anger still rang with truth.

He recalled the vision of her face completely lit with anger as she verbally served him his own ass on a platter. Even as her words had angered him, he had thought, *She's even prettier mad.* An urge to kiss her quiet had come in a rush. And it surprised him.

And when he grabbed her wrist to keep her from storming away from him, her skin had been soft and silky beneath his fingers. That had not surprised him at all. He figured a woman like Kaitlyn was soft and silky all over.

Especially that ass.

And in the last two weeks, they had made a game—or rather a challenge—of verbally topping the other. Barbs between them were the norm. He enjoyed their back-and-forth. It was a challenge to see if he could top her, like a chess match.

And there were plenty of opportunities, for the woman called him for the most simple things, which completely exasperated him. Changing lightbulbs. Asking if the complex offered maid services. Requesting he call the owner to have a pool put in. Stating her self-cleaning oven wasn't working . . . when, in fact, it was just that she didn't know how to do it. He had done more tasks and fulfilled more of Kaitlyn's oddball requests in the last two weeks than all the other residents combined since his time there had begun.

And the other residents loved ribbing him about Kaitlyn giving him such a hard time and keeping him on the go. The word had spread that they had started clashing, and everyone was sitting back to enjoy the fireworks.

They just didn't know he was two seconds from putting her over his knee to deliver the behind cutting she obviously never received when growing up.

One of the older tenants knew her family. They were a wealthy ranching family from right there in Holtsville. She was the only daughter *and* the youngest child. Everyone who knew the Strongs knew that the baby girl got what she wanted and when she wanted it.

That little tidbit offered to him plenty of insight on her attitude of entitlement.

And Quint swore to himself that if she tried to tip him one more damn time, he was going to lay hands on her behind.

An image of a nude Kaitlyn bent over a bed, with her buttocks high in the air, taunting in a sexy voice, *"Go ahead and spank it, Quint"* forced him to turn on his side and bunch up his pillow to force sleep.

Kaitlyn already bugged the hell out of him in his waking hours. He refused to let her dominate his sleeping hours as well.

Brrrnnnggg.

Quint's eyes popped back open at the loud and intrusive blaring of the telephone ringing. He snatched the cordless off the base before it could wake up Lei.

"Hello," he barked, glancing at his clock again. It was three o'clock in the morning.

"Uhm, hey, Quint—"

He stiffened at the sound of Kaitlyn's voice.

"This is Kaitlyn."

No shit, Sherlock, he quipped sarcastically in his head. He remained quiet.

"I just got home and my garbage disposal isn't working, and I poured hot water in it and now it's making a noise."

Quint sat up in bed. "Your what?" he asked.

"Garbage disposal."

Quinton dropped his head into his free hand. "You do realize everyone else in this building is asleep?" he asked.

"Humph. Not everybody! And I'm just gonna leave it at that and keep it none-of-my."

He frowned. "And keep it *what*?"

"None-of-my . . . short for none of my business . . . but I will say that old dude is dead wrong for creeping and sneaking and freaking like a little *rat*."

Mr. Hanson.

Again he was amazed by her ability to make him want to laugh with her and strangle her at the same time.

"On my way up, Kaitlyn," he said, and then hung up.

Quint pulled on some sweatpants and a wife-beater shirt before slipping on a pair of his athletic sandals and grabbing his mini toolbox.

"Where in the world was she out to until three in the morning? That's what I want to know," he muttered to himself as he left the apartment.

The September air was chilly at night and goose bumps raced up the length of his exposed arms as he rushed up the stairs. He had just reached the second landing when he spotted Mrs. Hanson unlocking her front door, obviously home from her night shift.

She was a medium-build woman, with a soft, pretty face and a ready smile. "Mighty *late* for a handyman," she teased with a little laugh. "Enjoy the rest of your night, Mr. Wells."

"Night, Mrs. Hanson," he said, hoping her work schedule kept her too busy from spreading the news that she had spotted him at Kaitlyn's door at that time of the night.

Most of the tenants didn't know how to keep a secret. He was surprised the news hadn't spread yet about her husband cheating with their married downstairs neighbor.

Kaitlyn opened the door before he could knock and reached out to grab his wrist to pull him inside and down the hall to the kitchen.

"See?" she said, waving her hand at the sink, which was indeed making odd gurgling noises.

Quint first allowed himself to take in her heavy makeup around her eyes and her hair styled in spikes. She wore a gold sequined suit, featuring shorts, and its short length was just shy of proving to the world she was a female. Her legs. Her full legs went on forever, and they were made all the more a sight to see in her skyscraper heels.

"You're quite *bright* tonight," he commented, slightly sarcastic, even as the sight of her made his heart pound in his chest. Hard. Fast. Undeniable.

Kaitlyn struck a pose. "I had to go all out. My friends threw me one helluva good-bye party. I danced all night. My legs hurt."

As he bent down to open the door to the cabinet under the sink, his eyes inadvertently shifted to take in her legs as she stood over him.

"Good-bye party? You should have invited me. That's one party I wanna be at."

"Well, tough, because I'm not going anywhere. They just think I am. Unfortunately, I'm stuck in this . . ."

Quint leaned back to look up at her.

Kaitlyn gave him the fakest of smiles. "Well . . . this *wonderful* establishment you run," she said, obviously exaggerating.

"This 'wonderful establishment' you're tearing up," he popped back, leaning forward to use his wrench to undo the trap on the kitchen plumbing.

"Whateva, Quin-ton," she said, stressing the syllables of his name.

"So where do your friends think you're going?" he asked, his voice echoing under the sink.

"Italy for school . . . but I don't want to talk about that."

He shrugged.

"Why do you hate me?" she asked.

Quint leaned back from under the counter and jumped back a bit to find her squatting down next to him. His eyes dropped down to her womanhood pressed against the seat of her shorts and between the backs of her full thighs.

"Kaitlyn, yo, you taking my picture," he said, averting his eyes as he felt desire for her flame up.

And that made him feel like a pervert.

And then that made him edgy and annoyed.

"Huh?"

"That means I can see your money shot. Stop sitting like that," he snapped.

She laughed. "There is nothing bad luck about *any* of that," Kaitlyn told him before she rose to her feet.

Quint finished loosening the trap and then rose to brush past her and empty the grease and bits of food into the garbage can outside her back door. She quietly watched him as he replaced the trap and then ran steaming hot water down the drain.

"You have any bleach?" he asked. "I mean, you do know how to wash clothes, right?"

When she never answered, he looked over at her and she was just standing there staring at him.

"The bleach."

"Do you have sex on the regular?" she asked suddenly. "You're very angry and abrupt, like a horny teenage boy with lots of built-up . . . frustration."

"Oh really?" he asked, turning to face her.

"Oh, most definitely," she assured him.

"So I look like the type of man can't get no play?" he asked cockily.

Kaitlyn applauded. "There's the cockiness that's been underlying all your bs from the jump street."

"Not cocky . . . confident. There's a difference," Quint told her as that energy they created during their sparring session rose up like sudden thunder in the skies. It felt familiar to him.

"Please don't let the fawning of women not used to good-looking men mess your head up," she shot back. "I've seen plenty as fine as you, and I have turned down better-looking."

Quint let his eyes leisurely roam her body. "You seem to be really focused on these looks," he said, rubbing his large hands against his smooth cheeks as he lifted his chin and posed for her.

"Humph. Negro, please. Not nearly as much as you are boo'ed up on yourself obviously," Kaitlyn said scathingly.

Quinton used his left hand to raise the hem of his T-shirt to expose his chiseled abdomen. "Go ahead. Rub it. See what a real man feels like."

Kaitlyn kept her eyes locked on him. "If only I

was as interested in touching you as you are used to touching yourself. Which brings us—what!—back to my original point of you being horny and frustrated."

Quint literally bit his mouth to keep from saying: *"Let me show you how good my dick game is."*

Or: *"I promise you, I got just what you need to shut you the hell up."*

Or: *"I'll have you crying for Jesus, with no Bible involved."*

Kaitlyn arched her brows and eyes at him, silently asking, *"What?"*

He did a five count. "The bleach?" he asked again. Some unnamed energy still crackled in the air around them.

Kaitlyn's eyes filled with triumph, and she looked smug as she turned to the small pantry in the corner to take out a bottle of bleach to set on the counter.

Quint snatched it up and poured a good portion down the drain to help cut the grease and buildup.

"Humph. If you scared, say you scared," she taunted.

He capped the bottle and set it on the counter before turning to face her. "Scared of what?" he asked in a low voice.

"I'm just saying in general. If you scared, it's no biggie, Quin-ton." She dragged out his name once more.

He took a step closer to her and it literally felt to him like the energy intensified. "What's there to be scared of?"

Kaitlyn licked her lips as her mouth parted a bit.

He wondered if she felt it too, because she released a small breath through her pursed lips.

"You talk a good game, Kaitlyn, but I see right through you," he told her, taking another step forward.

It was as if he were made of metal and she were the magnet.

"Oh really? Do tell."

Quint raised his hand and traced his finger along the deep vee created by her blazer. And just as he thought, her skin was smooth and silky.

When she shivered and gasped slightly, Quint had to fight the urge to ease his hand inside the blazer and trace a finger gently along her nipple to see her shiver again.

"I think you're so concerned about me being horny and frustrated because *you are*. Them rich boys don't know how to handle it. You too much woman for them. But me? I'll tear that ass up, and you know it, and you want it. Don't you?" he asked as he lowered his head to hers, inch by inch, until his breath fanned out against her face. He triumphantly watched her eyes glaze over.

Kaitlyn felt pure pressure surround them. She was breathless and light-headed as she looked up at the movement of Quint's lips as he spoke to her. Her nipples were hard and throbbing, rubbing against the silk lining of her sequined blazer as her chest visibly rose from her labored breathing.

When his lips were less than an inch above hers, she had to cling to the wall for support. Just then, Quint asked her in a soft whisper made to wreck any woman with the same power as D'Angelo's "Untitled (How Does It Feel)" video: "You want this dick, don't you?"

Kaitlyn had to bite her tongue from getting caught in the electric moment and whispering back "yes" as his finger again eased along the soft curves of her exposed cleavage.

The air seemed to crackle like lightning around them. She could smell the last remnants of his cologne or his soap or maybe just his natural scent. She was helplessly sandwiched between the pressure of his body and the wall.

In honesty she didn't know how this moment came to be, with her sharing such an intimate space with Quint at three in the morning. One more step up from either of them and their bodies would collide.

Mingle. Merge. Blend.

He was a fine man; of that, she couldn't deny. But somehow the line had been crossed, and she was completely lost in this world. Nothing made sense. Nothing added up. But everything in that moment felt right.

Alive. Vibrant. Energetic.

Does he feel it too? she wondered as her eyes dipped to watch him lightly lick his lips.

Or is this a ploy for me to reveal myself?

Kaitlyn locked her eyes with his as she brought her hands up in the thin space between them. She took him up on his earlier offer to touch his rigid abdomen. As she trailed her finger in the deep grooves, she enjoyed feeling his muscles clench from her stroke.

"Say you want me, Quinton," she whispered up to him, raising her chin just enough to place a soft, barely felt kiss next to his mouth.

One of her hands had shifted up, pressing her palm against his heart. She felt it pounding and wondered if the same life pulsed in his dick.

"Is it hard?" she asked, moving her hand from his

abdomen to slide it along the length of his dick, which ran down his thigh.

Quint stepped back from her. "You really shouldn't be feeling up men in your apartment this time of night," he said, turning to grab his toolbox.

Kaitlyn just shook her head. "The tables got turned and somebody couldn't take it," she quipped, pushing up off the wall to follow him leisurely to the door. "If you scared, say you scared."

Quint stopped.

Kaitlyn pulled up and stopped too.

Quint looked at her.

Kaitlyn placed her hands behind her back and looked up at him innocently, even as her pulse raced.

He opened his mouth, but then he closed it. He shook his head before turning and walking to the door.

"Don't dream about it," she called out behind him.

He turned again.

Her eyes stroked the contours of his face as she smiled smugly.

"You're really a Miss Know-It-All, huh?" Quint asked.

Kaitlyn shrugged. "I know men. I know you."

He nodded. "Too bad you didn't know that your sink doesn't have a garbage disposal."

Kaitlyn frowned.

"And next time you clog your sink, you're paying to have it fixed," he said, with a brief mocking salute before he walked out her door.

No garbage disposal? Is that possible?

"Where am I living, and why is this my life?" she said in a light wail as she locked the front door and turned off the lights. She then made her way to her bedroom and kicked off her shoes at the door. They landed on the floor with heavy thuds, which she hoped disturbed Quint.

Quinton Wells.

As she flipped the switch to illuminate her bedroom, she thought about just how hot that kitchen got when they were all up in each other's face and space.

"Whoooo," she said, fanning her neck and then between her thighs playfully.

"Quinton, Quinton. Umph. You surprised me," she said, undressing everything on her body. "Mama kitchen never got that hot when she had both ovens and every burner on the stove going," she continued saying aloud.

Kaitlyn made her way into the bathroom to use several wipes to clean the makeup from her face and then brushed her teeth. She didn't know if Quint's little stunt was real or just to prove a point because she taunted him. However, she couldn't lie that everything she felt in those heated moments had been real. Surprising and real.

Over the last couple of weeks since she moved in, Kaitlyn had struggled a bit in adjusting to her new lifestyle. The apartment managers at her old apartment had been almost like concierges of a five-star hotel. The residents' wishes were their commands. Things were different at No Name Commons—that's what she called it in her head.

And yes, she knew she called on Quinton quite a bit, but wasn't that his job?

And so she saw him frequently, but usually they were so busy throwing low blows at each other that she never considered that he could actually turn her on. And he had.

"You too much woman for them. But me? I'll tear that ass up, and you know it, and you want it. Don't you?"

With him giving her all that sexy vibe—and standing just a quarter of an inch from pressing their bodies together—for a moment Kaitlyn had widely considered ripping her blazer open and thrusting her lace-covered breasts to the sky as she roared, "Yes!"

But that was just for a moment—one crazy, fleeting moment—until she got her mind right.

And once she took the lead and gave him just as much sexy, he backed off, which led her to believe he hadn't meant it. He didn't really want it. She figured the next day his behind would be just as rude and insolent and barely tolerant as before toward her.

But for a moment he had her, and good.

He could've gotten her right there against the wall . . . or on the counter . . . or on the floor. . . .

Kaitlyn did a little shiver before she wrapped her hair with a silk scarf and took a quick shower to wash off the scent of liquor and cigarettes from the club. The feel of the hot steam and the pelting of the water from the showerhead against her body did absolutely nothing to cool the fire he unknowingly stoked.

She dried off and climbed between her crisp cotton sheets—but not before she retrieved her little friend from the velvet bag in her nightstand. "Tonight your name is Quinton," she joked as she turned it on and brought it to life in her hand.

Buzzzzzzzzzzzzzzzzzzzzzzzz . . .

Kaitlyn sighed as she pushed it down beneath the covers and between her legs to vibrate against her still-throbbing clit. She closed her eyes and remembered the feel of Quint's long and thick dick against her hand.

She and mechanical Quinton sang into the air in unison as she moaned deeply in pleasure. *"Mmmm."*

* * *

It was well after eight o'clock when Kaitlyn finally lifted her head from her plush pillows and looked out at the sun beaming through her curtains. She usually was an early riser—growing up on a ranch, where everybody beat the rooster's crow, she realized that was a hard habit to break.

She usually only slept in after a long night partying or a really explosive climax. She was fighting a wicked combo of both. Damn.

She rolled over onto her back and used the remote at the foot of the bed to turn on the flat-screen television sitting on the TV stand across from the bed. She had wanted it hung on the wall and called on Quint, but he quickly told her the owner of the building wanted nothing more than tiny tacks in the wall for picture hanging.

And that had led to another of their infamous verbal clashes.

At least it kept things lively.

Kaitlyn took another shower and made her way out of the apartment in jean leggings and a fitted black tee, with I'M VERY RICH, BITCH in Swarovski crystals à la reality-TV star NeNe Leakes. She stood beside the railing, trying to figure out what to do with her day.

She looked up as Quinton came up the stairs and eyed her.

She hated how her heart fluttered at the sight of him in long-sleeved dark blue T-shirt and jeans. Since he wasn't in his usual khaki-and-shirt attire, she had learned over the last two weeks that he was doing manual labor around the property.

"All dressed and nowhere to go," he said, walking past her to the last apartment on the second level.

"I can say the same about you," she finally shot back.

The thing was, he was right. She had absolutely nowhere to go.

With her bon voyage party thrown by Tandy and Anola last night, she was supposed to be heading to Italy, which meant the days of hanging out at their cribs were over. Without her credit cards or thick cash flow, shopping was torture.

Kaitlyn was punishing her parents, so she couldn't even go to the ranch to ride her horse. The rest of the family was working. Her mother was babysitting her younger nephews, and Kadina was in school.

She released a heavy breath as she eyed the traffic going by on the road beyond the trees lining the front of the property.

Kaitlyn knew there was no way she could make it sitting up in that little apartment all day. So what was the plan? It was becoming more and more obvious that she needed one.

CHAPTER 8

Kaitlyn pulled her vehicle onto the packed-dirt front parking lot of Donnie's Diner. Her father and brothers loved to come there for lunch. She was hoping to catch a late breakfast and get out before she ran into her father and had to muster the nerve and disrespect *not* to speak to him in person. Kaitlyn honestly didn't think she could pull that off.

And that's why when her niece occasionally spent the weekend with her, she purposefully avoided Kadina's tricky moves to get her to show up for one of their ritual Sunday dinner at her parents'.

She didn't spot any of their vehicles, so she made her way inside Holtsville's lone diner and put in her order for takeout.

"Here you go. Two specials for my two favorite customers. Enjoy, Mr. and Mrs. Johnson."

Kaitlyn looked on and smiled as she watched the waitress hand the elderly married couple glasses of iced mint tea and two plates of breakfast from her tray.

"Good morning, Mr. and Mrs. Johnson," Kaitlyn said with a little wave.

They waved back. The Johnsons lived not very far

from her parents' house, and the rear of their properties connected. Growing up, before she realized that she was not to do everything her elder brothers did, she and her siblings—excluding the hyperallergic Kaeden— had snuck onto the Jacksons' apple orchard. There they ate the juicy fruits from the trees until they all felt ready to bust.

They thought they were sneaky, but the Johnsons would always laugh about it with their parents when they crossed paths.

"You look especially pretty today, Kaitlyn," Sally said as she sipped her tea.

Kaitlyn batted her lashes. "Well, thank you. Thank you very much," she said playfully.

"How are your parents?" Clarence asked, a portly, dark-skinned man with low-cut hair as white as snow.

"They're good," she lied.

"I saw one of your brothers at the horse auction the other night. For the life of me, I don't know which one," he said around a bite of his food. His free hand was locked on his wife's ample thigh. "Hell, they all look alike."

Sally laughed and leaned back in her chair. "All good-looking," she said.

Kaitlyn smiled as he pretended to look offended, causing his wife to lean over and plant a kiss on his cheek.

"I heard you were sick recently. Are you feeling better, Mr. Johnson?" she asked as the waitress signaled that her to-go order was ready.

"I'm all better now," he said, looking at his wife with a twinkle in his eye. "Sally liked playing nurse."

The woman's caramel complexion shaded with a pink blush. "Clarence, you talk too much."

"And you love it."

"That I do."

Kaitlyn smiled as the couple, nearly ninety years old, leaned in for a firm kiss. She waved and left them alone, moving to the counter to pay for her order of French toast and bacon.

That would be her parents in another twenty years or so. In love with the same person for well over sixty years.

Was *she* ready to lock it in with someone for the next forty years? Hell to the no. Those "will I find love" questions weren't on her mind: Would she have someone to grow old with? Cherish memories with? Laugh and still play with? Build a family with?

Uhm. No.

But . . .

Kaitlyn could appreciate those who wanted it and found it.

And the Johnsons are cute. Too cute.

Maybe one day. But not now. Definitely not.

As she left the restaurant, she glanced back at the elderly couple one last time.

Maybe if I meet the right man, though . . .

"Take out?"

Kaitlyn stopped as Quint walked into the restaurant and stood before her. Close. Too close.

"Yeah," she said, moving past him to push open the door to the restaurant.

She felt his hand lightly touch her back, and she looked over her shoulder at him in question.

"No smart comment? No snappy comeback?" he asked.

As she looked into his eyes—those dark and deep eyes always seeming to brim with intensity—she remembered their interaction in her kitchen. It was her turn to run scared.

"That's it," she said, turning to leave.

Kaitlyn left the restaurant and climbed into her car. When she eventually pulled into her parking spot at the complex, she had absolutely no desire to spend her day—the entire day—just cooped up in her apartment.

Sliding on her shades, she lowered her convertible top, reclined her driver's seat, and said a silent prayer that the bird's aim was off as she chewed on a piece of bacon and enjoyed the feel of the sun.

"Can I join you?"

Kaitlyn looked left and then right before looking up. Over the rim of her shades, her eyebrows dipped to see Mr. Hanson smiling down at her. He was in nothing but his pajama bottoms.

"Call your wife and ask her," Kaitlyn called up to him before pushing her shades back down. "*Or* you can come downstairs and ask your girlfriend."

He chuckled. "I don't know what you talking about."

"And I don't care about what I'm talking about," she offered in an uninterested tone as she reached for another slice of bacon to chew on and closed her eyes.

She opened her eyes behind her shades a few moments later and was glad to see he was gone. It took everything she had in her not to tell him that his chest hair was so sparse and so prickly that it looked like a connect-the-dots sheet in a puzzle book.

He didn't work. He was barely cute. And he was cheating on his wife while she worked the late-night shift.

"Nope. Not even cute. No, thank you. I'll pass," she said aloud as she kicked off her patent leather spiked heels and kicked her feet over the side of the car.

The slight breeze felt good as she wiggled her toes

and considered just hitting the highway and driving until she was ready to turn around and come back.

Or maybe she could call an ex-lover for a steamy rendezvous. If DJ Jean from Paris called, she might just answer his call to amuse herself.

Or she could go and watch *The Young and the Restless* with Mrs. Harper and pretend a stuffed dead dog wasn't sitting in a dog bed. Staring. Not living. His physical form was locked in the crazy world of a little old lady who refused to accept that the dog was dead. And stuffed. And not listening to her.

"Man, bump this shit," she said, sitting up to pull on her shoes before she climbed from the car.

Quint pulled up and parked in the empty space next to her.

Kaitlyn spared him a glance as she gathered her purse and take-out container before raising the roof.

"You really like chancing it with the birds," he said as he came around the front of his truck.

Kaitlyn shrugged. "Bird shit woulda broke up the monotony."

Quint eyed her. "Is it okay to ask you something?"

Kaitlyn leaned against her car and eyed him from behind her shades as she pretended not to feel her pulse and her heart and stomach fluttering. *He really looks good in dark blue.*

"No insults. Not today," she advised him. "And last night never happened."

"No, you wished last night never happened."

Kaitlyn crossed her arms over her chest. "That's not a question."

"Okay. A'ight. What do you want to be when you grow up?"

* * *

Quint eyed Kaitlyn as he asked the question. He saw her visibly stiffen. "Seriously," he added.

"I am grown . . . or can't you tell?" she asked.

He allowed his eyes to travel along the length of her body. How could he not see that? And when he left her apartment in the wee hours of the morning, he found he couldn't release all the nervous energy he felt. He couldn't forget how being so near to her had made him feel.

He couldn't get past how soft her skin was to his touch.

The glazed look in her eyes.

The slight parting of her lips.

The shiver that raced across her body.

All of those moments came back to him until he did feel horny and frustrated, as she had accused.

He had meant to taunt and tease her; and instead, she had turned the tables to taunt and tease him.

"Say you want me, Quinton."

Caught up in that energy-filled bubble they had created, he realized that the words had almost tumbled from his lips. It took everything in him not to lift her up and press his body between her legs as they wrapped around his waist and he buried his head in her cleavage.

Quint blinked away an image of caressing her breasts and rubbing them before his fingertips brought her nipples to life.

"Uhm, physically . . . yes. But on other levels—"

Kaitlyn frowned. "What other levels?" she snapped.

Quint opened his own take-out container and lifted his cheeseburger to take a huge bite of it as he shrugged one shoulder. "Since you moved in here, I've seen you constantly on the go, partying it up, dressed like an A-list celebrity, but what else is there to know about you?"

Kaitlyn raised her shades. "Why do you care?" she asked, eyeing him.

"I don't."

"Then why ask?"

"Because you should care," he said frankly before taking another bite.

"Who says I don't?"

Quint set his container on the hood of his pickup. "Not 'who says' it. *What says* it. And what says you don't are your actions. That's what."

Kaitlyn pulled her tote up higher on her arm as she walked past him. "You are the most judgmental person I think I have ever met. Thing is, you really need to find somebody who gives a damn what you think," she told him over her shoulder as she climbed the stairs.

"It's your life," Quint called over his shoulder as he picked up the container and made his way across the parking lot to his office. He didn't spare her another glance as he unlocked the door.

He had more important things to concern himself with than trying to stop a woman from making a train wreck of her life. He only had one daughter to raise—he didn't need a second project.

Their little convo just reaffirmed for him that his physical reaction to Kaitlyn was just that—purely physical. She was another Vita in the making, no matter how much that offended her.

Hell with it.

He checked the answering machine for messages and shot his boss an e-mail updating him on the property. Through the window he saw the FedEx truck drive onto the property. He rose to his feet and looked out the door as the deliveryman made his way to his apartment's front door.

Quint made his way across the parking lot as the man knocked. He was holding a sizable box in his arms. Quint's eyes shifted up to take in Kaitlyn sitting outside her door in one of the chairs from her kitchen table. He ignored her.

"That's for me?" he asked the man.

The tall, fair-skinned redhead turned. "This your apartment?" he asked, his accent more Texas twang than Southern drawl.

Quint unlocked the door to prove it and then digitally signed for the box before looking down at the label.

"Have a good one," he called out to the man before backing into the apartment to set the box on the oversized coffee table.

It was from Vita.

Quint shook his head as he reached for his cell phone to call her. He ended the call before it connected when he remembered the five-hour time difference. It was just a little after 7:00 A.M. in Hawaii.

Lei's birthday was next week, and Vita had promised their daughter she was coming to visit. He hoped her sending this box wasn't because she wasn't coming anymore. That's what it had meant in the past. Big boxes filled with gifts would arrive a week before Christmas, birthdays, and other important events and milestones in Lei's life.

Quint walked the box into her bedroom and set it on the middle of her made bed. He spotted her Teen Nick calendar open to the month of October in the center of her wall of posters. She had placed a huge star around her birthday on the twenty-first and a circle around the seventeenth with *MOMMY!!!* written in pink Magic Marker.

He eyed the box as he left the room and closed her door securely.

He loved his daughter to death, but marrying Vita and choosing her to mother his child was the biggest mistake of his life. The absolute biggest. Sometimes he felt even more disgusted with himself than he did with his ex-wife.

Life was about choices.

Quint made his way back to his office. He started to look up to see if Kaitlyn was still sitting outside wasting her life away, but then he didn't. He busied himself going through the small stack of work orders for repairs in the various apartments.

The door swung open and he looked up, surprised to see Kaitlyn standing in the doorway. He leaned back in his chair and eyed her as she stood there glaring at him.

"You don't know me," she said.

"I know plenty like you," he said.

"The hell?" she snapped, stepping inside the building as the door swung all the way open. "It takes more than copping a free feel and getting a semihard to come out of your mouth to me any kind of way."

"Did I strike a nerve?" he asked.

Kaitlyn placed her hands on his desk and leaned over. "And what if I tell you what I see about you?"

Quint sat up in his chair and pressed his elbows to the desk as he looked up at her. "You taken a moment out of your life to pay attention to someone other than yourself to form an opinion? Then give it to me."

"You're an asshole."

"That's the best you got?"

"That's all the effort you deserve."

Quint's eyes flew over every aspect of her face. A beautiful woman. An even more beautiful mess. "And you're a spoiled heiress who is creating a life where she has no choice but to become a trophy wife so that staying pretty and dressing fly is all you have to fill your head with."

Kaitlyn stood up straight. "So it's my fault my parents have built a legacy for me."

"No, but it's your fault if you do nothing with it but shop and lounge all day," he countered.

The wind suddenly rustled the browning leaves as fall geared up to reign with the coming of fall. With a swift gush, which raised the corners of the papers on his desk, the door slammed shut.

Kaitlyn jumped and let out a surprised yelp as she turned to press her ass against the desk. "I thought somebody just bust off a round," she said, her hand pressed to her chest.

Quint caught a whiff of her perfume. It was the same that she wore last night. Soft and subtle. Teasing. Intriguing.

He shook his head to clear it. His thoughts shifted from the sight of her body in those formfitting leggings to the disappointment he just knew his daughter was about to experience. Again.

"Was being a manager of a low-level apartment complex the dreams you had for yourself?" Kaitlyn asked.

He looked up at her. "You are a beautiful mess."

Kaitlyn frowned.

Quint rose to his feet and came around the desk to open the door to the office. He waved her out.

Kaitlyn turned on her heels and took the few steps to stand before him. "You shouldn't dish it if you can't take it," she said, looking up at him.

"There's a difference between a low-blow insult and an observation," he told her, looking down into her eyes.

"Yes, and it depends on the viewpoint of the one being observed," she said.

He saw her eyes shift down to his mouth, and that made his heart pound as the wind carried her scent to him. His eyes drifted over her face, and it struck him how much of what he saw appealed to him. Excited him.

And he saw that she, too, felt whatever it was brewing between them. It was there in her eyes and in the quickened pace of her breathing.

But as much as something drew him, Quint knew he had to resist.

Kaitlyn Strong excited him too much, and passion like that could become addictive.

Kaitlyn turned and left the building.

He forced himself not to watch her walk away, but he felt the loss of her presence so close to him. He closed the door and reclaimed his seat, forcing his thoughts anywhere but on Kaitlyn.

He glanced at the time on his cell phone before he dialed his ex-wife.

"Yeah."

Quint frowned at the male voice. In two years that had never happened.

"Sorry. I was trying to reach Vita," he said. "Do I have the right number?"

"Who's this?"

"Quinton, her ex-husband."

His earpiece suddenly filled with rustling noises and lowered voices whispering before she got on the line.

"What do you want, Quint?" she asked, sounding extra salty.

"I got the box for Lei that you sent, and with you coming next week, I wanted to make sure you wasn't flaking out," he said patiently, not at all concerned with whatever relationship drama of hers he had just interrupted. His concern was their daughter.

The line remained quiet. Too quiet.

"What is it this time, Vita? Huh? Your man don't trust you long enough to leave his sight?" he asked, already dreading breaking the news to Lei. "Hell, bring him along. I just want you here for our daughter."

"Tell Lei to call me and let me know if she loves her presents," she said, sounding far too light and bright and jovial.

Quinton rubbed his hand over his bald head and wasn't surprised at the beads of perspiration that coated his hand. His dome always sweated when he was heated—in sex or in anger.

"You haven't laid eyes on your daughter in two damn years. He was worth you ruining our marriage, but is he worth you ruining your relationship with your daughter?" he asked in exasperation, slamming his hand on the desk.

"Oh, okay, then. Bye," she said before ending the call.

At first Quinton could do nothing but stare at the phone. He dialed the number back, but he already knew it would go straight to voice mail.

He turned his chair and leaned back against the wall as he kicked his Timberlands up on the desk. He purposefully thought back to the days they had lived together as a family. Had Vita shown signs then that she could one day become the type of mother to leave her child behind? He couldn't go so far as to say she didn't love Lei. He just believed she loved *herself* more.

Quint stayed reflective and lost in thoughts, glad that none of the residents or any business intruded on him. He was surprised when he heard the sound of the school bus pulling to a stop in front of the complex. The laughter and noises of children soon followed.

It took less than five minutes before the office door opened. Lei was standing there in her white polo shirt and khaki pants, with the gold shoes that Kaitlyn gave her. In her hand was the box from her mother.

He looked up at her heart-shaped face and his gut literally clenched at the look on her face.

"She's not coming, is she?" she asked, stepping farther inside to drop the box on the desk, next to his feet.

Quint sat up straight and swung his feet down to the floor as he reached across the box and cupped her hand.

"No, baby, she's not coming. She's gonna call you later to explain," he said gently.

"'Kay," Lei said. She tucked her chin to her chest as she fingered the box before picking it up into her hands and turning to leave.

"Hey," Quint called out to her. "You okay?"

"It's not like she works, or she doesn't have the money to come or send for me, 'cause she always sending me stuff," she answered, without turning around, and then walked out of the office.

Quint picked up his cell phone and tried Vita's number again. Voice mail. Sometimes he wished she had just disappeared for good and had never contacted

Lei because the ups and down of her lies and disappointments might affect their daughter far worse.

Later that evening Kaitlyn was on the phone listening to her niece, Kadina, tell her about an upcoming fashion show at her school when there was a soft knock at her door. She climbed off the couch and opened the door, not at all surprised to see Lei standing there. But she was surprised at the preteen's sad expression.

"What's wrong?" Kaitlyn asked, stepping back to open the door and reaching for her wrist to pull her inside gently.

Lei just shrugged her shoulders.

"Kadina, let me call you back," she said into the phone.

"Okay. I have to give the baby a bath, anyway."

Beep.

Kaitlyn crossed her arms over her chest as she walked over to where Lei sat, slumped on her sofa.

"Ooh. Don't frown. You'll have wrinkles before you're thirty."

"I just talked to my mom and she said she wasn't coming for my birthday again."

Kaitlyn's heart tugged.

In the days since she moved into the apartment, the little girl came to visit her often, and a few times she alluded to feeling neglected by her mom. Kaitlyn never knew quite what to say then . . . or now.

"She just messed up my whole birthday."

Kaitlyn sat down on the sofa next to her. "Lei, you *never* let anybody steal your joy," she said gently. "It's your birthday. Your day. And you're becoming an official teenager. Come on . . . that is way too fly to let anybody stop you from enjoying it."

Lei looked up and smiled a little. "I'll like being a teenager," she said, her eyes brightening.

Kaitlyn snapped her fingers. "Of course. It separates the little kids from the young adults, and that's too fabulous for words."

Lei sat up a bit straighter.

"Are you having a party?"

Lei shook her head. "I told my dad I didn't want one because I thought I would spend the day with my mom," she admitted, sounding disappointed again.

Kaitlyn rose to her feet. "Where's Quint?" she asked.

"Probably in his shed," Lei said.

"That big building in the back?" Kaitlyn asked, pointing her thumb toward the rear of the apartment.

Lei nodded. "That's his carpentry shed. He brought it from his house so he could build things while we're living here," she said, picking up the *Vogue* magazine Kaitlyn had been flipping through earlier during her day of boredom.

Carpentry shed?

His house?

Build things?

Kaitlyn opened her mouth to ask the many questions running through her mind, but she decided against it. It really wasn't any of her business.

"You head home. I have some things I have to take care of," Kaitlyn told her.

"Yes, ma'am." Lei set the magazine back on the sofa.

"You can have it. I'm all done with it," Kaitlyn said, already heading for her kitchen.

"Thanks, Miss Kaitlyn."

Moments later the front door closed behind her.

Kaitlyn left out the back door and paused on the balcony to look down at the metal shed. Indeed, the windows were lit. She had never really paid attention to the shed and just assumed it held tools. All the while it was Quint's hiding place.

She jogged down the stairs as the leaves of the trees rustled from a breeze or from the sudden movements of their inhabitants. She paused on the bottom of the steps, oddly remembering being a teenager sneaking with a boyfriend into the woods for a first kiss, and then being scared shitless by the sounds of rustling trees because she thought one of her brothers had caught them.

Kaitlyn smiled.

Growing up on Strong Ranch had been fun for a kid. She had been way more fearless and rough like her brothers. Back then, she hadn't cared about walking barefoot through grass heated by the summer sun, or riding bareback on her horse, or skinny-dipping in a cool pond.

But those days are over, she thought, trying to remember the last time she rode the horse that she had received for her sixth birthday. It had been years.

Kaitlyn continued down the stairs and across the paved yard to Quint's shed. She knocked on the metal door lightly and stepped back in case it swung out.

And it did.

Quint looked down at her; his handsome face was filled with surprise.

Kaitlyn was surprised by her nervousness. There wasn't much that rattled her. Not much at all. Except this man.

"I hate to interrupt you," she said, looking past

him briefly into the shed. "Uhm . . . I wanted to talk to you about Lei."

For a moment Kaitlyn actually thought he was going to send her on her way.

"Can we talk in here?" he asked. "Is that okay?"

Kaitlyn looked past him again. The shed was no more than ten feet by ten feet, and there was a large worktable in the center and several carved wooden frames in another corner. Along the back was an armoire partially covered by a large white drop cloth. Amid these items there wasn't much space left.

But she stepped inside and pulled the metal door closed behind her.

CHAPTER 9

Quint turned his back to the door as he set his tool on the center of the huge piece of wood before turning back to face her. He was so tall that his head completely blocked the ceiling light and caused the interior to darken. She came up to stand beside him. And in the few seconds after she did, it was hard to deny the intimacy of being side by side with him in a place so small and contained. And warm.

"You did that?" she asked.

Quint nodded.

"I didn't know you were so clever with your hands," she said, looking up at him.

And Quint looked down at her. The light from the ceiling illuminated his eyes. "Oh, you didn't?" he asked, kind of flirty and cocky.

Maybe an offhand reference to her reaction to his touch in her kitchen?

Kaitlyn's body tingled as they continued to stare at each other.

"No, I didn't, Quin-ton," she said lightly and teasingly, hoping to lighten the mood. She was the first to look away as she lightly traced her finger along the grooves of the wood.

"My grandfather taught me to work with all types of wood when I first moved to South Carolina from New York," he said.

Kaitlyn's eyes filled with understanding. "Oh, that's why you're so rude. It's an East Coast thing. You're not a country boy," she said.

"And that's a bad thing?" Quint asked. He smiled and his dimples deepened in his chocolate cheeks.

Kaitlyn completely lost her breath at the sight of him.

"I don't believe in stereotypes," he said, picking up one of the tools lying on the untouched center of the wood.

"Funny, you seemed to have attached quite a few to me," she said.

Quint glanced briefly at her over his broad shoulder. "I think you've attached quite a few to yourself."

Kaitlyn held up her hand. "Not another lecture, please," she said. "I have a father and four older brothers for that."

"Oh, so I'm not the only one telling you to grow up—"

"An-y-way," Kaitlyn said loudly, cutting him off with a wave of her hand. "I wanted to know if I could organize a pajama party weekend for Lei and a few of her friends."

Quint rose to his full height with his slashing eyebrows dipping as he eyed her. "Did she ask you to?"

Kaitlyn moved to sit on the wooden stool by the door. "Did you make this too?" she asked before sitting on it.

"Yes," Quint answered patiently.

"You're really good," she said, lifting the drop cloth to sigh at the sight of the armoire with Lei's name engraved on the front doors. "Is that for her birthday?"

When Quint didn't respond, she looked over at him. He was standing there, staring at her.

"Kaitlyn, can you focus?" he asked.

Kaitlyn's natural instinct was to flash one of her beguiling smiles, which usually got her whatever she wanted from a man. Any man. Except Quinton Wells. So why bother?

"I'm focused. What's up?" she asked, sitting up straight on the stool as she crossed her legs.

His eyes dipped down to take in the move.

Kaitlyn arched an eyebrow. She knew the leggings she wore put emphasis on the hips and thighs she inherited from her mother. Had Quint noticed? He was rude and judgmental at times, but he was still a man.

"Did Lei ask for a pajama party?" he asked again.

Kaitlyn uncrossed and then crossed her other leg, but this time Quint missed the move as he focused his attention on his carving.

"No, no, she didn't," she said, sliding back off the stool as she eased around his body to stand on the other side of the table. "She was looking sad about her mom not coming, and she's turning thirteen, and I thought maybe something extra girlie and extra fun would be needed to focus on what's really important . . . her birthday."

"She talks to you a lot, huh?" he asked.

Kaitlyn nodded as she bent slightly to study the intricate details of the carvings. "Girl things. PMS. Boys—"

"Boys!" Quinton said sharply, his handsome face alarmed.

"Yes, and clothes. School. You know, things a little girl does not want to tell her daddy."

"She's not old enough for some little boy to be sniffing at her skirts," he said sternly.

Kaitlyn twisted her lips. "But she doesn't wear skirts," she said.

"You know what I mean."

Kaitlyn rolled her eyes. "Don't worry, Quint. Lei is not interested in the grungy little boys in class. She's more worried about which one of Mindless Behavior is the cutest each week."

"Mindless Behavior?" Quint asked.

Kaitlyn sighed as she picked up one of the tools. "Four cute little boys who sing in a group."

"Oh." Quint looked up at her and then reached out with his hand. "Careful, that's really—"

Kaitlyn cried out as the blade of the tool sliced into the flesh of her index finger when she lightly touched it. She instantly dropped it as her blood began to seep from the cut.

"Shit," Quint swore as he stepped over and held her hand. He studied the cut. "I hope you don't need stitches."

The combination of Quint's nearness and the thought of stitches made Kaitlyn's knees give out a little bit. She leaned her hip against the table for support as Quint released her long enough to jerk off his long-sleeved tee. He wiped up some of the dripping blood before tearing off a strip of the bottom with his teeth to bandage her finger.

Kaitlyn barely felt the steady throbbing of her wound as she closed her eyes and dragged her suddenly parched tongue across her lips to keep from the total impact of Quint's now-bare upper body. The man had the physique of an Olympian.

His body is bananas.

"I need to keep a first aid kit back here," he said.

Kaitlyn opened her eyes and looked down at his hands applying the pressure before she looked over at his body again.

"I grew up on a horse ranch. I know better than just picking up tools. I wasn't thinking. I was distracted. . . ."

Her words faded off as she looked up and found Quint's deep-set eyes on her.

"By what?" he asked.

"Huh?"

"What distracted you?"

Kaitlyn couldn't look away from him. "You," she admitted softly.

His eyes deepened in intensity.

"No, I meant—"

The rest of her words were swallowed into his mouth as Quinton dipped his head to cover her mouth with his. The first feel of it was softness before he wrapped one arm around her waist; then he swiftly lifted her body up to hold against the length of him as he first touched her lips with his tongue.

A shiver raced across Kaitlyn's body and she moaned in hunger as she brought up her uninjured hand to press against the back of his bald head.

"Oh, my God," she moaned into his open mouth in between a dozen small kisses, which were electric and fevered and urgent.

Every pulse point on her body ached and throbbed. Her heart pounded. Their chemistry was off the charts, and she honestly wondered if she had ever felt something *so* intense and *so* wicked.

Quinton backed them up until her back was pressed against the chilly metal of the shed's back wall. Her gasp was a mix of the shock of the cold mingled with the heat they created. She broke their kiss to take in deep breaths as they stared across the short distance at one another.

She brought her hand up to press against his chest.

And she loved that he seemed as affected as she was.

Glazed eyes.

Pounding heart.

Arousal. Desire. Want.

Quint used his strength to lift her body higher against the wall. Her small but plump and pert breasts were now sitting in his face.

Kaitlyn arched her back and raised her shirt above her head to fling it onto the wood shavings covering the floor.

"I knew you wore some sexy shit," he said low in his throat as he took in the black sheer bralet. The lingerie did nothing to hide that her areolas were large and brown, and her nipples were thick and hard as they strained against the material.

"So you thought about me in some sexy shit?" she asked.

Quint didn't answer. Instead, he dipped his head and sucked her nipple hotly through the material.

"Oh, my God. *Yes!*" She sighed as she jerked his head back and freed her nipple to completely tear open the front of her bra.

The move shook him as he looked up at her in surprise. He increased his intensity before rubbing his smooth face against her cleavage. He moaned as he extended his tongue and flickered it against her nipple.

Kaitlyn's clit pulsated as heat infused her body.

Quint turned his head to press his face against her other breast before tracing the outline of her entire areola before circling inside the bumpy brown skin of it, until his tongue dragged against her taut nipple.

Kaitlyn cried out.

"I wanna be inside you," he whispered against her skin as he let her body slide down his.

She gasped at the feel of her hard nipples against his hard, contoured chest. "Quinton," she sighed in pleasure as his hands massaged the fullness of her buttocks as he pressed kisses to the side of her face.

Kaitlyn tilted her head up; and as if synced into her desire, Quint kissed a trail to her throat before pressing his lips to her racing pulse.

"Yes," she whispered with each kiss. Each and every kiss. "Yes . . . yes . . . yes."

Quinton gently jerked her leggings down around her hips.

She felt the cold metal of the wall against the bare flesh of her ass and her eyes opened, jarring her from the sexual daze she was in. Even with her heart pounding, she shook her head and struggled for her composure.

"I can't do this. We can't do this. I'm not sexing some dude *in a shed,* and we not even dating, going out, chilling. No! No-no-no-no-no. I am not going out like that. *No.*"

Quint let his head fall back as he released a frustrated breath through his mouth as he held up his hands and stepped back from her. "Hey. No problem. 'No' means *no.*"

Kaitlyn jerked her leggings back up and snatched her shirt from the floor. She slid it over her head with wood chips stuck to it and all.

"Nothing like that. Definitely not nothing like that. I just . . . I got caught up in the moment. I can't front—you sexy as fuck, but I just never did one-night stands. That's not me."

Quint turned from her, and Kaitlyn knew he was waiting on his erection to die down.

"I'm not a tease. I just didn't think," she said into the silence.

Quint grabbed his shirt and held it over his crotch before he faced her. "Hey, don't apologize and explain. It's cool. Honestly, I'm glad that one of us came to our senses. Even though I know it woulda been hella good, it woulda been a mistake because I'm not looking for a relationship."

"Yeah . . . yeah, you right," she said, covering up her disappointment as she moved past him to the door of the shed. She had to get the hell out of there . . . ASAP! "So . . . uh . . . uhm . . . Lei's slumber party?"

Quint wiped his face with his hand. "That's cool. I understand she rather hang out with her friends than chill with her pops," he said good-naturedly.

"Okay." Kaitlyn turned and opened the door.

"Kaitlyn."

Her heart pounded in her chest as she turned.

"Just let me know how much you need to throw her a really nice party," he said as the light cast shadows against his chest.

"Sure," she told him, and then hurried to leave the shed and close the door behind her.

She allowed herself a moment to lean back against the door. When she stopped Quint, she had foolishly thought they could spend a little time together and get to know each other first. But he just admitted that sex was all it would have been for him.

She felt even better for not letting things go too far, but it was never an easy pill to swallow when any man saw you as the jump-off/one-night/no-strings-attached chick. That wasn't Kaitlyn at all.

Not even a week of spending time in romantic Paris had made her give up the panties. There was no way she was handing over her goodies that easily to any man.

Not even Quint Wells—the man with the body that seemed to be chiseled in stone.

Was his dick just as hard as the rest of his body?

Kaitlyn allowed herself a deep shiver at that thought as she finally made her way over, to climb the rear staircase.

Quint's dick was hard.

He was a man of honor and would never press himself on any woman, but he couldn't lie and say he wasn't disappointed as hell when Kaitlyn put the brakes on. Suddenly pulling away all of her goodies had made his heart pound just as heavily as the excitement of knowing she tasted and felt just as good as he knew she would.

Soft breasts. Tasty, dark chocolate nipples and large areolas.

The memory of them kept him hard, and Quint busied himself cleaning his tools. However, as he stroked the long tool inside the towel, he couldn't help but take the seemingly innocent move and replace it with his tool stroking deeply inside Kaitlyn, with her legs wrapped around his waist.

Quint's dick strained against his boxers, and he tossed the tool and cloth across the worktable.

Her sexy brassiere. Her even sexier open and uninhibited reactions. The moans. The cries.

"Oh, my God. Yes!"

Quint placed his hands on his waist and looked down at his erection. His dog was definitely on the hunt for a cat. Kaitlyn's cat.

Would he have sexed her right here in his shed and put in work too? Yes. But he would have regretted it if she regretted it later, because she was looking for more than sex.

And that's all Quint had to offer her.

In hindsight he couldn't let his desire for her cloud his judgment.

Their chemistry could get addictive. And now that he knew that he had been wrong to assume she was the rich party girl down for one-night fun—he really couldn't go there. Kaitlyn Strong was off-limits.

Quint grabbed his cell phone and shot a quick text off to Joni: U Busy?

Bzzzzzz . . .

He opened the incoming text from her: NO. U COMING THRU?

And it was simple and easy with her. They hadn't hooked up in weeks and barely called or texted each other in the interim. Joni knew the rules and played by them. Hell, she helped set them.

Quint left his shed and locked it. The fall winds whipped around his bare chest. He glanced up at Kaitlyn's kitchen window. The light was out. *What's she doing?* he wondered before continuing around the front of the building to enter his apartment.

Lei was lying on the couch, reading a book. She looked up and then did a double take at his bare chest.

Quint shook his head. "Don't ask," he told her over his shoulder, on the way to his bedroom to grab another shirt.

Coming back into the living room, he pulled the

shirt on over his head. "Lei, ask Mrs. Harper if you could sit with her for a couple of hours."

"She can stay with me."

Kaitlyn?

Quint finished jerking his shirt over his head and found Kaitlyn sitting next to Lei on his sofa. His heartbeat picked up the pace double time.

"I was just telling Lei about her birthday pajama party," Kaitlyn said, avoiding his eyes. "I thought you were still out back."

Lei bounced off the chair and came rushing at Quint to throw her arms around his waist. "Thank you, Daddy," she said sweetly.

And that made his heart tug. He loved his daughter, and he had to admit he appreciated Kaitlyn stepping in to make her feel better about her mother not coming.

"Thank you," he mouthed over Lei's head.

Kaitlyn smiled weakly and rose to her feet. "So, anyway, we can go upstairs and plan while your dad . . . makes a run," she said, with an arch of her brow, before she continued to the door. "Just come up when you're ready, Lei."

"I'm coming now. Bye, Daddy," she said.

Quint followed them out the door and made his way to his Ford truck. Behind the wheel he looked up to see Kaitlyn glancing over her shoulder at him before she entered her apartment behind his daughter.

Starting the car, he headed out of the parking lot and drove the short distance to Joni's. He pulled into the driveway in front of the small brick home she rented from the Jamison twins, two of the most successful privately owned home-building contractors in the state. In the last few years, the brothers had gotten into acquiring homes, repairing them, and then renting them out or flipping them for profit.

Before he could climb out of his vehicle, the door of the house opened and Joni filled the doorway in nothing but a short tee and boy shorts. She smiled at him as he came up the walkway and the small front steps.

"Hey, stranger," she said, wrapping her arms around his neck to press her mouth against his—and her thick curvy body too.

Quint had to admit that Joni had one of the best bodies ever. She worked out five days a week; and not only was she thick, but she was solid and well toned—and she knew it. She was soft where she needed to be soft, and firm where she needed to be firm.

"I was just thinking about you," Joni whispered against the corner of his mouth as he closed the door behind them.

"You was?" Quint asked as he gripped her hips and pulled her closer to him as she suckled his neck . . . in the same spot Kaitlyn had just hotly licked him less than thirty minutes ago.

"I can't do this," he said, raising his hand to undo her arms from around his neck as he stepped back from her.

He couldn't get riled up by Kaitlyn and then come use Joni's body to get it off. Even though he knew Joni wouldn't care, that wasn't the kind of man he wanted to be. Especially with Kaitlyn now babysitting his daughter.

For him that felt like a low-life move. Something for an immature man or a man in his early twenties. Not him. Not a grown-ass man more than happy to be over thirty, and full grown physically and mentally.

"Something . . . *wrong*?" she asked, with a swift glance down at his zipper.

"No. Noooooooo. Nah, I'm straight," Quint said. "I just changed my mind."

Joni shrugged and dropped down on her sofa to pick up her TV remote. "No problem," she said nonchalantly.

Quint eyed her. He was used to Joni being real-laid back in their dealings, but this complete uncaring was odd at best. Like psychopath odd. Or she-had-another-dude-lined-up-to-replace-you odd.

Giving her one last glance over his shoulder, he left her house and made his way back to his vehicle. As he started his truck and reversed out of her yard, he felt completely unsettled.

He was on the edge of being in trouble.

As Joni had pressed her body to his, kissed his mouth and then his neck, all he could think was he had never felt as much electric chemistry with any woman like he had with Kaitlyn. He had compared Joni and Kaitlyn—one woman he bedded quite often in the past to one woman he had never slept with— and Joni had lost. He had turned down good sex because his thoughts were on the woman who had turned him down and frustrated him at every turn.

All of that spelled nothing but trouble for him, and trouble was Kaitlyn Strong.

Kaitlyn tossed and turned in her bed. She kicked the sheets off her body for a few moments and then reached out in the darkness to pull them back up over her. She sat up in bed to snatch off the silk scarf holding the short curls in place. Then she thought about not having the money in her budget for the month to hit the hairdresser's, so she climbed out of bed to find the scarf on the floor and retie her head.

She was completely frustrated and out of sorts.

A man like Quinton Wells was nothing at all like what she usually favored. He was brash and outspoken and brutally honest. He was rough around the edges. He cared nothing about designer clothing and the latest fashion for men. She couldn't see him strolling through Paris or jetting off to some foreign land.

Quint reminded her of her brothers. Hardworking, simple men who could be found in their boots and jeans putting in sixty hours a week or better to take care of their family—except Kaeden, who favored suits and indoor activities, but he still lived an uncomplicated life with Jade.

She had nothing against her brothers, and she loved them all, but she had always seen their lives as boring and ordinary. She had always thought she was the adventurer. The dream seeker. The one to see the world and live in it. She always had more in her life than Holtsville, South Carolina.

And so although she loved her brothers, she could never imagine dating a man like them . . . a man like Quinton Wells.

But she could also admit that of the few boyfriends she had over the years—the ones blessed enough to make love to her—she had never experienced the kind of wild abandon that Quint had created in her. He made her tingle from her toes to the small and fine hairs on the back of her neck.

Quint made her feel like there was a door inside of her that had never been opened. And behind that door was true passion. A wildness. A lack of inhibition.

"Them rich boys don't know how to handle all

that. You too much woman for them. But me? I'll tear that ass up, and you know it, and you want it. Don't you?"

Kaitlyn rolled over in bed and pounded her pillow.

The truth did hurt.

She wasn't a virgin to sex, but she was a virgin to passion.

The feel of Quint's tongue on her nipples had damn near brought her to an explosion, and she could recall some full-blown sex acts that hadn't elicited near a response from her.

But Kaitlyn didn't do casual sex, and she wasn't quite sure she was sold on even wanting to date Quint.

Rock. Hard place.

And she hated—absolutely hated—that it bugged her all night that he headed out. It was quite clear that it was none of her business, but had he gone to another woman to finish what they had begun, but she had ended?

She flipped over in bed again before kicking off the covers and making her way to the kitchen to pour herself a glass of wine. She left the kitchen and made her way out the front door, being sure the door was unlocked, before she stood out on the balcony. In her old apartment she would have been able to faintly hear the lake's movement. She missed the peace it used to give her.

Her current view couldn't compete.

Kaitlyn sighed.

Moments later she heard: "You can't sleep either, huh?"

She looked down to see Quinton now standing on the sidewalk, looking up at her.

First she felt a thrill of excitement at the very sight of him in his beater tee and pajama bottoms.

And then she thought of him making love to another woman less than an hour after sucking her titties and she had to fight the urge to pour her wine down on his face.

Finally she just shook her head and took a sip of wine.

Quinton looked down at his feet and then back up at her. "Wanna talk?" he asked.

It tugged at her heart that he sounded so unsure, when he was usually so confident.

"What's to talk about?" she asked, even as that familiar excitement he caused coursed over her body.

He started to say something, but then he closed his mouth before he turned and headed up the stairs. "Stay there!" he called up to her.

Kaitlyn just sipped her wine and hoped the effects kicked in so that she could finally sleep. Deep sleep. Colored-dreams sleep. Don't-hear-the-alarm-go-off sleep.

Quint came to stand by her at the rail. "I apologize for earlier and the other night," he began.

Kaitlyn looked down in the center of her wine goblet and swirled it, as if she were a professional wine taster. "Well, the previous time I taunted you and we were playing one-up on each other—so no apologies, and then this time I will accept your apology for assuming I'm a one-nighter," she said, cutting her eyes over at him. "That is what you thought, right?"

Quinton reached up and brushed her bangs off her face.

Kaitlyn trembled.

"I did assume that," he admitted, dropping his hand. "But I'm man enough to admit when I'm wrong."

"So no worries," she said.

Quint was silent.

So was Kaitlyn.

"With the way Lei's mom dropped out of her life . . . I'm not interested in getting into a relationship with anyone," he said suddenly.

Kaitlyn nodded and took another sip of her wine. "Just 'wham bam, thank you, ma'am,' huh?" she asked into her glass.

Quint smiled. "Not all rude and whorish like that, but yeah. Kinda," he admitted.

Kaitlyn glanced over at him. "And as much as I can admit you turn me on—"

"Oh yeah?" he asked, looking at her.

Kaitlyn made the motion to flip her hair over her shoulder, but then she remembered she cut her hair over a year ago. "You know that already. Just like I know—*Just. Like. I. Know*—that I do it for you, Quinton," she said with the utmost confidence.

"Oh yeah?" he asked again.

Kaitlyn turned to face him as she braced her hip against the railing. "Oh no?" she countered.

Quinton bit his lip to keep from smiling as she continued to eye him like she *dared him* to deny it.

"I want you," he admitted.

Kaitlyn toasted his honesty before she took another sip. "But you and I would never work, because I respect you putting Lei first, and I hope you respect that I don't do casual sex. Soooo . . ."

"Here we are," Quinton said, his eyes enjoying the feast of her beautiful face lit by the moon.

She really is pretty, he thought.

"'Here we are the two of us together,'" she sang off-key.

Quint laughed. "What you know about Atlantic Starr?" he asked.

"'Secret Lovers' is classic," she told him.

"True, true," Quint agreed.

They fell silent again.

Kaitlyn took another sip of her wine as she cast him a look. "I know you have friends, right? I mean, there's not too many grown men that are celibate."

"I have friends," Quint admitted. "Willing friends."

Kaitlyn nodded. "And was one of those *willing* friends extra willing tonight, Mr. Wells?" she asked before tilting her head back to finish the last of her wine.

Quint looked up at the moon and then back over at her. "I didn't make love to another woman tonight, Kaitlyn," he said softly but firmly.

She believed him. "You and I would be *so* good," she added as she turned to sashay back into her apartment.

"Damn good," he called behind her just before she closed the door.

CHAPTER 10

Kaitlyn fell back against her door as soon as she closed it. She closed her eyes and tilted her head back as she waited for normalcy. Everything felt like it was on overload.

"I want you."

She smiled softly as his words seemed to float over her body like the caress of his hands. Quinton Wells made her completely breathless. Completely.

His beauty was evident.

His physique was flawless.

His touch was electric.

His smile was charismatic.

The man had her *all* the way gone.

And the fact they both admitted it—but accepted that it couldn't be—made her want him all the more. The temptation of it was addictive.

She pursed her lips and pressed her hand to her neck to feel her pulse rapidly racing against her fingertips.

It would have been so easy to turn and tell him to come inside her apartment and then inside her.

So very easy.

So very, very easy . . .

* * *

Kaitlyn turns and opens the door, surprised to see Quint still standing there outside her door, leaning against the railing, as he looks up at the stars and the moon.

"Quint," she calls out softly, enjoying the feel of the night breeze as it drags itself across her naked body.

He turns. At the sight of her nudity, he stands up straight as his eyes miss not one detail of her body: the soft roundness of her shoulders and the dips of her collarbone; her small breasts plump and full; her hips and strong legs; the perfect pear-shaped beauty, with a body meant to be caressed, tasted, and stroked by a man.

But not just by any man. Him. Only him.

Kaitlyn blinks and in a moment he is as naked as she is, and standing before her. She raises her hands above her head with the hint of a smile and thrusts her breasts forward.

"Suck them," she directs him.

And he does.

Bending to glide his hands up her body to cup her breasts, he guides his mouth to one and teases the other with his fingertips as he backs her into the apartment. Wildly he licks away. The tip of his tongue flickers with speed and agility.

Kaitlyn feels like she is high. Floating. On a trip.

"Yes. Yes. Quint . . ." She moans as he kisses a trail to her breasts; she lets the passionate onslaught begin again, until her clit begins to throb and literally aches for release.

But not yet. Half the fun of a mind-blowing climax is the ride to get there. They are only just beginning.

She gasps as he pushes her body against the wall and bends his knees slowly as he moves his kisses to just below her breasts . . . and then her stomach . . . her navel . . . both hips . . . the plump and juicy shaved mound of her pussy . . . her thighs . . . the back of her knees. And all the while his hand stays locked on her breasts. Kneading. Teasing. Gently massaging.

Kaitlyn shivers against the wall, completely over-whelmed by the combined methods of his passion: his hands, his mouth, his tongue, his words.

Praise sings against her heated flesh.

"Your skin is so soft."

"I can smell your sweet pussy."

"Your legs are thick as shit."

"Damn, you sexy."

"I can't wait to stroke inside you."

Kaitlyn bites her bottom lip and looks down at him with sex-crazed eyes. She turns to face the wall, loving the feel of the coolness against the side of her face, and presses her nipples against the surface as she pops her hips to stick her full ass up.

Before she could even ask, Quint slaps her but-tocks.

Whap!

And again. Twice.

Whap! Whap!

Kaitlyn releases a shaky breath, which is a release of pure pleasure.

The first feel of his tongue at the small curve of her back makes her pant. And when he uses his hands to spread her cheeks to kiss her intimately, before licking a trail down to lick her pussy, she flings her head back and cries out.

He presses into her and scoops her ass up higher

as he sucks her pussy lips before sweetly biting each of her cheeks.

"Mmm. Good?" He moans out his question.

She turns and lifts one leg up on his shoulder as she circles her hips and brings her hands up to squeeze her own nipples.

"This is better," she says, looking down into his face.

Quint keeps his eyes locked on hers as he shifts his head to kiss her plush inner thigh. And then the crease of her leg. And then her moist pink clit that is swollen and pulsating in arousal.

He smiles wolfishly before he flickers his tongue against it.

Kaitlyn uses one hand to cup the back of his smooth bald head as she makes tiny circles with her hips, which brings her clit against his tongue.

"Oh, that feels so good," she admits hotly.

He sucks her clit into his mouth.

Her knees buckle and he grasps her hips to hold her upright as he sucks away.

Kaitlyn shivers and bites her bottom lip, closing her eyes.

When she opens them, they are in the middle of her bed with Quint stroking deep inside her from behind as his fingers dig into the flesh of her ass.

"Beg me for this dick," he demands.

Kaitlyn looks over her shoulder at him. "Please. Harder. Harder," she begs.

Her wish is his command, and his strokes deepen until she could feel the soft curls of his hairs brushing against her buttocks.

Kaitlyn blinks again.

She is riding him backward aboard the deck of a yacht.

She blinks again.

They are on a deserted island at the edge of the turquoise sea as Quint kneels in the wet sand, stroking away like a well-oiled piston inside her. She lays on her side, facing him, with her leg across his body and on his shoulder.

She blinks again.

Quint has her body pressed against the base of the Eiffel Tower. His buttocks clench as he makes tiny circles with his hips, sending the length of his dick up against the tightness of her walls as the thick base glides back and forth over her clit.

She blinks again.

They are back in her apartment. His body braces against her front door as Kaitlyn braces her knees on either side of him against the door as she rides him. Furious and fast. Quint's mouth teases her nipples. His tongue circles her areola.

"I'm coming. Yes, I'm coming!" *she shouts as a fine sheen of sweat coats both their bodies.*

"Ssssh, you too loud," *Quint whispers up to her. His eyes stay fiercely locked on her as he enjoys the passion on her face, the feel of her entire body shivering against him, and the tight spasms of her walls against his dick as she comes and coats every inch of him with her juices.*

Kaitlyn cries out again as she wraps her arms around his head and hotly licks his lips.

Knock, knock.

Quint pauses at the sound of the knock against the door.

Kaitlyn continues to ride away against the length of him, too caught up in her white-hot climax to stop for anything.

Knock, knock.

Quinton covers her mouth as her sex noises continue to fill the air.

"The neighbors, Kaitlyn. Somebody's knocking. . . ."

Somebody's knocking.

Somebody's knocking.

Knock, knock.

Knock, knock.

Kaitlyn's eyes opened and she jumped forward off the door as she was jerked from her sexual fantasy. Her wine goblet crashed to the floor from the sudden movement as she struggled for composure. Her face and neck felt flushed. Her clit throbbed. Her panties felt moist. Her nipples were hard.

Swallowing hard, she stepped away and then rose up on her toes to look out the peephole.

Quint.

Kaitlyn dropped back down on her feet and looked down at her nipples, hard and thrusting against the thin material of her T-shirt, which she was wearing to bed. She opened the door and instantly crossed her arms over her chest as she looked up at him.

"Yes?" she said, clearing her throat as she pictured him naked and hard.

"There's broken glass on the floor," he said, stepping inside to begin picking up the pieces.

"Thanks, I have it," she said, reaching down to pull at his strong arm.

Kaitlyn paused at the feel of the dips and grooves of his muscles under her touch. Everything about him was hard. Everything.

"Get the broom for me to get the little pieces

before you miss and cut your foot," he told her, look-ing up briefly.

Kaitlyn released him and stepped over the mess to dash to the kitchen. She took a moment to grab the kitchen counter and breathe, deeply and slowly, as she pressed her thumbs to her revealing nipples.

"You got it?" he called down the hall to her.

She grabbed her broom and dustpan from the pantry. "Coming," she called back before retracing her steps down the hall.

Kaitlyn outstretched her arm to hand him the items.

Quint's eyes shifted from them to her breasts, and then traveled up to her eyes. "You a little cold, huh?" he asked, smiling.

Kaitlyn said nothing as she continued to hold out the broom.

Quint brushed past the broom. "Uhm, I'm not Geof-frey," he quipped.

"Who?" she asked, completely lost.

"This isn't the *Fresh Prince of Bel-Air* and I'm not your butler. Don't give it to me. Use it," he stressed, his hands filled with the larger shards of glass as he carried them into the kitchen to throw away.

Kaitlyn made a face as she quickly swept the entire area and brushed the tiny remnants into the dustpan.

"Oh, you do know how to use it," he teased from behind her.

"Ha-ha," she said dryly before easing past him to dump the glass into the garbage can outside her back door.

"Can I help you with something?" she asked, coming back into the kitchen.

Quint bit back another smile.

"Another late-night repair?"

They both turned and looked out the door at Mrs. Hanson, smiling at them as she shook her head.

"Y'all have a good night," she teased before she continued on to her apartment, two doors down.

Kaitlyn and Quint eyed each other.

"She swears we're dealing," Kaitlyn said.

"I know."

"She is so nice," Kaitlyn added.

"I know that too."

Kaitlyn moved to the door to close it. "Her husband tried to holler at me," she said as soon as the door was closed. "Did you know *that*?"

Quinton frowned deeply. "What?" he snapped.

Kaitlyn nodded. "The same day I was minding my own in my car in the parking lot," she said. "Talking 'bout, can he come sit in the car with me—"

"Like he don't have enough on his plate," Quinton muttered under his breath.

"Exactly," Kaitlyn stressed.

"I don't respect cheating," Quint said, turning to look up at the picture of Kaitlyn hanging on the wall beside him. "Just end the relationship and save everyone the heartache."

Kaitlyn walked over to stand beside him and peer up at the homage to herself as well.

"True," she agreed.

"Is that a weave?" he asked.

"No," Kaitlyn stressed.

Quint glanced at her face. "The shorter hair brings out your eyes more, but why'd you cut it?"

Kaitlyn shifted her eyes to him and then playfully

posed. "It's just hair. It'll grow back, if I let it," she said. "Just like it would all be silver, if I let it."

That obviously surprised him.

"My whole family is prematurely gray. We get it from our dad," she told him, moving over to pick up one of the picture frames on her nightstand to show him . "On men? Sexy. On a twenty-something young lady? Witchlike."

Quint looked at the photo and then up at Kaitlyn as she smiled sadly.

Kaitlyn missed her family. She spoke to her brothers and went to their homes, when she knew her parents weren't there. She missed the entire family getting together for Sunday dinner after church, birthdays, and holidays.

"What are you doing here, Kaitlyn Strong, youngest daughter of the wealthy ranching Strong family?" he asked.

Kaitlyn chuckled as she looked down at the group photo taken at Zaria and Kaleb's wedding. Everyone was smiling and huddled close together to make sure they all fit. It wasn't a good feeling to think she didn't fit in the family picture anymore. She swallowed over an emotional lump in her throat. She didn't miss Quint's eyes dipping to her throat to take in the innocent move.

"Honestly?" she asked.

"Yes," Quint said with enthusiasm as he smiled at her. "Curiosity is killing me."

"My parents were pissed I spent, like, thirty grand at one store when I was in Paris this summer, and they lowered my monthly budget to 'teach me a lesson.'" Kaitlyn did the air quotes with her fingers, her sarcasm clear.

Quint eyed her incredulously. "Kaitlyn, you do understand some people don't make thirty grand in a year?" he said slowly.

"Yes, I understand that . . . but not *my* parents," she countered.

Quint wiped his mouth with one of his large hands. "Okay, maybe your parents make that in a month and you blew it in an hour?"

Kaitlyn widened her eyes. "You know nothing about what my parents make," she told him, turning to set the picture frame back in its spot.

"Okay, but do you?"

Kaitlyn didn't answer him. She didn't mean to. Of course she knew nothing about her family business matters. Why would she?

"Listen, all I know is I've lived where I wanted, bought what I wanted, vacationed wherever I wanted, and it was fine—"

"On their expense?" he asked in disbelief.

"Yes," she answered with emphasis.

"And how old are you?"

Kaitlyn didn't answer, and she didn't mean to . . . again.

"My point is, all of a sudden they pull the rug from under me and I had to move from James Island to *here*—"

"James Island, huh?" Quint said with a steep whistle.

Kaitlyn's eyes lit up and she reached for his wrist. "And it was right off the water, with real hardwood floors and a gourmet kitchen and ten-foot-high ceilings with crown molding."

Quint chuckled.

Kaitlyn eyed him. "Did I tell a joke? What's funny?

You see Kevin Hart somewhere?" she asked, pretending to look around her.

"You know, the answer to getting everything you want is real simple," he said.

"Oh yeah? What, Mr. Know-It-All?" she asked.

"Get a job, Kaitlyn," Quint said. "Get a *J-O-B* and pay to play."

Kaitlyn frowned at him. "Good night," she said, dismissing him.

"So what are you going to do?"

"Not speak to my parents until they understand the injustice they have put upon me," she answered, pressing her slender hand to her chest.

"Kaitlyn," Quint said gently. "You're willing to turn your back on family for money. Because that is what you're doing."

"No, I'm not."

"Yes, you are."

"No, I'm not."

"A'ight," he said, holding up his hands as he briefly held up his square shoulders. "Look, I originally wanted you to let me know what-all you need for the sleepover. I can pick it up when I go to town in the morning."

Kaitlyn was happy for the change of subject. "I can do a list. I'll have it for you in the morning. I can tell you, lots and lots of snacks. A few movies. Maybe a karaoke machine. I have plenty of makeup and nail polish for them to play with."

"She's twelve."

Kaitlyn eyed him. "Quinton, I'm not taking Lei and her friends out for a ho stroll and putting them out to work. They'll be right here in my apartment."

"That's my baby girl," he explained.

"And she's beautiful and becoming a young lady,"

Kaitlyn said, gently guiding Quint toward the door. "Boys are gonna sniff around her, regardless if you keep her in sneakers and jeans or not. Thing is to teach her not to fall for their shit, and I can help with that . . . as you know."

Quinton paused to look at her. "Ha-ha, funny."

Kaitlyn smiled. "You know, you really should just unass a card and let *me* take Lei to the store."

Quint laughed out loud. "No offense, but I am not turning *you* loose with my card," he said dryly.

Kaitlyn opened her front door. "Good night to you and your wack joke. I'll have the list for you in the morning."

Quint turned suddenly and their bodies slightly touched. "Thanks again, and good night, Kaitlyn."

Her heart beat erratically as she closed the door on him and his overwhelming presence.

In the days that followed, Quinton couldn't deny that his daughter was excited and happy about her pajama party. Now, instead of talking about Kaitlyn all the time, she filled his brain with every one of her friends who promised they were coming. Quint was happy to see her happy. Lei meant everything to him.

And that was why he kept peeling off the cash to give Kaitlyn as she put her all into making sure Lei's party was "*the* perfect sleepover jammy jam"— whatever that meant.

That morning, as soon as Lei left for school, he used a dolly and a lot of sweat and muscle to take her armoire into her bedroom. He positioned it in the empty corner where her dollhouse once sat. He stood back to watch his handiwork.

It was large enough with plenty of shelves to hold

whatever she wanted, but not too big to overpower the room. He even relented and followed his initial idea to install a lock and skeleton key. Just a little privacy for a new teenager.

My little girl is growing up, Quinton thought, remembering the day she was born and how proud he felt as he held her for the first time. How much he wanted to be a better father for her than his had been for him.

Her first steps.

The first time she called him "Dada."

Her first day of school.

Even the appearance of her menstrual cycle last year.

He shook his head at how much that shook him, but they got through it together—and a trip to her pediatrician's office for a nice chat with the nurse about her new feminine responsibilities helped a lot.

Quint picked up the brightly wrapped gifts from where he set them on her bed earlier and slid them inside the armoire and locked it, leaving the key in the lock. Her birthday wasn't until that Sunday; but with her sleepover that Friday night, he decided to give her most of her gifts early.

Glancing at the time on his cell phone, Quint left her room and then their apartment. He climbed into his Ford pickup and reversed out of his parking spot. He hit his brakes at the sight of Kaitlyn already up and tying dozens of pink and silver Happy Birthday balloons to the railings.

He fixed his eyes on her face and found it squinted in intense concentration to be cute as hell. The friends Lei invited were catching the school bus to the complex with her; and Kaitlyn obviously wanted everything ready for them. He couldn't deny that she really seemed to like Lei and that earned her his respect.

He put his truck in park and climbed out of the vehicle. "You need any help right now?" he called up to her.

Kaitlyn looked up and then down at him. She smiled brightly.

The sight of it warmed him more than the summer sun could.

"I might move my sofa into the guest bedroom to make more room for the sleeping bags," she said.

"I gotta make a quick run and I'll come right up," he told her.

"Going to see a *friend*?" she asked, winking.

Quint just smiled and climbed back into the pickup. Even though both agreed that they couldn't act on their chemistry, nothing about the way they excited each other had weakened. In fact, it had seemed to intensify. Something about wanting someone so close, but not being able to have that person, made the desire crazy intense.

And it didn't help that they often found themselves flirting a little or sharing long looks, or they caught the other enjoying certain body parts too tempting to ignore.

There had been many a night he would wake up from a dream that she had dominated, or it was even worse when he would lose focus on a project and realize he had been thinking about Kaitlyn.

Something she said that was funny.

Something she did that baffled the hell out of him.

With each passing day it could be either of the two or both. There were many, many moments he swung between wanting to swat her bottom, like she was a misbehaving child, or kiss her like the woman she very clearly was.

Turning off the main road, he decided to take the back roads or side streets to Walterboro. As he passed Joni's house, he shook his head at the sight of the car pulled up close behind hers. She had texted him a few times, inviting him to come and give "it" to her, but he never responded.

Something about her nonchalance at him not going through with the sex threw him off. It made him think maybe she wasn't all there. He hadn't wanted the drama of an argument, but for a woman not to even question why was odd to him.

So he wished her and her new lover well—*if* he was all that new.

His cell phone vibrated on his hip and he reached for it as he pulled to a stop sign. He felt annoyance at seeing his ex-wife's number. Answering the call, he ignored the car behind him blowing its horn. He lowered his window and waved his arm for them to go around him. "Listen, Vita. We've been over for years. I don't ask you for any financial help for our daughter. There is no emergency with her on this end. Lei has her own cell phone for you to call her. There is no reason for us to talk," he said, completely sick of her and her drama.

The line remained quiet.

He frowned. "Vita?" he said.

Still nothing.

Beep. Suddenly the call ended.

Quint tossed the phone on his passenger seat before checking for oncoming traffic as he slowly eased the Ford F-250 around the corner. He had a feeling that his ex-wife was up to her old tricks, and she had her old boy on the prowl for evidence.

Not his problem.

The last person Mr. Hawaii needed to be worried about was Quint. He and Vita lived thousands of miles apart. They were divorced—at his doing. And he wouldn't make love to his ex-wife again, even if she were blessed with a brand-new vagina.

Somebody tagging that ass, but it ain't me, brah.

He pulled his vehicle onto the paved drive of his brick home. Before he hopped out to start his quarterly inspection of the two-story brick home and half an acre of land, he allowed himself a moment to miss it. He didn't get sentimental over many things, but outside of Lei this house was a major accomplishment.

When he decided to end his marriage, he had made the choice to let Vita and Lei remain in their home. He took nothing but his clothes and moved into his own apartment. By the time a year rolled by, and the divorce was final, he had saved enough money to put a down payment on his own house. Outside of regular child support and the barest of living expenses, he saved every cent he could.

He and his Realtor searched for months for the right home, in the right neighborhood, with enough room for Lei to play safely in the yard. This one was a perfect fit; and the day he closed, he felt more excited than he had in the moments just before he had sex for the first time at age thirteen.

Vita had actually sued him for child support through the court system when he moved into his new home. She couldn't care less that he had given her a generous amount, free and willing, every pay period. And the judge had agreed; because based on his salary, the amount that was set was lower than the amount he had volunteered to pay.

That still made him smile.

He paid what the court ordered and put the rest of his voluntary payment amount in a bank account for Lei, which he still contributed to.

This house was a major accomplishment after walking away from everything and starting over alone.

And in another year or two, when he felt more comfortable about leaving Lei home alone, he planned to give his tenants advance notice, resign from his job at the apartment complex, and use his savings to pay his mortgage until he found a higher-paying job.

Soon he and his daughter would be moving back home.

The next evening, after all her friends were picked up by their parents, and Kaitlyn fell asleep from the sheer exhaustion of cleaning up from a twenty-four-hour slumber party, Lei gathered up all her presents and made her way downstairs.

It was Saturday, and her father's day off, so she wasn't surprised to find him vegging out in front of the television, watching sports. It did surprise her that he was asleep. Not bothering to wake him, Lei moved quietly into her room and set all of her presents inside the pretty armoire he had built for her. She loved it. She loved all her gifts!

She grabbed her diary and her fingers scribbled furiously as she wrote about watching movies, singing karaoke, their spa treatments and makeup sessions. All the snacks. Fruity and slushy drinks. Games to win prizes. Her cupcakes.

Kaitlyn and her dad had really gone all out.

She rubbed her fingers through her newly curled bob, courtesy of Kaitlyn and her flat iron. She bit the end of her pen before she wrote: *Kaitlyn would make the BEST stepmom ever. Maybe my dad thinks so too. Fingers crossed.*

She lay back on her bed and smiled at the thought of that.

CHAPTER 11

Three weeks later

Kaitlyn looked over at Kadina and Lei giggling as they looked at swimsuits in the trendy boutique located on King Street in Charleston. She was glad that her neice and Lei were just a year or so apart and could enoy hanging out with each other. Now, what either one planned to do with swimwear in the fall was completely in *their* minds. Ever since Lei asked her to invite Kadina to her sleepover, the two had become thick as thieves.

They were driving her crazy, playing music and singing along to videos on YouTube, so she decided to take them shopping.

More like window-shopping.

After paying her parents for car note, insurance, utilities, and groceries, she had three hundred dollars left over in her allowance. And in this shop on King Street, where even the panties started at fifty dollars, three hundred meant nothing. Absolutely diddly-squat.

She pushed back the hangers on the rack and stopped at a leather dress with lots of detail. It was the perfect dress for a Vegas party. It was a put-the-spotlight-on-me kind of dress. Deep vee. High skirt. Body-hugging leather.

Kaitlyn's mouth literally salivated.

"We just got it in, Ms. Strong."

She turned and found Xena, the boutique owner, standing behind her.

"I think that one is your size too. A size eight, right?" she asked, stepping forward to ease the dress and its wooden hanger from the rack. "Should I put it in the dressing room for you?"

Xena and her small staff knew Kaitlyn well. She used to be a regular customer, and the old Kaitlyn, with unlimited spending potential, would have nodded her approval of the idea and shopped on. This new Kaitlyn knew there was no way she could spend eight hundred dollars on a dress. She just didn't have it.

And that was embarrassing. She felt her cheeks flame.

"I'm really just letting my niece and her friend look around a little bit," Kaitlyn said, trying to sound casual.

Xena nodded. "I'll tell you what. Let's still set you up, and if you or the girls see anything, you won't have to wait for an open dressing room."

Kaitlyn just nodded and continued to browse around the store. She looked up and happened to spot Anola and a tall man, whom Kaitlyn didn't recognize, strolling up King Street. Kaitlyn's glossy lips dropped open at the charcoal tweed blazer she wore with matching shorts, patterned tights, and a fierce pair of booties.

"Love, love the outfit," she said as she pressed her face against the glass and watched her bestie strut with the confidence she felt waning from herself.

When Anola and her male companion neared the storefront, Kaitlyn gasped and squatted down to the floor.

Please don't let her come in. Please don't let her come in. Please, God, please.

"Aunt Kat?"

Kaitlyn popped one eye open and looked up at her niece and Lei looking down at her. She smiled and rose to her feet, glancing over her shoulder to see Anola and the man had breezed right on past, on their way to continue enjoying the fabulous life Kaitlyn used to have.

"I dropped something on the floor," she lied.

"Just checking," Kadina said before pulling Lei's arm for them to rush over to the accessories.

Kaitlyn glanced at her watch. She was giving them ten more minutes, maybe treat them to a faux cocktail ring, and then they were headed to somewhere fast and cheap for lunch. She turned and eyed one of the salesclerks arranging an outfit to put on a mannequin in the other storefront window.

Kaitlyn walked over to her, frowning slightly at the color combo and overuse of accessories. The oatmeal light wool and lace sleeveless dress was young, fun, a little edgy, and very stylish, with its lace top and attached wrap skirt, which was at best midthigh, depending on the wearer's height. She could see herself wearing it for a fun day of shopping at someplace ultrastylish.

"Do you have that in an eight?" she asked.

The clerk looked on the rack and handed it to her with a smile. She laid it atop a table of folded designer shirts. Quickly she moved about the store and pulled a pair of matching sandals with straw heels rimmed in brown leather with gold grommet. She selected a leather wrap bracelet and a simple long gold chain with a smoky quartz amulet.

Kaitlyn stepped back to observe her handiwork and enjoyed the rush she felt. The clerk glanced at Kaitlyn's outfit and then back at her own.

Xena walked over to join them. "I love those shoes with it, and the single gold chain isn't as busy against the lace. You always have good style," she said, already reaching across the table to pick up all her items. "You hardly ever needed Justine's help."

Kaitlyn opened her mouth to tell the woman not to put the things in the dressing room for her, but she just closed her mouth. She walked over to where the girls were trying on accessories.

"Okay, ladies, pick out one cute thing. Don't go crazy, and let's go get something to eat," Kaitlyn said.

Xena breezed past her. "Too bad you're not looking for a job, because we need a new stylist to replace Justine," she said as she started to refold some of the jeans on display.

"No, no, I'm good," Kaitlyn said. "But thanks for the compliment."

"We're ready, Miss Kat," Lei said.

They both held out their choices. A turquoise ring for Kadina and a stack of beaded-and-wooden bracelet mix for Lei.

Kaitlyn carried the items to the register. "That's it for today. I don't want to go on a shopping spree in front of them. You know?" she said.

"I understand," Xena said, coming around the desk, which held the antique cash register. She placed the small items in two separate bags, with the Adorned Boutique logo on them.

Kaitlyn couldn't believe how hard it was for her to unpeel those two fifties from her wallet.

I hate my life.

"Hey, Garcelle," Kaitlyn said as she followed Kadina into their kitchen. "My brother home?"

Garcelle looked up from the pot she was stirring. "No, he went hunting with your dad and brothers," she said, bending to take a sip from the serving spoon before she rinsed it and set it back on the stove.

Kaitlyn squatted down to press her face into Karlos's neck as Kadina held him in her lap. The thick and solid toddler of almost two years giggled and released a little sigh of contentment, which made Kaitlyn melt as she rose and took him in her arms.

"Aww, Auntie loves you."

"A baby looks good on you," Garcelle said, glancing over at her sister-in-law and son as she closed the refrigerator door.

Kaitlyn looked alarmed. "Please! I can barely take care of myself," she said. "I haven't been shopping in weeks. I'm growing out my hair because it cost too much to get it trimmed and styled every week. And I let Kadina give me a manicure because prior to that my nails were naked."

"I did a good job!" Kadina protested as she popped grapes in her mouth.

"Gwapessssss," Karlos said, reaching out his hands to Kadina.

"Yes, you did," Kaitlyn agreed, but then shook her head at Garcelle when her niece was busy mashing grapes to feed into her brother's mouth.

"I saw that, Aunt Kat," Kadina said in a droll tone.

"Well, Kaitlyn, you're a smart girl," Garcelle said. "You've even been to college. Why not find a job? I think that would help your parents see that you're trying, and maybe they will even help you more."

Kaitlyn rocked her body back and forth as she let her chin rest on the soft and bouncy curls of Karlos's head as he pressed his face against her chest and nestled his plump thumb between his lips. "To be honest, I'm really thinking about it, because I thought Mommy and Daddy would cave by now. So I guess they really are cutting me loose."

Kadina grabbed her heart-shaped rhinestone purse and quietly left the room. Kaitlyn's eyes followed her before she shifted her gaze to Garcelle.

"It's really bothering her about you and your parents not speaking," Garcelle stressed. "I mean, *really* bothering her."

Kaitlyn said nothing as she pressed kisses to Karlos's cheek as he lightly snored.

"I bet everyone would be so happy to see you at *iglesia* and then Sunday dinner tomorrow," she said gently, obviously not wanting to seem like she was pushing.

"Iglesia?" Kaitlyn asked.

Garcelle looked apologetic. "Church. *'Iglesia'* means *church,*" she said, smiling, as she wiped her hand and came over to take her overgrown son into her arms. "We're having a cook-off to see who makes the best stew *estofado.*"

That word Kaitlyn knew because she had eaten one of Garcelle's stews before, a delicious *estofado de pollo.*

"Can I taste it?" Kaitlyn asked.

"It's not ready yet, but it will be . . . tomorrow,

chica," Garcelle said on her way out of the kitchen to put Karlos down for his nap.

Kaitlyn could just imagine the fun her family would have with their cook-off tomorrow, and she would be home, alone, counting pennies or day-dreaming about the fun she had in Paris—the last trip she would ever take, it seemed. She moved over to the stove and lifted the lid from the pot. Her mouth watered at the sausages, jumbo shrimp, bite-sized chunks of chicken breasts, real lump crab meat bubbling away with vegetables in a deep and rich tomato-based broth.

Kaitlyn's mouth literally watered.

Garcelle breezed back into the kitchen and gently took the lid away, to ease it back down onto the pot.

"I talked to Kade. They're on their way here."

Kaitlyn looked up in alarm, feeling like her short hair actually did shoot up to stand on end. "Is my dad with them?" she asked.

Garcelle gave her a chastising look and didn't answer.

Kaitlyn grabbed her keys. "I gotta go, anyway. I got something to take care of."

"Kaitlyn," Garcelle chided.

"What? I do have something to take care of," she insisted, already walking out of the kitchen, with a wave of her hand in the air.

She was climbing into her car when Garcelle stepped out onto the porch, looking like a mix of Beyoncé and Shakira. Kaitlyn lowered the window as her sister-in-law walked up to the car with a small container, which she pressed into Kaitlyn's hand, along with a few folded hundred-dollar bills.

The money she gave back. The steaming container of stew she kept.

Kaitlyn gave her a smile. "You know you're my favorite sister-in-law," she said, smiling.

"We all are, whenever you're with each one," Garcelle said. "We all talk. We're onto you."

"But you love me," Kaitlyn said playfully as she put her vehicle in reverse.

Garcelle nodded and placed her hands on her ample hips. "We *all* do," she stressed.

Kaitlyn just waved and reversed into a mini arc before pulling out of the yard and onto the road. With a final toot of her horn, she accelerated away from Garcelle and Kade's home. She felt proud of herself for refusing the money.

And that surprised the hell out of her.

Hitting her family up for money had meant nothing to her before. She felt like she was the baby of the family and they wanted her to have a fun life. And fun costs. So why not ask and receive?

But now, she felt like it was begging, and that made her feel uncomfortable. Why? Who knew? But it did.

As she made her way back to her apartment, Kaitlyn's eyes kept darting to the small bag from the boutique, which one of the girls left in her vehicle. By the time she parked next to Mrs. Harper's pink vehicle, she reached for her cell phone and dialed the number to the boutique.

"Adorned Boutique."

Kaitlyn closed her eyes. "Xena, please. It's Kaitlyn Strong," she said in a rush before she backed out.

"Please hold, Miss Strong."

What am I doing?
Am I crazy?
Is this what desperation feels like?
Hang up. Just hang—

"Hello, Miss Strong. Did you change your mind about those items you saw today?" Xena asked. "I can have them charged to your account and shipped out to you."

Kaitlyn licked her lips as her heart sped so fast and hard in her chest that she thought she might pass out.

"Actually, I was thinking about the position you mentioned earlier. I think it might be fun," she said, proud that she sounded intrigued and not completely desperate.

"Really?"

"Sure. Why not?"

"Well, we're looking for longevity. I don't want you to take a position here and move on after a month or two," Xena said gently.

Translation: *We do not have time for a flaky rich girl looking for something to break up the monotony before the next interesting thing comes along.* Or at least that's how Kaitlyn interpreted it.

Is that how people see me?

"Let me talk to Lyle—my co-owner—and if he agrees, we'll call you in to talk to both of us together. All right?"

"Okay, I look forward to hearing from you," Kaitlyn said, completely aware that their "talk" was an "interview."

Whatever.

The fact was she needed more income than her allowance allowed; and if her family hung in there with their plan, then even that money would disappear in a few months.

Kaitlyn Strong swallowed the fact that she *absolutely* needed a job. It was becoming clearer and clearer that the safety net provided all her life by her family was slowly fading away. She couldn't believe her family would just toss her aside like this.

That's how she felt, and it hurt.

She bit her lip and shook her head as she brushed away the tears that filled her eyes and raced down her cheeks.

Kael Strong missed his daughter.

Long after church service was over, and the family all met up at the house for dinner, he made his way down to the barn and stopped at the stable, where Kaitlyn's all-white horse, Snowflake, was housed. The horse moved forward and Kael raised his hands to rub her nose and feed her carrots.

Although it had been a few years since Kaitlyn gave the horse the time of day, Kael still thought of Snowflake as hers. He remembered the look on her face at her sixth birthday party when the all-white foal with a long white mane was walked out to her. She took just a second to hug her father close around the neck before she raced off to ride the young horse—still in her party dress and all.

He smiled.

Kaitlyn was his only daughter. His baby girl. After his wife—she was his heart.

The one to make him laugh.

The one to say wild and unexpected things to keep things lively.

The pop of red in a black-and-white day.

Kael missed that. He felt no anger that she had severed ties with him and her mother. He was patiently waiting for her tantrum to be over.

But in the meantime life sure was a lot less interesting.

"Good game, Q."

Quint nodded to his teammates, Justin and Kyle, as they walked off the indoor court of the recreation center. They had just won their three-on-three pickup game, and Quint felt rejuvenated from the physical exertion.

"Thanks," he said, his shirtless chest still heaving as he grabbed the towel from his bag and wiped the sweat from his face.

Aware of the chill in the air, he quickly pulled on his sweatpants over his knee-length basketball shorts and then his hoodie before sliding the strap over his head across his body.

"We're headed to my house to watch the football game," Justin said, also throwing his hood up over his head as they all left the building.

"I might ride over later. My daughter is cooking dinner for me," Quint told them as he unlocked his truck and threw his bag onto the passenger seat.

"You know where I stay, so just come over," Justin said. "We'll all be in the garage, to stay out of my wife's hair."

"A'ight." Quint climbed into his vehicle and started the engine.

The ride back to Holtsville took all of ten minutes, but during the entire ride his thoughts were on Kaitlyn. He hadn't seen her much during the last couple of weeks. He'd even asked Lei what was up with her, but she didn't know.

Maybe she's spending time with a new man, he thought.

He thought about Kaitlyn flashing her pretty eyes and flirting with another dude and he frowned. Deeply.

As he turned his Ford F-250 into the parking lot of the complex, he spotted her flashy red car parked in the space in front of his door. As he pulled into the spot across from her, he wondered if she was home. His eyes shot up to her door as he made his way to his apartment.

He couldn't believe he actually missed her.

Unlocking his front door, he paused, surprised by the sound of voices and giggles from the kitchen. Lei was supposed to be next door at Mrs. Harper's until he got home.

"Lei?" he called out.

"In here, Daddy," she called back.

He strode into the kitchen to find Lei and Kaitlyn in bright pink aprons looking at him over their shoulders as they stood at the stove. He was surprised by his reaction to having Kaitlyn suddenly reappearing in his life—and in his home. He had to force his eyes away from her smiling face. It felt too much like sunshine right after a bad rain.

"What are you two up to?" Quint asked, coming over to stand behind them and peer over their heads at the pots on the stove.

"We cooked," Lei said as she stirred a pot of yams.

That he recognized.

Kaitlyn stirred something white as it bubbled over onto the stove.

Quint made a face. If that was rice, then he could only pray for how it ended. Rice was best cooked if left alone.

"We made steak, rice, yams, and macaroni and

cheese," Lei said with pride. "I invited Miss Kaitlyn to eat dinner with us. Okay, Daddy?"

He looked over at Kaitlyn. She slightly lifted her eyebrows as she eyed him back.

"That's cool," he said as Kaitlyn turned back to the stove.

His plan had been to guide Lei through cooking her first meal.

"I didn't know you could cook, Kaitlyn," he said, reaching up to remove his hood as he took a seat at their kitchen table.

"Me either," she said, sounding excited.

Quint bit back a smile. These two were going to make praying before a meal *even more* necessary.

"Well, I'm going to wash the funk off me before we eat," he said, rising to his feet to leave the kitchen.

He happened to glance back over his shoulders and he absolutely caught Kaitlyn's eyes zoned in on his buttocks. He cleared his throat as she shifted her eyes up to meet his. If Lei wasn't present, he would have asked her if she enjoyed the view. Instead, he enjoyed the flush of color to her cheeks as he chuckled and walked to his bedroom.

Closing the door behind himself, he rushed out of his clothing and boxers, feeling the kind of nervous excitement of a child waiting on Christmas morning. Kaitlyn had him on edge—especially in the V-necked, formfitting sweater she wore, with even more formfitting leggings and thigh-high boots.

His dick stirred as he made his way across the room to his bathroom.

"Don't," he said, looking down at it. "She's off-limits."

Easier said than done.

He hopped into the shower and enjoyed the feel of

the water pelting against his body as he inhaled the steam, which swirled around him. It brushed against his body like a whisper. Like the soft kiss of lips.

Full pouty lips that were perfectly shaped.

Kaitlyn's lips.

He remembered the feel of them on his neck.

Or the sight of them open and panting as the things he did to her made her breathless.

Or the feel of them as he kissed her.

Shaking his head, he felt his gut clench as his dick hardened and hung away from his body like a strong arm. He tilted his head back and took the thickness into his hand as he tried to fight the image of Kaitlyn suddenly on her knees in front of him, with the water beating down on her head as she took his dick into her mouth.

"Shit," Quint swore, catching himself stroking the eleven inches of length. He even considered finishing the job and getting *some* relief.

Kaitlyn strutting her fat ass around in those damn leggings in front of me can get real crucial.

But he didn't give in to the temptation as he grabbed his soap and cloth and vigorously scrubbed every inch of his body. This was not his first time imagining the woman showering with him and seducing him. Kaitlyn could get to be very distracting.

Finishing up the shower, he walked into his bedroom, with just a towel loosely slung around his hips. After putting on his deodorant, he had to catch himself from putting on cologne and pulling out an outfit. That was overboard and would be obvious. He could just see Kaitlyn giving him teasing and knowing looks as he strolled back out there in a cashmere sweater and dress denims with hard-bottom shoes on.

Instead, he settled on no cologne, a little coconut oil on his bald scalp, a pair of jeans, and a V-necked tee.

When he made his way back to the kitchen, the ladies were setting bowls of food on the center of the table. Kaitlyn turned to grab a glass from the top shelf of the cabinet. Quint had to fight not to take in the way her sweater rode up and exposed the small of her back, just above the rim of her tight leggings.

Damn good sight.

Quint stepped over to her and was instantly hit with that subtle but sexy scent of her perfume. He easily reached for the glass to hand to her as he looked down at her, looking up at him.

"You're welcome," he joked.

Kaitlyn gave him the hint of her smile. "Thank you so much, Quin-ton," she whispered up to him.

And he shivered. Literally, stood there—a grown man—and felt himself shiver from softly spoken words from her.

Like a bitch.

Quint got the hell away from her and turned, surprised to see Lei looking at them and smiling like she had won the lottery.

"You sit here, Daddy," she said, tapping the back of the seat at the end of the table.

He eyed her suspiciously as he bent his tall, muscled frame onto the chair as she took the seat at the other end, leaving the seat in the middle for Kaitlyn. The seat directly adjacent to him.

And her scent was there again, making his head feel cloudy as she sat down. She felt like a drug he was trying to kick, and he was failing and still jonesing bad for her.

And he was beginning to realize that his feelings were more than sexual. He didn't know when or where or even why, but he cared for Kaitlyn. He missed her when she wasn't around. He enjoyed the sight of her smile. He hated to see her upset or disturbed. He felt protective of her.

Somehow this woman, who he thought was a replica of his ex, proved him wrong and had gotten under his skin and into his heart. And he hadn't wanted or expected that at all.

Lei held out one hand to Kaitlyn and the other across the table to her father.

Kaitlyn slid her hand into Lei's and then turned to look at Quint as she offered her other hand to him.

Quint took Lei's offered hand first before he finally slid his hand into Kaitlyn's. She closed her fingers around his and her index finger ended up lightly pressed against his wrist. On his pulse point. He wondered if she felt it pounding as hard as he felt his heart racing.

As Lei said grace, Quint was *so* aware of that crazy energy between him and Kaitlyn. It seemed to have a life and a heartbeat and a pulse all its own. And the pace of it all quickened to a dizzying speed whenever they made contact. Quint didn't uncoil the tension from his body until his daughter said "Amen."

His eyes shot up when he thought Kaitlyn purposefully stroked his pounding pulse before she released his hand. She just looked away from him and turned to Lei as his daughter rose to scoop a little of everything onto everyone's plate.

"Now, be honest, Daddy," Lei said as she reclaimed her seat.

Quint picked up his fork as he looked down at his plate. He wasn't a gourmet cook, but from looking, he knew what needed what. The yams could use more cinnamon and butter. The rice could've taken less water. The steak needed more cooking time. The mac and cheese could use more milk.

But nothing smelled or looked inedible.

"I'm sure it's delicious, baby girl," he told her, picking up his fork to dig into the steak first. "Thank you."

"Miss Kaitlyn too, Daddy," Lei said, giving him a meaningful stare.

"Thank you, Kaitlyn."

They both eyed him as he raised his fork to his mouth. He paused and shifted his eyes from one to the other. With one last deep breath, he slid the food into his mouth.

The saltiness of the meat made his eyes bug before he caught himself. He chewed and smiled at them. The meat was a lot more tender than it looked, though.

Kaitlyn bit back a smile. "I didn't realize your meat tenderizer was seasoned, and I had already put a lot of seasoning on it," she admitted.

Quint swallowed and reached for the glass of juice next to his plate. "Not bad," he admitted, taking a deep sip. "A little salty but not bad."

They all resumed eating. Like he thought, neither was ready for a chef position; but it was edible, if not delicious.

He looked up when Kaitlyn started choking.

"You all right?" he asked, reaching out to pat her back lightly as she set her glass back down on the table.

Kaitlyn nodded as she continued to cough. "It went down the wrong hole," she said.

Kaitlyn and Quint looked at each other and said "Pause" in unison before they laughed.

"You okay, Miss Kaitlyn?" Lei asked.

"I'm good."

Quint removed his hand from her back and tried not to notice that the outline of her bra proved to be just as skimpy as the one she wore that night in the shed.

Her nipples looked so damn good against the black lace.

"I got a job," Kaitlyn said suddenly.

It was Quint's turn to choke, but he held up his hands that he was fine when Kaitlyn moved to swat his back.

"That's good," he said as she eyed him.

"Yeah, they even gave me a better position than the one I wanted," she said, pushing around the food on her plate. "After I met with the owners to be a salesclerk/stylist, I was offered the position as the majority owner's assistant and to help with the buying for four stores he owns."

Quint puckered his forehead. "So you got a promotion without even trying?" he asked, sounding skeptical.

Kaitlyn shrugged as Lei rose to take their plates.

"I think they didn't want to offend me by *not* giving me a job, because I spent so much money there, but I also don't think they wanted to trust putting me in the store, in case I quit after a month or something."

That made no sense to Quint, but what did he know about the mind-set of rich folks?

"And your boss is a dude?" he asked.

"Lyle? Yes," she said. She set her chin in her hand as she looked at him. "Why?"

"Just asking," Quinton said, rising from the table. "Is he married?"

Kaitlyn rolled her eyes heavenward. *"No,"* she stressed. "Why?"

"Just curious about old boy, that's all," he said, trying to sound nonchalant.

"We didn't have time to make dessert," Lei said.

"We can ride to Dairy Queen and get some ice cream," Quint offered. He looked down at Kaitlyn, who still sat with her chin in her hand, watching him. "Care to join?"

She tilted her head to the side before she rose. "No, but thank you. I have to drive some files to my boss's house later."

Lei looked disappointed.

Quint grunted.

Kaitlyn threw her hands up in exasperation. "Now what, Quint?"

"Lei, go get your coat," Quinton said as he walked behind Kaitlyn to the front door. "And, Kaitlyn, just be sure this great deal is all business and no pleasure."

"Not every man within two feet of me wants to screw me," she drawled before turning to head up the stairs.

"Now *that's* a bunch of bullshit," he said, enjoying the view as she walked away.

Kaitlyn never stopped her ascent up the steps, and soon the sound of her front door closing echoed.

CHAPTER 12

"I'm headed to lunch, Kaitlyn. I should be back around two."

Kaitlyn looked up as her boss, Lyle Turner, strolled past her desk with his usual flair. Blond hair lying just right. Clothes pressed and styled to perfection. Skin perfectly tanned, even as the fall season reigned in South Carolina.

"Enjoy," she told him, glad he was leaving the downtown Charleston offices and not watching her like a hawk.

And she learned in the weeks that followed that around two probably meant that he was done for the day. His equally gorgeous male lover, whose skin was as smooth and dark as black opal, would keep him tied up for the afternoon.

Her job was to look pretty, dress well, answer the phone, and take messages when he didn't ask her to accompany him to fashion shows or designer show-rooms for her opinion on the latest trends. She was handling the job just fine, and even enjoyed it. And she was learning even more about the fashion and retail industry than just shopping up a storm. He owned four upscale boutiques—two in Charleston, one in Mount Pleasant, and another in Charlotte, North Carolina—and he wanted her to start presenting ideas for items to be carried in all of them.

She just wished the government didn't snatch so much in taxes. Kaitlyn opened the envelope with her first paycheck. She was paid every other week—a concept she had struggled to understand—and she had not counted on losing such a chunk.

Taxes were no joke; and Quinton said that at the end of the year, she had to file tax returns and possibly pay more!

Ugh!

She looked out the clear glass window at the beautiful sight of historical Charleston. Lyle's offices were located on the upper level of a beautiful four-story building on King Street. The brick building had a façade that matched the history of the surrounding neighborhood. It was a nice view. The offices were plush and stylish. All of the best eateries and shops were in walking distance, and she got to talk fashion on the regular.

The life!

Because she knew she had checks coming—and her parents were still covering her expenses for the next few months—Kaitlyn had splurged a little. A few new wardrobe staples. A pair or two of sensible kitten heels for those days she didn't feel like strutting in four-inch heels. Her hair cut and dyed and laid to the side. New makeup. Mani and pedi.

She was completely back to the old Kaitlyn, or was she?

Kaitlyn twirled in her seat and reached down into the infamous Hermès bag, which had started it all, to pull out her cell phone. She crossed her legs in her

A-line navy linen skirt, with leather piping detail. She hit number five on her speed dial roster. Parents first. Then Kade. Kahron. Kaleb. And Kaeden.

"Yes, little sister," he said.

"Hiya, Specs," she said playfully as she pulled out her compact and tube of bright red lipstick.

"Ever since you cried to Ma about us teasing you about that streak of white hair by calling you—"

Kaitlyn stopped applying her lipstick and sat up straight in her chair. "Don't you say it," she warned.

"Skunkie," he finished without a bit of pause.

Kaitlyn snapped her compact shut and was pretty sure she cracked the glass. "Okay, no more nicknames," she said quickly.

Kaeden laughed.

"An-y-way," she stressed. "I need a full list of all my bills."

The line stayed quiet.

Kaitlyn tapped her bright red fingernail against the mouthpiece.

"Hello?" she sang into the phone.

"Sorry, you shocked me. You never asked that before. Ever," Kaeden said.

Kaitlyn picked up a pen and pulled forward a pad. "Just give it to me."

And he did.

At times she cringed. At other times her eyes widened. But still, she scribbled away.

And then he gave her the total monthly expenses.

Kaitlyn gasped.

"It would have been much higher with the rent you used to have."

Kaitlyn set her chin in her hand as she looked at the list of bills and looked at her check. She fell back in her chair and fought the urge to slump down.

"Kaitlyn, you there?" he asked.

"Yeah. I'll call you back," she said, ending the call.

The door to the outer office opened and she looked up. Her face filled with surprise to see Quint stroll in. She rose to her feet and came around the desk to meet him.

"What are you doing here?" she asked, thinking he looked really handsome in a charcoal peacoat over a sweater of the same color, paired with dark denims.

He looks hella good.

Quinton looked around the office. "I was downtown handling some business and I thought I'd come by and take you to lunch."

Kaitlyn looked confused. "Me? You want to take me to lunch?" she asked.

Quint walked over to her desk and then looked down the hall behind him. "Yes. You can't eat with me?" he asked, turning to study her.

Kaitlyn locked her hands behind her back as she gazed at him.

Well, just like the night she first told him of her job, Kaitlyn thought Quinton was a little jealous. And she liked the idea of that.

She liked it a lot.

Quinton Wells was an extraordinarily handsome man, with the kind of body a man had to put work into to receive. He was a good father. He was helpful; and once they got past their initial dislike of each other, she found him to give good, solid advice. She enjoyed being in his company and the way they taunted each other while flirting shamelessly. She loved that he didn't pursue his desire for her, because he knew she would want more from him.

That made him honorable.

Plus he was sexy as hell.

And she liked him. She liked him a lot. Enough that she wanted more from him than he thought he was willing to give.

"Well, Lyle usually insists we eat lunch together. He said we look good together," Kaitlyn lied, crossing the room to pass Quint and letting her hand trail across his chest as she circled him. She came around him to lean on her desk.

Quint shoved his hands into the pockets of his coat. "You do know he can't force you to go out or do anything you don't want to do?" he asked, looking down at her with his dark, deep-set eyes.

Kaitlyn batted her long lashes at him. "Quinton, I know the difference between sexual harassment and courting," she said. "In one I feel I have no choice. In the other I do."

"So you're being courted?" he asked.

Kaitlyn had to bite the inside of her cheeks to keep from smiling. Quint was salty and trying not to show it.

"Don't I deserve to be courted?" she asked.

"Of course."

"I don't see anyone else trying to do the job . . . do you?" she asked, sitting back in her chair to look up at him.

He paced the brief length of her desk before turning to press his hands against her desktop as he leaned down to face her.

"Who else would you want to do the job . . . or are you stuck on old boy back there?" he asked, lifting his strong chin toward the hall.

Kaitlyn leaned forward until their faces were inches apart.

"Is this another one of our dances, Quinton?" she asked him softly, the air around them crackling like static energy. "Another back-and-forth? Another challenge? Another chess move?"

His eyes dropped to her mouth.

"You don't want me, but you don't want anyone else to have me either," she said boldly.

"Oh, *I want you,*" Quinton stressed.

"In bed. Yes. But in your life, Quinton? Do you want me in your life?" Kaitlyn asked, ignoring the steady pulsing of her clit.

This wasn't about *that*.

It was all about her heart.

The entire time Quint stared down at Kaitlyn, he had to fight the urge to kiss her. He wanted nothing more in that moment than to taste her mouth—the way a man kisses the woman he cares about during a hello or good-bye.

And he had begun to think of her in that way: *the woman he cared about.*

He was proud of her for finding a job, even if she sang the praises of her handsome boss at every given moment. And the more he thought of another man having her, the more he realized that he wanted Kaitlyn for himself. He couldn't remember the last time he felt jealous and threatened.

All he could think of was her boss, Lyle Turner, making moves on Kaitlyn and his jealousy pushed him over the edge. Just last night she stopped by their apartment to give Lei a huge pink rose arrangement, bragging that she had enough floral arrangements from *Lyle.* It took everything he had not to childishly kick it out the door like a football.

For the rest of the night, he was tormented by images of Kaitlyn—*his* Kaitlyn—and this faceless, wealthy man who seemed to be more about socializing than business. That night before he finally dozed off to sleep, he promised himself he was giving in to his curiosity about the man and would ease on down to downtown Charleston.

How could he not admit to himself that his feelings for Kaitlyn were beyond that of apartment manager and tenant, or even the good friends that they had become?

Although she and Lei had a close relationship, what effect would it have on Lei if they didn't make it?

But what effect could it have on her if they did?

Could he risk losing Kaitlyn because he was afraid to take a chance?

"Do you want me in your life?" Kaitlyn asked again.

"Every day it's getting harder to picture you *not* in it," Quint admitted, as so many different emotions burst inside his chest like fireworks. He felt excited and nervous and anxious and even a little afraid. But mostly . . . he felt happy. And outside of the love and joy he received from his child, it had been quite some time since he felt that way.

Her eyes melted and that tugged at him. He gave in and pressed his mouth to hers.

"We've been fighting this for a minute, huh?" he asked her as she used her thumb to wipe the lipstick from his mouth.

"Yesss!" she exclaimed, pushing back and rising from her seat to come around the desk to him.

Quint placed a hand on her waist, and it felt natural and easy to him. "So we're not fighting it anymore?" he asked, his voice deep and serious.

Kaitlyn shook her head. "I'm not."

He nudged his head toward the hall.

Kaitlyn stepped up close to him and pressed her hands to his smooth face before she kissed him.

"He has nothing on you," she promised him.

Quint's lips still tingled from her kiss and the touch of her thumb as she removed the lipstick.

"You look really beautiful," he admitted.

Kaitlyn twirled away from him dramatically and then struck a pose in her crisp white shirt with the bell sleeves and elaborate high neck, with a side bow.

"Who me?" she asked before starting to vogue.

He smiled at her goofiness, but then he looked around.

"Where's your boss?" he asked. "I really can use some lunch."

Kaitlyn stopped midpose. "I have to pass on lunch. I'm sorry," she said as she walked back up to him.

"Okay. I did just drop by unexpected." Quint reached for her hand and rubbed his thumb against her pulse. "How about dinner when you get off?"

"A date?" she asked, smiling.

He liked that he caused that smile. "Yeah, a date. You game?"

Kaitlyn nodded. "Definitely. I should be home by six."

He bent down and pressed a kiss to her cheek before he allowed himself a quick inhale of her perfume.

"See you then," Quint promised, giving her hand one last, light squeeze before he turned and walked out of the office.

He was glad that she couldn't see the smile on his face. He couldn't wipe it off to save his life. Even as he jogged down the stairs, he found he was still smiling like a fool.

Hell with it.

He stepped out of the building and onto the street

and chanced a look up to find Kaitlyn already standing at the window. She was casually leaning against the windowsill with her arms crossed over her chest. He smiled, thinking she looked like a mannequin.

Quint wondered what her thoughts were as he turned and walked the short distance down the street to where his vehicle was parked. When he came to Kaitlyn's job, his goal had been to check out her boss, but he was leaving with a date planned for that night. It felt like bungee jumping—that mix of exhilaration and anxiety.

And it was not all based on Kaitlyn making the wrong move. He hadn't been in a relationship since Lei came to live with him. The expectations were higher. The rules were different. Did he still know how to play by them?

Time to get my shit together.

Kaitlyn's assumption that her boss would not return for the day turned out true. But she remained there answering calls and taking messages until five o'clock on the dot, and not a second later. She had been so anxious to get home that she got pulled over for speeding, but a smile and an innocent face led to nothing but a warning . . . and her easing up off the gas pedal.

She turned this way and that in the full-length mirror of her converted guest room. The black satin shirt had long blouson sleeves and a deep plunging neckline that emphasized her small but plump breasts and cleavage. She paired it with high-waist, wide-leg black pants and sky-high, peep-toe shoes. A wide leather cuff with gold accents encircled one wrist, and oversized gold hoops swung from her ears.

She placed extra emphasis on the eyes with smoky makeup; less emphasis on the mouth with sheer gloss for less messy kisses.

She twirled again as she imagined Quint's reaction, but midspin Kaitlyn really took in the contents of the room. The wall of shoes. The designer clothing and handbags. The jewelry. All of it.

Courtesy of her parents.

Kaitlyn picked up the Hermès bag and pulled out her paycheck and the notepad holding her list of bills. She had to shake her head. It would take two of her paychecks, plus some, to take over all of her bills alone. She glanced at the Hermès bag and then around the room again, looking at all of her things.

Things that were costly.

Things that went out of style and had to be replaced to be relevant.

Things that were completely out of her new income bracket.

Things she shouldn't have expected her parents to pay for on her whim.

Kaitlyn looked pensive.

She worked eighty hours to make what she had once spent on a pair of shoes. There was no way she could see blowing two weeks' worth of work like that.

And her father's wealth hadn't come from boardroom decisions made while he was dressed in a white collar. He had worked from sunup to sundown on that ranch; and now that he was retired, her brother Kade had stepped in to do the same. Every penny earned was coated with their blood, sweat, and tears.

Everyone in her family worked hard. Everyone— even her in-laws. Everyone—except her.

She turned and looked at her reflection in the

mirror from where she sat, but only for a few seconds.
It was all she could take of herself.

Knock, knock.

Quint.

A bright spot in a dark moment. Her heart pounded
as she rose to her feet and grabbed her small, sequined oval clutch. She smiled at the thought of him
and the first step they were taking to be together.

And the idea of it made her happy.

He was a good man. Nothing at all like the men she
usually dated, but there he was—along with this amazing chemistry—and she wanted to explore both much
more.

Kaitlyn headed out of the room and down the
narrow hall to the front door. With one last smooth-
ing of her hair, with a surprisingly shaky hand, she
opened the door.

Quint felt like a ton of air was pulled from his
body as he caught the first sight of Kaitlyn standing
in her doorway. She was glam and gorgeous and
giving him a mix of sensuality and maturity that he'd
never seen before.

But then she smiled and everything about her was
familiar.

The makeup and the clothes, which perfectly emphasized her shape, were just extras to her natural
beauty: the playful twinkle to her almond-shaped
eyes, the healthy bronzed caramel glow of her complexion, the flirty hint of a smile on her lips, the
now-familiar scent of her perfume, the smoothness
of her neck that begged to be nuzzled and kissed.

All of it created the perfect picture, and Quinton

felt completely ready for everything the night had to offer.

Kaitlyn's face filled with pleasure at the sight of Quint standing there in all black, from his tailored blazer and silk shirt to his flat-front pants and shoes.

The dark coloring suited his skin's chocolate complexion and made his angular features all the more fierce and sexy. His deep-set eyes seemed brighter. His smile seemed more vibrant; his aura more alive.

Kaitlyn felt completely taken aback by him.

It was almost like seeing him for the first time all over again, and all she could do was smile.

"One . . . two . . . three . . ."

"Have fun!"

Quint and Kaitlyn jumped in surprise and turned in the middle of the parking lot to find almost every resident of the complex standing in the doorways, waving them off on their date. Lei smiled bigger than all of them as she stood next to Mrs. Harper, who dutifully held on to her Fifi.

Both of their eyes took in each and every smiling face before Quint lightly grabbed Kaitlyn's wrist and guided her to the passenger side of his truck.

"I see the word has spread," he said.

Kaitlyn nodded and then smiled as she said, "The only one we know for sure *didn't* spread the word was Fifi."

Kaitlyn chanced a glance at Quint as they both enjoyed their dinner in a quiet corner at the rear of the seafood restaurant. She found his eyes already on her from across their table. That flustered her. It made her wonder about his thoughts.

"What's on your mind?" she asked.

"That we should have done this a lot sooner," Quint readily answered.

Kaitlyn felt her cheeks warm. "I agree," she said, reaching across the table to lightly stroke the back of his hand.

Quint sat back a bit in his chair as their waitress brought them their desserts: coconut cheesecake for him and a sorbet fruit medley for her.

"Tell me more about growing up on a ranch," he encouraged her as soon as the server stepped away from their table. He found he enjoyed looking at all the different emotions on Kaitlyn's face as she retold stories of her adventurous youth as the only sister with four brothers.

And she held back nothing. Everything she felt was expressed in her demeanor. If the moment was sad or playful or joyous or triumphant or disappointing, it all showed across her face.

Quint honestly felt like he could sit there and watch her all night.

Meanwhile, Kaitlyn watched Quinton over the rim of her wineglass as he settled back against the leather booth. He was waiting for her, and she was completely baiting him.

"Yes, Quinton. I will teach you how to ride a horse . . . if you're serious . . . and if you mean a *real* horse," she said, setting her glass on the table as she finally answered his question.

When Quinton covered his wolfish grin with a

hand, she knew he had meant a ride that included a bed and her sitting astride his body. She could ride horse or man quite well. The movement of the body was the same on man or beast.

They both shared a long look.

Kaitlyn was picturing herself sitting on Quint's lap as he sat in a chair. They both were naked and sweaty and out of breath as he gripped her hips. She rode his dick like she was in a race and had a finish line in her sights.

They both suddenly looked away.

As Kaitlyn fanned herself with her napkin, she didn't miss Quint shifting uncomfortably in his seat. She kicked off her shoe and eased her foot across the short distance, and found his dick hard in his pants. She stroked the length of it with her toes before Quint reached under the table to grab her foot.

"That's not gonna help me leave this restaurant," he told her.

She smiled as she eased her foot back across the short distance.

Quint had driven Kaitlyn the hour drive to Savannah, Georgia, for their first date. It was his favorite restaurant and he wanted to share it with her. She surprised him by suggesting they drive to River Street and take a walk on the city's beautiful waterfront.

Several times they stopped to enjoy the sounds of jazz music coming from one of the many bars lining the street. At other times they stopped and browsed the carts and stalls of vendors who were still out and selling their wares. As they came to the railing to look out on the moon glinting against the water, Quint stood behind her with his hands on the railing on either side of her.

The music seemed to dim to background noise as they both focused on the water gently lapping against the wall, and the boats in the water cruised softly by their view. There was a calm and natural feel to the moment as Kaitlyn leaned back against Quint's chest and felt secure as he tilted his head down to press a kiss to her temple.

On the ride back from Savannah, Quint looked over at Kaitlyn as she fell quiet. He was surprised to see her sleeping in the passenger seat. Gently he pulled off the road and eased out of the car to open the passenger door to use the controls to lay her seat back flat. Her eyes fluttered open for a second and she softly smiled up at him before she drifted right back to sleep.

Once he was back in the driver's seat, Quint let his hand rest comfortably on Kaitlyn's knee as he drove with his other hand. He learned a lot about her, and he enjoyed that they talked when they needed talk. Likewise, they were quiet and comfortable with each other when they needed to be as well. Although that crazy, sexual energy was there pulsing around them, it was good to see that there was more to share with each other than the physical.

Kaitlyn shifted suddenly in her sleep and let out a tiny snore.

Quint's eyebrows lifted in surprise; he chuckled, finding the little show of imperfection endeared her to him even more.

Kaitlyn was stirring awake as she felt the vehicle turn a corner and come to a stop. Sitting up, she stretched a bit in her seat as she looked over at Quint as he parked in front of the complex.

"You let me?" she asked, massaging her neck before she tried to fluff life back into her flattened hair.

"Sleep *and* snore," he told her, leaving the car running and the heat on to beat off the chill in the October night air.

Kaitlyn looked affronted. "I do *not* snore," she insisted.

Quint chuckled. "Okay, you make little noises in your sleep every so often."

She reached across the short distance to pinch him. "Ha-ha."

Quint settled back against the door and looked over at her in the semidarkness.

"Good date?" he asked.

Kaitlyn nodded. "Great date. Maybe even the best date ever," she admitted, surprised by her honesty. Quint made her want to sweep away all the games and stand in truth about her feelings.

"Same here," he agreed.

Kaitlyn thought she would literally swoon.

"And the best is yet to come," Quint added.

Kaitlyn side-eyed him. "Tonight?" she asked.

Quint held up his hands. "Not sex—I mean, not that I wouldn't like to finish the foreplay we've been having all these weeks—*but* I meant even more dates. Even better dates."

Kaitlyn felt her heart race as she nodded in agreement.

"You ready to go in?" Quint asked.

Her eyes shifted up to her door and then down to his. Going in meant leaving him behind and she wasn't prepared for that.

"I'm not ready to say good night," Kaitlyn admitted softly as she looked over at Quint.

"What are you ready for, Kaitlyn?" he asked. His tone was serious and his eyes questioning as they moved about her face.

"You."

Quint shut the engine off and left it to come around the truck to open the passenger door. He said nothing as he held his hand out to her.

Kaitlyn pushed aside her nerves and stoked her confidence as she took his hand and let him help her from the vehicle. Together they climbed the stairs to her apartment, and she closed her front door securely behind them.

CHAPTER 13

Quint pulled Kaitlyn into his arms as soon as the door closed behind them. The feel of his hands against the curve just above her buttocks made her shiver as she raised her hands to press against his shoulders before slipping her hands beneath his collar to slide the blazer from his body.

They brought their heads together, but they came just short of their mouths being less than an inch apart. They both stared at one another for long, electric-filled seconds before they shared one brief kiss, and then another, and then another. And another.

Quint moaned in the back of his throat before he slid his hands up to her back and jerked her forward to deepen their kiss with his tongue. He enjoyed the taste of hers as he first circled it with his tongue; then he suckled hers gently into his mouth in an insidious back-and-forth motion, which made the strength leave Kaitlyn's knees. He held her more tightly against his body, not wanting the taste and feel to leave him.

Kaitlyn began to undo the buttons of his shirt with shaking hands. She fought the urge to tear the silk from his body. She just wanted it gone so that his body could become her playland. With rushed movements she pushed the shirt down the length of his muscled arms and back, until it fell completely away and landed on top of his blazer in a puddle around his feet.

She broke her lips free from the kiss as she pressed her moist lips to the deep ridge between his pecs. The moan she released was like she had just drunk water to quench a thirst. She dipped her knees to drag the clever tip of her tongue inside the length of that groove before she kissed a trail to one hard and tight brown nipple, which she licked hotly before blowing a cool breeze on it through pursed lips.

Quint hissed in pleasure.

Kaitlyn sucked the damp nipple into her mouth as she smoothed her hands over his rigid abdomen before undoing his belt. Then his button. Then the zipper. She jerked the pants and boxers down his narrow hips to just below his hard buttocks and then took his hard and curving dick into her hand to stroke.

"Oh shit," Quint cried out at the first feel of her smooth hand against him.

Kaitlyn smiled and stepped back a bit; it was still hard and pulsing in her hand.

"You like that?" she asked, her voice thick with desire.

He nodded and began to move his hips against the motion of her hand as he closed his eyes and tilted his head back against the door.

Kaitlyn moaned and licked her lips as she looked down at his dick; she felt the heat and strength of it. His skin was smooth and dark—darker than the complexion of his abdomen and thighs. But the tip was a shiny milk chocolate, made all the more glistening by the occasional drizzle of his fluids. The hairs surrounding the wide shaft were black and tightly coiled.

"You gone make it nut," Quint said roughly, reaching to hold her hands and stop the back-and-forth motion.

She looked up at him. "You don't want to nut for me?" she asked.

Quint looked down at her, locking his eyes on hers with intensity. "Not until I'm in you," he told her thickly as his chest heaved.

Kaitlyn's clit jumped at that.

She stepped back and released his dick, and began undoing her clothes.

"Jack it," she ordered in a heated whisper as her eyes took in the sight of his muscled body pressed against the door. His thick thighs strained against the ridge of his pants as he bent his arm to squeeze and tease the top length of his dick.

She smiled a little and licked her lips as her lids hooded her eyes as she flung her shirt away and attacked the bothersome side buttons of her high-waist pants. He patted his dick solidly against the palm of his hand, and Kaitlyn laughed a little at the move as she released a shaky breath. She shook her head at him, enjoying that he had no more inhibitions than she did as he eyed her.

Quint missed not one detail of her body. Not the way the strapless lace bra cupped the tips of her breasts and barely constrained her nipples. Not the way her bikini rode low on her hips. And his dick jolted in his hand when he saw that the soft mound of her pussy was completely hairless against the black lace. It made the desire to taste her rise in him like a hunger.

He released his dick and kicked his legs free of

his pants and boxers to stride across the room. He used one arm around her waist to turn her body around and pull her back against him. The full cheeks of her bottom perfectly cupped his dick and held it upright as she circled her hips. Her head fell back against his shoulder as she let loose a heated sigh.

Quint pressed kisses along the length of her neck and brought his hands up to jerk her bra down and free her breasts. He cupped them in his hands, kneading and massaging the soft flesh, as he gently rolled her nipples between his fingers.

Kaitlyn bit her bottom lip and heaved a sigh. "Yes, Quinton. *Yesss.*" She was moaning, bringing her hands up to circle his neck as she felt light-headed from his touches.

Quint suckled the base of her neck and eased one hand down her stomach to palm and squeeze her whole pussy through the thin lace. His dick hardened at the feel of her clit throbbing against his thumb.

"Can I eat that pussy? Huh? You want me to eat that pussy?" he asked. His voice was deep in his throat as he grabbed the rim of her panties and worked them over her hips.

As soon as she nodded and let him know that she wanted him to taste her, Quint turned Kaitlyn around, grabbed her waist, and literally turned her upside down in one fluid move. Her breasts pressed against his stomach and she felt his cool breath against her pussy as her stilettos flailed in the air. She shrieked and wrapped her arms around his body. This was a first for Kaitlyn.

Quint never lost his cool; he was in total control. For him Kaitlyn's body weight was nothing.

"Hold on," he told her. He shifted up his hands to

cup her buttocks tightly, hitching up her body and holding her securely.

Kaitlyn barely had a moment to feel alarmed at being turned upside down as she felt the kiss of his lips against her clit before he sucked it deeply. She cried out as her body shivered and heat filled her stomach as her toes tingled. She reached up to grip the back of his arms for extra stability as he evidenced his strength and passion.

Quint suckled, licked, and ate her with a slow thoroughness. He moaned as he sucked her clit so deeply that she knew he enjoyed it just as much as she did. He plunged her core with his tongue and circled the walls leisurely as if he wished it were his dick.

Kaitlyn pressed heated kisses against his stomach as she freed one hand to reach and pull downward on his erection with a slow, unmethodical twisting motion that made him stumble backward a bit as his knees gave out. She was surprised that she wished she could take him into her mouth to suck, but she couldn't be that daring—that bold—yet. Not yet.

Quint took one last suck of her clit and kissed her moist, thick lips before he turned her right side up and let her body unhurriedly ease down the length of his body. And when they were eye to eye and breathing in each other's exhaled air, and the electricity seemed to crackle like lit wood, they kissed. First small puckers in between small smiles. And then deeply, with heated stares.

Kaitlyn couldn't care less that she tasted her own juices on his mouth and tongue. It was a testament to his ability to please.

"Mmmmm," she moaned as he flickered the tip of his tongue against hers.

Quinton squatted down with his strong, defined

thighs and picked up his pants before walking them down the hall to her bedroom. Kaitlyn wrapped her legs around his waist and her arms around his neck as she kissed him from one shoulder to the other, enjoying the slight tingle of his sweat against her mouth and tongue.

He kicked the bedroom door closed and eased her body down onto her pretty bed before he stood back to admire her body like it was a work of art. Kaitlyn preened under his attention as she sat up to undo her bra and flung it at him.

Quint caught it with the same hand that held his pants. He pressed his nose against the lace as he kept his eyes locked on her. And he was rewarded with Kaitlyn pressing her heels into her bed and playing in the slick folds of her core as she arched her back and thrust her hard nipples upward like twin peaks.

Quint's mouth watered as he rushed to pull out his wallet and a condom. He grabbed his shaft and worked the tight latex down the length of his hardness as he came to climb onto the bed beside her. He bent down to suck her whole breast into his mouth as his tongue flickered against her nipple.

"You like that?"

Kaitlyn nodded with a little moan in the back of her throat as she raised her hand to wipe her juices on her nipples.

"Suck 'em some more," she demanded softly.

Quint didn't hesitate. His hand replaced hers between her thighs as he tasted the juices on her nipples. His eyes watched the rapture on her face as he slid his middle finger deep inside her and circled it around her walls.

Kaitlyn cried out and raised her hips slightly to make tiny circles.

Quint withdrew his fingers and sucked them clean. "Come to the edge," he told her, rising from his knees to stand on the side of the bed as he massaged his hardness.

When she had her buttocks on the edge, he spread her legs wide and tapped the tip of his dick against her clit before massaging it.

"Oh shit," she gasped, her fingers tightly grasping the covers of her bed.

His dick strained against the edges of the condom at the rush of need he had for her. At first, he wanted to impress with his skill and technique, and he planned to position her body in a pretzel-type fashion that would shock and awe her as he sexed her. But Quint felt a shift deep within him as his eyes traveled from her face down to her fleshy rose, which sprouted open before him the more she spread her thighs as a welcome to her body. The innermost portal to her soul. The ultimate connection.

And he was ready to be with her. In her. Connecting.

But it was more than sex and bravado, more than wanting applause and accolades.

So he lay down on her and pressed his hardness inside her tight, moist, hot core. He gathered her body into his arms and felt a rush of passion and emotion at the feel of her skin pressed against his. His heartbeat pounded in unison with hers.

Their eyes connected as mirrors to their souls. Their hands explored each other's bodies. Their lips pressed. Their limbs entwined. Their hips moved in splendid unison as they made love . . . as they got lost in each other.

Their pace was slow and achingly tender. Emotional. Satisfying.

"No," he begged, easing his dick out of her a bit. "I don't want it to end."

Kaitlyn looked up at him with eyes glazed with every drop of passion he had evoked from her.

"Quinton," she whispered into his mouth in between dizzying kisses. "Quinton, please."

And he did sacrifice the delay of his own climax as he kissed her and plunged his dick deep within her. Quint worked his hips as he pressed her down into the softness of the bed with each delicious thrust. He felt the spasms of her walls against him, pulling his own seed from him. He covered her mouth with his own to smother her uninhibited cries of passion and release.

And soon he felt the heat and force of his own release as his dick pulsed against her walls with the force of each spasmodic release of his nut into her. Then it was her mouth that swallowed his hoarse cries as she worked her hips beneath him to drain him of seed, energy, and power.

They stayed locked together, long after their zenith, as they listened to their ragged breathing echoing in the air.

"No regrets?" Quinton asked as he lay with his head pressed against her bosom and listened to the beat of her heart.

Kaitlyn stroked the contours of his back and his head as she answered in complete honesty in a voice barely above a whisper: "No regrets."

Hours later, Kaitlyn grinned as she lay propped against her pillows, with Quint lying propped against her as she stroked his chest and sat with her chin gently atop his head.

"I hate that you have to go," she admitted.

He tilted his head back to look at her. "I don't have to . . . if you don't care about the entire complex knowing I spent the night."

Kaitlyn mused that over as she lightly patted his rock-hard chest. "For Lei. I'm not ready for Lei to know that," she said. "Too much to explain about what we did all night. I want her to do as we say—"

Quint appreciated that her priority was his daughter. "And not as we do," he finished for her.

"Right."

He brought his hands up to top hers and squeezed them before picking up her hands to bring to his mouth to kiss.

"I better get up then," he said, his regret clear. "The sun will be up in a couple of hours."

Kaitlyn fought the urge to reach for him as he climbed from between her legs on the bed.

"Maybe we can do something with Lei later," she suggested as she climbed from the bed as well.

He paused in pulling his pants up over his bare ass and limp—but still thick—member to eye her nudity.

"I have to run some errands this morning, but we can all do something when I get back?"

"That works for me because I have an important matter this morning—after my nap," Kaitlyn said as she grabbed her robe from the back of the bathroom door. It was her thick terry cloth she wore after showers to dry off. It was fuchsia and furry. She found Quint side-eyeing her comfort.

"What?" she asked, looking down at it.

Quint just shook his head and took her hand in his as they left her bedroom.

"That's a good idea about taking Lei somewhere,

because she's gonna be mad I didn't wake her up from Mrs. Harper's house—"

"She can't be scared, because they have one helluva guard dog," Kaitlyn joked.

"Kaitlyn," he said, his voice chiding as he scooped up his boxers and shoved them into his pants pocket and grabbed his shirt and blazer to pull on.

"I'm just saying the dog freaks me out."

Quint reached the door and pulled her body against his before he playfully swatted her behind and kissed her.

"Call me when you get back home. Okay?" he asked.

She answered by nodding. As he walked out the door, she watched him until his head disappeared as he descended the stairs. She stepped back inside her apartment and yawned.

"Y'all look good together."

Kaitlyn poked her head back out the door to see Mrs. Hanson leaning against the wall by her door, smoking a cigarette in her nightclothes. She eyed the woman in open curiosity.

"The hubby hates for me to smoke inside," she explained with a shrug.

Kaitlyn felt her ire rise at her neighbor's hubby. She had to bite her lips to school her that any man who didn't work—because he *chose* not to hit a lick at a stick—to help pay the bills didn't get to dictate a damn thing.

"You should be sleeping after working all night," she said instead.

"Can't sleep," the woman admitted. "Sometimes things sit heavy on your chest and your mind that you just can't shake 'em long enough to sleep."

Kaitlyn placed the dead bolt on to keep her door from locking as she walked over to her neighbor. She didn't miss the way the woman turned her face—but not in time for Kaitlyn to see that her eyes were puffy from crying.

"Are you okay?" she asked, stopping in her tracks because she didn't want to intrude.

Mrs. Hanson smiled at her as she flicked away the ashes on the cigarette she had stopped smoking.

"Quint is a good man. You hold on to him," she said. "They hard to come by sometimes."

And Kaitlyn knew then that Mrs. Hanson's sadness was her husband. Maybe she suspected more than the rest of the residents thought she knew.

"Thank you," Kaitlyn said, turning to head back to her apartment.

She heard the woman sniffle, and Kaitlyn's heart broke.

"Mrs. Hanson . . . sometimes you should come home early from that job of yours," Kaitlyn said, not turning to face her, before she hurried into her apartment.

As soon as she undid the dead bolt and closed her door, she stood there with her head pressed against it, waiting for the woman or her husband to come and confront her for her meddling.

That knock never came.

Quint felt like he couldn't stop yawning—or smiling.

He was sex beaten and tired, but he had promised to deliver the custom frame to his widow client in Summerville. It had to be there in time for her to place the painting of her deceased husband in it for a memorial service she was having the next day.

That done, his check was in his pocket. It was a nice hefty fee for the custom work, and she had loved it. Definitely a win-win.

As he steered his truck back toward Holtsville, Quint turned his radio up loud and bobbed his head in beat to Jay-Z and Kanye's "Otis." He even sang along with the Otis Redding chorus: "Please her, don't tease her."

Quint was in a good mood.

For the first time in a long time, he was taking a chance on love, and he felt damn good about Kaitlyn. He thought about flipping her upside down to eat her and he sang the chorus a little bit louder, "'Please her, don't tease her.'"

After making love to her, they had fallen asleep. He had awakened to find Kaitlyn straddling his body nude and massaging him to hardness. That led to round two, and he had to admit that time he did pull out a few tricks.

He stroked his dick inside her as she lay on the bed, with her legs held together over one shoulder. He held her luscious ass up high in the air as he pumped away until his body was dripping sweat down onto her. She was coating every one of his delicious inches with her cum.

Quint shook his head and released a heavy breath as he shifted in his seat to give his suddenly hard dick more room in his pants. The entire night had been epic. Kaitlyn and their crazy vibe had solidified her in his life. Not just for the amazing sex, but also for her concern for Lei, her ability to make him laugh and not take life so seriously, and the way he could talk to her and feel like she listened and gave a damn about what he was saying.

He was ready to see her and couldn't wait to find out what their plans were for the afternoon. As he made the left turn by the gas station, he fought the urge to call her. She had her own errands to run and he was patient.

Quint steered into the parking lot and parked. He felt like doing a dang-on New Edition dance move— he was in such a good mood.

"Hi, Mrs. Harper," he said cheerfully as his neighbor exited her apartment with Fifi under her arm.

She winked at him. "Good date, huh? About damn time," she said.

"Thank you, Mrs. Harper," Quint said, his broad smile re-forming his face to a boylike quality as he unlocked his front door and breezed inside the apartment.

But he soon felt like he was kicked in the balls as he eyed his ex-wife, Vita, rise to her feet in his living room.

What the fuck?

"Daddy, Mommy's back. She moved back to South Carolina," Lei said excitedly.

But his eyes never strayed from that of his ex-wife. Just a cloud over what he thought was going to be a good day. He had to fight the disappointment he felt, because his daughter was happy.

Vita walked over to him, looking like an older version of their daughter. Lei was her spitting image, even down to her thick and curvy frame. Nothing about her had changed: long, flowing hair, lots of flash, overdressed and in impossible heels, nails too long for any real job.

"Don't I get a 'welcome home,' Quint?" she asked, making a move as if to hug him.

"Welcome back," Quint forced out as he eyed Lei looking at him expectantly. "When did you get back in town?"

Vita dropped her hands when he didn't open his arms for the hug. "This morning. I'm staying with a friend until I get my own place."

Quint's gut clenched and he hated the fear that claimed him. "So Hawaii didn't work out?" he asked. Translation: *You got dumped?*

Vita's eyes glittered as she looked up at him from her petite height. "No, it didn't, but I'm fine with it." Translation: *Back up out my business.*

He literally bit his bottom lip to keep from throwing her a verbal jab alluding to her propensity to cheat. He didn't doubt that Mr. NFL caught her doing dirt and sent her packing so fast that her head spun. She had to tuck her tail and return to South Carolina.

And now she was here in his home; when for over two years, she couldn't muster the strength or desire to come and visit her child.

Quint wondered what the sudden reappearance of Vita Wells meant for *his* life.

Kaitlyn parked her car, but she sat in it for a long time and looked out at the home she grew up in: this was the home where she had been blessed with lots of love and family; the home where she knew she could always come back.

Kaitlyn quite honestly was embarrassed and ashamed about how she had pulled away from them, how she hadn't spoken to her parents in weeks. How could she face them now?

But she missed them. She ached for them.

She massaged her eyes with her fingertips as she released a heavy breath filled with her nervousness.

"Auntie Kat!" Kadina screamed, sounding as if she had seen the teen group Mindless Behavior.

Kaitlyn looked up as her niece turned and ran back in the house so fast that her ponytail whipped across her face. She took one final breath and left her car as she heard Kadina's voice screaming like a fool through the house: "Auntie Kat!"

By the time she made it to the steps, the front door opened and her mother, Lisha, stepped out. She was holding baby Kasi on her hip and toddler Karlos by his hand as four-year-old KJ squeezed past her to stand in front of her.

"Come on and help with your nephews," Lisha said, smiling at her daughter. "I'm trying to get myself ready for making Sunday dinner."

Kaitlyn climbed the stairs and reached for Kasi. She blew air bubbles against his cheek as they all made their way inside. Kadina was so excited that she was snapping her fingers and dancing as she kept knocking Kaitlyn with her hip.

"I'm making lima beans and fried chicken," Lisha said as she continued into the kitchen.

Kadina took Kasi from Kaitlyn. "Come on, y'all, let's go play Xbox 360," she said, using her legs to guide her two rambunctious cousins into the den as she motioned for Kaitlyn to follow Lisha into the kitchen.

And Kaitlyn did, rubbing her fingers through her short hair and then down the length of her jean leggings as her heels clicked against the hardwood floors leading to the kitchen. She removed the studded leather jacket she wore as she eyed her mother at the kitchen island, cutting up pieces of chicken on a thick plastic cutting board.

"Don't just stand there. Rinse those beans for me," Lisha said.

Kaitlyn felt relief and was able to relax her spine as she made her way to the sink to wash her hands. Lisha Strong was a no-nonsense woman, and Kaitlyn knew that this show of normalcy without all the dramatics was her mother's way of saying, "All is forgiven. Now let's move on."

"You look happy," her mother said from behind her.

Kaitlyn looked over her shoulder. "I am," she admitted.

"What's his name?" Lisha asked knowingly.

Kaitlyn hung her head, surprised by the heat she felt rising to her neck and cheeks. "Quinton, but everyone calls him Quint—"

"The sexy landlord guy . . . who, I thought, was reported to me as *married,*" Lisha said.

Kaitlyn chuckled. "I just told my sisters-in-law that because they wanted to play matchmaker."

Lisha set down her knife and came over to the sink to stand beside her daughter as she washed her hands. "Did some matchmaking on your own, huh?"

Kaitlyn leaned her head against her mother's shoulder for a few seconds before she filled her in on *most* of her first date with Quint.

With her high heels left at the front door, and her feet snuggled into a pair of her mother's knee-high leather riding boots, Kaitlyn drove one of the four-wheelers from the main house to the barn.

Her eldest brother, Kade, looked up as she pulled to a stop. His surprise gave way to approval; she saw this in his handsome face as she climbed from the four-wheeler with a wave. It was Saturday and her brother was on the ranch working, and undoubtedly had been there since before sunup.

And maybe because he had always been a second father figure in her life, due to the age gap, and now that he ran the ranch after her father's retirement, his anger over her spoiled ways had been more palpable than the other brothers'.

"Hey, Bubba," Kaitlyn said, walking up to him and hugging him close as he dwarfed her with his six-foot-five height.

"Whaddup, kiddo?"

Kade avoided touching her with his dirty hands; but in that moment Kaitlyn wouldn't have cared, because she could've used one of his strong bear hugs.

Her mouth opened in surprise as one of the ranch hands led Snowflake out of the barn toward her. The horse was already saddled and ready to ride. For a moment Kaitlyn was taken back to her birthday party and the joy she had felt as the beautiful white horse was led to her.

"I saw the boots and figured you wanted to ride her," Kade was saying from somewhere behind her as Kaitlyn walked to her horse and stroked her muzzle.

"Hiya, Snowflake," she said as the horse nuzzled her hand. Kaitlyn wished she had carrots or sugar cubes to feed her.

"He's over on the west end of the property."

Kaitlyn glanced over her shoulder at her brother with a nod before she placed a foot in the stirrup and climbed up onto the saddle with ease. She grabbed the reins as Snowflake shifted a bit back and forth. Once Kaitlyn felt comfortable, she squeezed the flanks with her thighs and steered the horse in a semicircle before she guided it to a gallop away from the barn and toward the outer ends of the property, which totaled hundreds of acres.

As she rode the horse down the trail, Kaitlyn was taken back to a childhood spent exploring the woods with her brothers. Sometimes she had to force them to let her tag along, but they always did. They always let her have her way.

That thought made her smile.

Since before she could remember, her brothers had always been her protectors; and having four of them sometimes meant she had to get crafty to keep them from injuring a suitor she was interested in. She had to be slick and stay creative. Her true freedom didn't come until she left home for a brief stint at the College of Charleston. And that's where she had met Anola and Tandy.

Kaitlyn missed her friends, setting them aside because she was afraid of them judging her. It really was simple. If they had judged her new living circumstances, then they weren't friends to hold on to, anyway. But she should have given them the opportunity to show her what they were made of.

Kaitlyn pulled up on the reins as she spotted her father sitting on his horse at the edge of the small pond and looking off into the distance. As she edged Snowflake forward, she let her eyes absorb the regal silver-haired man who had sired her. One of the horse's hoofs snapped a branch.

Kael turned.

Kaitlyn gripped the reins more tightly as his eyes opened in surprise before he turned his horse and galloped toward her. She covered her mouth with her hand as her emotions flooded her. Her mother, she cherished. Her brothers, she adored. But her father— her father was her everything.

"Kat," Kade said. He bent over to squeeze her hand when he reached her.

"Hi, Daddy," she said, leaning over in the saddle to press a kiss to his cheek and to be surrounded by the scent of his Old Spice cologne and the outdoors. Familiar. Warm. Missed.

"You over it now?" he asked, patting her back.

"Yes, sir," she answered, using the side of her hand to wipe her eyes as she sniffled.

"Good."

Kaitlyn straightened up in the saddle.

"I want to finish checking the fences," he said, turning his horse and heading back to the trail, knowing that his daughter was going to follow.

And she did.

Quint looked up as Kaitlyn knocked on his office door briefly before she stepped into his office. His spirits were instantly lifted at the sight of her. He rose to his feet to come around the desk and pulled her close against his body.

Instantly her hands came up to hold him back tightly. "What's wrong?" she asked. "I'm sorry I took longer than I said. I was at my parents'."

Quint stepped back from her and braced against his desk as he held on to her hand. "Good. They were happy to see you?" he asked.

Kaitlyn nodded hesitantly. "Yeah . . . but we can talk about that later. What's wrong?"

"Vita, my ex-wife, is back."

Kaitlyn's mouth shaped into an O.

Quint pulled her forward, and Kaitlyn held him close as she pressed kisses to his brow. In that moment it was everything, and enough.

CHAPTER 14

One month later

"How do I look?"

Kaitlyn smiled as she turned to smooth her hands over Quint's chest in his cashmere sweater, which he wore with denims.

"You look good enough to be late for dinner," she said, playfully wiggling her eyebrows at him before she stroked his face.

"Nah, nah. Much as I love it—and I do love it—I am not letting you make us roll up late to your parents'," he said, stepping back from her as he picked up his cell phone and keys from his dresser.

"Your loss," Kaitlyn teased him.

Quint's cell phone vibrated in his hand as they left his bedroom. He looked down at it. "It's Lei," he said, stopping in the hall as he answered the call.

"Tell her I said hello," Kaitlyn whispered as she eased past him to walk to the door of the apartment.

"Happy Turkey Day, Daddy."

Quint smiled broadly as he leaned in the open doorway of her bedroom. "Same to you. Y'all up cooking?" he asked. A literal pain hit him in his gut, knowing that he was spending the holiday apart from her. Their first apart in years.

Vita had settled into a townhome in Charleston and had taken to getting Lei nearly every weekend since her return. And when Lei asked if she could spend Thanksgiving with her mother, since he had Kaitlyn and her mom was alone, he agreed. He couldn't deny his little girl much, anyway.

"We're going over to someone's house that Mama knows," Lei said. "And that's fine, because I want some *good* food."

He laughed at that. "Kaitlyn said to tell you hello."

"Tell her I'll be home Sunday night, and ask her to bring me a plate from her mother's and to tell Kadina to call me."

Quint smiled. "I will."

"Love you, Daddy."

"Love you too."

Quint gave Lei's room one last look before he turned and left the apartment. He wanted his child with him, but he knew he couldn't be selfish and keep her away from her mother, because he would never want his ex-wife to do the same to him. Still, he was human and could admit his faults; and he just couldn't deny that life was much easier when Vita had her behind in Hawaii.

He locked the apartment and then crossed the parking lot to join Kaitlyn in his truck. She was already in the passenger seat. "Ready?" he asked as he started the engine.

"Yes. You?" she asked, looking pretty in an orange turtleneck sweater dress with a cropped leather jacket, which was the color of caramel.

He leaned over and tasted her lips before steering

the vehicle out of the parking spot. As he drove, Kaitlyn settled back in the passenger seat as he reached over to rest his hand comfortably on her thigh. He squeezed it gently.

The last month with Kaitlyn had been good. Really good.

After work they would have dinner at his apartment or at hers, with Lei always there to complete the circle and regale them with stories of her school day. At night they enjoyed a movie or just watched the news as they lounged together. They had settled into a comfortable relationship, which was still heavy with their desire for each other.

Most times they couldn't wait for Lei to go to bed before they snuck away for an hour in Kaitlyn's apartment and got lost in one another.

But it was the weekends when their relationship really flourished. If they didn't have other plans, they were together. Sometimes just lounging around the house together. Other times they explored Charleston, Savannah, and Beaufort together. But always, the nights were there. And those nights he spent holding her and sleeping with her cuddled against his body were the best.

Quint looked over at her as she mouthed the words to some song playing on the radio and his heart swelled. She looked at him and reached over to smooth her hand over his bald head before she rubbed his neck and went back to gazing out the window.

I love her.

And that thought—that realization—shook him. His grip on her thigh tightened as his heart felt like it was being squeezed in his chest.

I love her.

She glanced at him again, and the words almost tumbled from his lips. He swallowed them back.

"I wish Lei could've gone with us. She and Kadina haven't seen each other much since Vita moved back," Kaitlyn said, pouting her mouth.

"Yeah, me too," he said, swallowing a lump in his throat as he looked out the windshield at the road ahead.

"Too bad Kadina is a little older and at the high school this year, or they could see each other at school."

Quint eyed the deserted trash dump site ahead. With one more glance at Kaitlyn, he steered the truck off the road and put it in park. He saw Kaitlyn eye him curiously. He climbed out of the vehicle and came around to snatch open the passenger door.

"The hell?" Kaitlyn shrieked, eyeing him like he was crazy.

Quint pulled her out of the truck and pressed her body against the Ford. He lowered his bald head to taste her lips a dozen different times and ways before deepening the kiss with every bit of emotion he felt for her.

He felt Kaitlyn's body weaken as she kissed him back with matched intensity. As his tongue flickered against hers, he felt her body shiver, and her moans echoed inside his mouth. His dick stirred between them and he reluctantly kissed her lips one last time before he stepped back from their heat.

Kaitlyn was panting. Her peach gloss was smeared over her mouth, and her hands were splayed against the side of the truck as she eyed him in desire and surprise.

"Damn," she gasped.

Quint cleaned the sticky gloss from his mouth with

his thumb as he eyed her. The urge to kiss her and to somehow express his love for her had overwhelmed him. He smiled at her and shook his head, completely shaken by the fact that this woman whom he once considered a beautiful mess had eased her way into his heart.

"Everyone take your seats," Kade Strong announced, his eyes and his smile bright as he called his family into the spacious dining room.

Kaitlyn smiled as she watched Quint pick up KJ as they all made their way into the dining room. Her nephew had instantly taken to Quint, who tossed the little boy like a football into the air as he laughed with childish glee.

"I think I want a son," Quint whispered to her after he settled KJ into his seat at the kids' table before sliding into his own seat beside her at the long and wide table.

"Today?" she asked playfully, reaching over to place her hand on his thigh.

Quint just chuckled.

Kaitlyn smiled at him and raised her finger to ease it into one of his dimples.

"Awwww!" The women around the table all sighed.

Kaitlyn snatched her hand away and blushed. She had completely forgotten there were people around. She had been lost in the Kaitlyn-and-Quint bubble.

He massaged her back comfortingly and she felt the slight tension ease from her body, just like *that.*

It felt good to be there with him, and around her boisterous family too. And he seemed to fit just fine. That was asking a lot from her overprotective brothers, inquisitive father, curious mother, and nosy sisters-in-law. But he took it all in stride.

Her life and the way she viewed it were so different; and although she was proud of herself, her job, and the fact that she had taken on paying her own rent and car note, she knew her change in outlook had a lot to do with him. A whole lot.

"Kaitlyn. Kaitlyn?"

"Huh?" She drifted from her thoughts and found everyone at the table staring at her.

"What are you thankful for, Kat?" her father asked.

"Uhm, I'm thankful for my family, my new life, and my new man," she admitted.

"Thank you, baby." He leaned over and kissed her cheek.

Her brothers rolled their eyes teasingly. Her sisters-in-law and her nieces—including Kaleb's stepdaughter twins—all sighed.

Quint reached for her hand on the top of the table and stroked the back of it with his thumb, even as he talked to her brothers about football.

Kaitlyn looked up and found her father's eyes on them. She gave him a reassuring smile and was glad when he nodded in approval.

Quint looked around at the vast acres stretched out before them as he walked alongside Kaitlyn. It was nice to get away from the crowd and have her back to himself for a few minutes before they returned to the main house.

"Where are you taking me?" he asked.

Kaitlyn bumped her shoulder against his before

she turned and walked backward. "Are you afraid, city boy?" she teased.

Quint eyed her. "I'm from the city. That's true. But I left being a boy behind a long time ago. But then you know that, right?" he shot back, with a meaningful stare down below his belt.

Kaitlyn just arched an eyebrow before she turned and dashed off to run inside the barn. She paused at the door and looked back over her shoulder at him briefly before she disappeared inside.

Quint followed behind at a slower pace as he marveled that Kaitlyn was so comfortable traipsing through grass and dirt in her heels. Yet another facet to her. As he entered the stable, he was thankful that the scent of the housed horses was not strong. It was clear that the horses, like the rest of the impressive ranch, were well taken care of on a continual basis.

His eyes widened in surprise to see Kaitlyn nuzzling her face against the nose of a white horse. Even though Kaitlyn had told him about her horse, he still didn't expect to find her so close to it, reaching her head and hands over the door to its stall. He walked up and reached out to lightly pat the horse's strong neck.

"So this is Snowflake?" Quint asked.

Kaitlyn nodded with pride. "Isn't she beautiful?" she asked, reaching into the pocket of her leather jacket to pull out slices of a carrot. She placed one in the middle of her palm and spread her hand out flat, with her fingers angled down toward the ground.

Quint watched as she held her hand a few feet away and the horse reached its head out to take the carrot slice into its mouth.

"Good girl," Kaitlyn said, stroking the flat area between its eyes.

It surprised him again when Kaitlyn didn't turn up her nose in distaste or run to wash her hands. Instead, she set another carrot slice in her hand and repeated the process.

Kaitlyn laughed when she looked over and saw the odd expression on his face. "I did grow up on a ranch, you know," she reminded him.

Quint eased his hands into the pockets of his denims as he leaned against the wall of the stall and studied her. "So which one is really you? The glamour gal, with her high heels and a job in fashion, or the country girl, who loves feeding horses and eating chitlin'."

Kaitlyn pointed her finger at him. "Don't sleep on my mama's hog mog and *chitterlings*," she said. "You shoulda tried 'em before you knocked them."

Quint shook his head. "There was too much fried turkey and ham available for me to need *chitterlings* on my plate."

Kaitlyn just laughed.

"So which one?" he asked.

"Both," she answered without hesitation, as if the question had remained on her mind as it did for him.

Quint fell silent and just watched her patiently feed the horse the carrots, one by one. It was a comfortable silence. They had shared many of them in the past month, and he knew they would share many more in the months—and, hopefully, years—to come.

"Did I ever tell you that when I watch you carving or building something from wood that I think it is the sexiest thing I have seen in my life?" she asked suddenly as she walked over to the deep sink at the end of the stable to wash her hands.

Quint's eyes dropped down to watch the movement of her buttocks in her dress as she did so.

"No, I don't believe you have ever told me that," he said, his voice deep.

She nodded. "Why don't you start a business doing it, you know?"

Quint raised his thick eyebrows. "I don't need an actual business for you to get hot watching me work my wood."

He jerked his head up and she whipped her head to look over her shoulder at him with mischief in her eyes.

"Pause," they said in unison.

"But seriously," Kaitlyn said, wiping her hand with paper towels that she had yanked from the metal dispenser on the wall. "You're really, really good, and I think you should consider doing it more. Maybe not full-time, but take on more. I can help, if you like. I'm pretty good with wood."

Thankfully, they both let that "pause" moment pass.

"You really think so?" he asked as she came up to wrap her arms around his waist and leaned back to look up at him.

"Yes, I think I'm very good with—"

"Not that," he said, pressing a kiss to her forehead. "Do you really think I can get a strong hustle going?"

Kaitlyn eyed him in the utmost seriousness. "I believe that you, Quinton Wells, can do *anything* you set your mind to do," she told him.

Quint liked the faith and confidence she had in him. And he believed her. That made him believe in himself a little more.

"I'll think about it," he promised.

Kaitlyn undid her arms from around his waist and reached for his hand to lead him down to the last stall. "Now I have something else for you to think about," she said, grabbing one of the freshly laundered saddle blankets from the shelves before pulling him into an empty stall.

Quinton stopped short and then tugged on her hand and pulled her body against his.

"We can't do this," he said, even as he felt the pulse running along the length of his dick, which picked up the pace.

Kaitlyn flung the blanket over her head as she licked and then lightly bit his bottom lip. "You're right. Why get on that hard floor when there's a perfectly good stool for you to sit on," she said, using her hands to pull down on his shoulders until he bent his knees and sat on the stool.

Quint eyed her as she pulled her sweater dress up around her waist and eased her bikini panties down over her hips. He licked his lips at the sight of her bald pussy as she straddled his hips, but she sat back on the top of his thighs as she straddled him to reach down and undo his belt and zipper. Soon his dick was in her hands and she was stroking him to hardness.

And it felt good. Damn good.

"Kaitlyn, we can't," he protested, sounding weak even to his own ears.

She reached up under her dress and pulled a condom from her bra.

"Oh, so you planned this?" he asked thickly, looking down as she tore the foil and worked the latex down the slight arch of his long thickness.

Kaitlyn said nothing as she rose up on her toes and then shifted forward to guide her pussy down onto him slowly, adjusting to the feel of him pressing against her walls. She winced and gasped in pleasure until all of him was planted deep within her. The very base of his hardness pressed against her clit and she already felt herself near an orgasm.

"Oh shit," Quint gasped, tightly holding her hips as he stretched his legs out before him. She was tight and wet and already pulsing against the length of him.

Kaitlyn pulled the front of her sweater dress over her head as she began to work her hips back and forth, sending her core gliding up and down the length of him. She guided his mouth to her cleavage and felt her walls spasm as he sucked at it hotly. She grasped the door to the stall tightly as she rode him. Each thrust of her hips rammed the chair and his back against the door, making a loud slamming noise.

Bam!

Quint used one hand to free her breast to suckle her nipple as the pace and force of her thrusts picked up.

Bam!

Bam! Bam!

Kaitlyn let her head fall back as she gripped the door tightly enough to crack it as she enjoyed the feel of his mouth and the sliding, gliding motion of her throbbing clit against his hardness. The added intensity of them being caught kicked everything up a notch.

Bam! Bam! Bam!

Quint opened his eyes as her breasts jiggled in his mouth. He wondered if anyone could hear them. Between his moans and her hip work, even the horses had to be curious as to what exactly was going on in stall number ten at the end.

Bam! Bam! Bam! Bam!

"Kaitlyn," he managed to say, even as he enjoyed her ride.

"What?" she asked, lifting her head to look at him.

And ride him harder. Their slamming echoed inside the stable.

Bam! Bam! Bam! Bam! Bam!

"Kaitlyn!"

"What?" she asked softly, looking at him intently as she licked her lips.

Quint's body went stiff as he felt his climax coming on like a storm.

BAM! BAM! BAM! BAM! BAM!

"Don't worry," Kaitlyn whispered to him. "I'm coming with you."

BAM-BAM-BAM-BAM-BAM-BAM-BAM-BAM-BAM-BAM!

They cried out hoarsely as they both felt the white-hot explosion firing off inside them and pushing them far over the edge of caring who heard.

Kaitlyn and Quint walked up to the main house together, still playful and caught up in the afterglow from another heated coupling.

"Thank God, those horses can't talk," Quint quipped.

She laughed as she slid her arm through his. "Ain't that the truth."

They neared the porch and Kaitlyn grimaced to see her mother, sisters-in-law, and the twins, Meena and Neema, all lounging on the porch as the sun was just beginning to set.

"Uh-oh," Quint said under his breath as they climbed the stairs to the sound and sight of the ladies' whispers and nudges against each other.

Kaitlyn knew Quint was glad to leave the porch and head inside to wherever the men were gathered around the television. She started to do the same, but

Bianca leaned over and tugged on the front of her dress.

"The shape is gone, boo. What happened?" Bianca asked, with a sly look up at Kaitlyn.

"Are all the sweet potato pies gone?" Kaitlyn asked as she sat down next to Meena and crossed her legs.

The ladies laughed and shared knowing looks at her swift—and obvious—change of subject.

"I made a plate for you, Quint, and his daughter," Lisha said as she rocked in her chair. She pulled her wrap closer around her arms as the wind began to turn chillier as the sun took its heat with it.

"Thanks, Mommy."

The front door opened and Quint stepped out onto the porch. Kaitlyn looked up at him and she could tell he was angry. She rose to her feet, thinking somehow one of her brothers and he had gotten into it.

"What's wrong?"

"I have to check on Lei, so I have to go," Quint said, reaching in his pocket for his keys.

"I hope everything is okay," Lisha offered.

"Yes, ma'am," he said. "Kaitlyn, if you want to stay with your family, I can come back for you."

Kaitlyn nodded. "Yeah. Okay. If you don't need me. As long as Lei isn't hurt or anything?"

Quint nodded. "No, it's not *her*," he stressed.

Vita.

So far, Kaitlyn had avoided meeting her, and she didn't mind keeping it that way. But she frowned at all of the long, big-eyed stares the ladies were giving her.

"I'll walk you to the car," she offered as they began to whisper.

The hell?

"Lei just called, and her mother wants her to move

back in with her," Quint said before he climbed into the driver's seat.

Kaitlyn felt her shoulders slump under the weight of his words. She knew that the news affected him, and that made her ache for him. Lei was his heart.

"Kat."

She turned and was surprised to see her mother coming down the stairs to stand on the bottom step with a plastic bag holding the to-go containers. Kaitlyn frowned in confusion.

Lisha motioned for Kaitlyn to come to her.

"One sec, Quint," she told him before walking up to the foot of the stairs.

He gave her mother another wave before closing the driver's door and starting the truck.

Lisha pressed the bag into her daughter's hand. "See you Sunday?" she asked.

"But I'm not go—"

"Yes, you are," every woman on the porch said in unison.

Kaitlyn leaned to the side to look past her mother at her family. Each one's look conveyed: *Don't be stupid.*

She opened her mouth, wanting to defend Quint:
I trust him.
We give each other space.
This is about his child. I'm minding my own.

"Baby, are you serious about this man?" Lisha asked.

Kaitlyn straightened her body to look up at her mother. "Yes. Yeah. Yes. *Yes,*" she stressed.

"Then you be by his side when he's going through something. You be his spine. The backbone. We're family. We love you. And we've done proved, we ain't going nowhere," Lisha advised.

She leaned over again to look at the women. They all waved her bye-bye.

"Oh . . . okay," Kaitlyn said, turning to head back to the pickup.

"You changed your mind?" Quint asked after she climbed up into the truck and closed the door securely behind herself.

"Yeah. If that's okay?" she asked.

"I prefer it," he said, patting her thigh reassuringly before he circled out of the yard and down the long drive. "I didn't want to force you to leave your family for my drama."

They were right. Humph.

"I'm good. I'm full. We got to-go plates. Now let's go check on Lei."

Quint steered with his left hand and opened his right one to her, palm side up. Kaitlyn took the hand into the middle of both of hers and squeezed them as she looked over at his handsome profile.

"Did she already say she wanted to live with her mom?" Kaitlyn asked.

Quint shook his head. "She asked me to pick her up so we could talk about it."

She squeezed his hand a bit tighter between hers. "What are you going to do?"

"Hell if I know," Quint admitted. "Vita is her mother. She carried her. She still has the C-section scar. But for two years she just checked out on our daughter—maybe because she was confident I would step up, or maybe she's just as selfish as I think she is. To be honest, I don't think it's fair that she messes up her life, and now she wants to come back and mess up ours."

Kaitlyn nodded in understanding.

"It's some real bullshit, you know?"

She looked down at their entwined hands as she felt him tighten his grip—seeking *her* comfort. If she had remained behind with her family, he would have taken this ride to Charleston *alone* and dealt with his raw emotions *alone*.

And there was no need for that when he had her.

"Prepare yourself, baby," Kaitlyn said with a little hesitance, "because if she wants to talk about it, then she's thinking about it."

Quint glanced over at her for a second before refocusing his eyes on the road. He said nothing else, but he left his hand sandwiched between hers; and Kaitlyn made sure that she never let it go.

The next morning Quint stood leaning in the door frame as he watched Kaitlyn help his daughter pack her clothes. He kept the sadness from his face, even as he felt as if his very heart were being plucked from his chest. He didn't want Lei to feel guilty for her decision to move in with her mother.

He didn't want to let her go . . . but he was.

Lei was old enough to decide for herself, and so Quint was respecting her wishes.

"Don't forget your shoes," Kaitlyn said, picking up the two pairs of sequined flats she'd given her.

Lei shook her head. *"Oh no,"* she stressed. "My mama would wear them, so I'm leaving them here."

Quint's gut tightened and his jaw clenched in annoyance. He had to bite his tongue not to snap out, "Why the hell are you going to live somewhere where you can't even take your damn stuff?"

Behind Lei's back Kaitlyn motioned for him to smile. He forced one to his lips, but he wouldn't be surprised if he looked like a damn clown.

A horn blew. He pushed off the frame to walk to the door and open it. Vita's new cherry red Miata was parked next to Kaitlyn's red Volvo. He shook his head, thinking himself once a fool for letting material and exterior bullshit fool him into thinking Kaitlyn was anything like his ex-wife.

He had been wrong.

"Lei, your mom," he called back to her as he began carrying her suitcases from beside the front door. "Open your trunk, Vita."

She eyed him as he passed by her driver's-side window before she leisurely unlocked the trunk and then lowered her window. "I guess you'll be moving back into that big, old house," she called out the window behind him.

Quint frowned, already on guard about her intentions. He said nothing as he slid the large suitcase and book bag into the empty trunk. Knowing Lei had another large suitcase, he left the trunk open before he walked back toward the apartment.

Vita suddenly swung her door open, blocking his path. She turned and sat sideways on the seat as she looked up at him. "I said . . . I guess you'll be moving back into that big, old house of yours," she said.

Quint worked his shoulders in agitation as he eyed her. "What does that have to do with you?" he snapped, losing his patience and desire for false niceties real fast.

"Plenty," she stressed. "Because you might want to rethink it, since you'll be back on child support. ASAP."

And that was the other shoe that he had been waiting to fall. Quint eyed her and didn't bother to hide his distaste for her. It was sad that he couldn't stand the sight of a woman he thought he once loved—the woman who had bore his child.

The front door opened. Lei and Kaitlyn stepped out, and he watched as his woman hugged his daughter and kissed her cheek. He shifted his eyes back to Vita; his ex-wife took in the show of affection as well before she smirked.

Quint backtracked and went around Kaitlyn's car to reach them. "Wait until I tell you what she just said to me," he whispered to Kaitlyn when Lei walked over to greet her mother at the car.

Kaitlyn rubbed his arm. "I'll be inside," she said, turning to walk back into the apartment with a final wave at Lei.

Quint knew she wanted no part of the drama. He couldn't blame her. He wished *he* didn't have to deal with it either.

CHAPTER 15

Two months later

Kaitlyn parked her car in the small parking lot
beside the boutique. She opened the vehicle's back
door to pull out the garment bags her boss had asked
her to bring to Xena, his co-owner of Adorned. She
closed the door with a bump of her hip and turned.

"Kaitlyn?"

Ain't this some shit? She smiled as she eyed Anola
and Tandy walking toward her in the parking lot.

"Oh, my God!" Tandy shrieked, rushing over to
Kaitlyn to hug her, with Anola arriving close behind.

"When did you get back from Italy?"

"Did you buy the most amazing clothes?"

"Did you hook any cuties?"

"Did you get a chance to lie out . . . because you
don't look bronzed?"

Kaitlyn's head spun as she looked back and forth
from each of the fab divas as they shot questions at
her like the paparazzi. She held up a hand to stop
the barrage.

They both clamped their mouths shut.

Kaitlyn's lips moved, but no words emerged as she struggled with continuing her lie or shaming the Devil with the truth.

"I have to be honest," she said. "I didn't—"

Anola's Nicki Minaj ring tone sounded off, and she visibly jumped as she dug into her black patent tote.

It was Kaitlyn's turn to clamp her mouth shut.

"Is that Ursula?" Tandy asked, leaning over to look down at Anola's phone.

Kaitlyn's face filled with disbelief.

"Yes. We gotta go," Anola said, carelessly dropping the phone back into her bag. "Kaitlyn, there's a Botox party at Ursula Griffin's."

"You totally know Ursula, right?" Tandy asked. "She's the daughter of that newscaster from Channel 4. They just moved in next to Anola and her parents and she has the best closet in the—"

"Botox?" Kaitlyn asked, her brow puckering as she completely cut off the Ursula Griffin bio. "I don't need Botox, and neither do either of you."

They both eyed her like she was an alien. "So you don't want to go?" Tandy asked, looking confused.

Kaitlyn shook her head. "No, I'm good."

"Let's all hook up for sip and shop tomorrow," Anola said, leaning forward to air-kiss each of Kaitlyn's cheeks. "We have so much to tell you."

Tandy air-kissed her as well. "Yes, we have *lived* since we saw you last."

"So have I," Kaitlyn said, even though she knew they spoke of living in completely different ways.

Kaitlyn had found love, grasped at her maturity, and earned the respect of her family. She loved her friends, but she knew they spoke of parties, fashion, and scandalous gossip.

"We gotta run," Anola said, pulling Tandy by the wrist to her white BMW Roadster.

"Call us," Tandy called over her shoulder.

Kaitlyn waved them off and made her way out of the parking lot and into the boutique. Just as she pushed the glass door open, they pulled out of the parking lot, blew the horn, and then sped off down King Street.

Kaitlyn felt like she hardly even knew—or understood—them.

Quint stood back and observed his handiwork on the crib he was commissioned to design and build as a surprise for an OB-GYN's wife. They had struggled for many years to conceive, and the doctor wanted a unique and sturdily built crib that they planned to pass down through their family for the generations to come. He got the job off a referral from the widow for whom he had done the custom picture frame.

In fact, he got that job and two more. He was swamped. He yawned as he began cleaning his tools. He was exhausted. Between his work at the apartment complex, the increased carpentry work, carving out quality time with Lei, and still making time to devote to his relationship with Kaitlyn, Quint was beat.

Quint hadn't been running or gone weight lifting in weeks. Although he missed the physical exertion, he was enjoying working—and making good money— from his craft. So much so, he was seriously considering walking out on faith and leaving the job at the apartment complex behind to focus on building a real business of his custom cabinetry.

He took the job to be able to be there for Lei, but

that was when she was living with him. Now that she was back living with her mother, he could speed up his plan to move back into his house and live off his savings while he focused on woodworking. He had only delayed the move so far because he wanted to make sure his ex-wife wouldn't fly the coop again and leave him to willingly rearrange his life to suit his daughter living with him.

Quint glanced at the time on his cell phone. It was well after nine. He finished up in his shed and locked it securely, glancing up at Kaitlyn's rear windows to see her apartment was still dark. He made his way to the front of the property, and her car was nowhere to be seen.

Usually she got home from work around six and she would call him or come back to the shed to sit with him as he worked. He frowned.

Did something happen?

As he unlocked the front door and entered his apartment, he called her cell phone. Relief flooded him when she answered the call.

"Hey, baby," she said cheerfully.

The background chatter was so loud that he barely heard her.

"Hey, I was just checking on you when I didn't see your car," Quint said, turning on the lights as he made his way to the kitchen to grab a bottle of beer from the fridge.

"Oh, I'm at my parents'. Everyone in my family was here, just cutting up," she said.

"Tell Quint I said chill out. You good," he heard one of her brothers holler out in the background.

Quint smiled. "Just wanted to make sure you were safe."

"Aww, thanks, babe. My mama already made you a plate. We had baked spaghetti."

The mention of food made him remember that he hadn't eaten and his stomach grumbled in protest as he dropped down on the couch and turned on the television. "I can use it. Thank her for me."

"Be there soon."

"A'ight." Quint ended the call and tossed his cell phone on the chair as he flipped through the channels. He had barely settled on an old Richard Pryor movie before his cell phone vibrated.

"Yeah," he said.

"Hey, Daddy."

He smiled. "What's up, Lei?"

"Nothing. Just got done with my homework."

Quint put the TV on mute with the remote as he noted the odd inflection in her voice. "Everything okay?" he asked.

"Yeah. I just wanted to call you before I went to bed. I know you miss me," Lei teased.

"I damn sure do."

"I miss you too, Daddy."

He thought of his little girl toddling toward him as she took her first steps. "Movie night?"

"Definitely."

He was still smiling when they ended the call. Lights flashed against the wall of his living room. He rolled off the couch to look out the window at Kaitlyn parking and then climbing out of her car to pull shopping bags from her trunk. Many, many shopping bags. All glossy and designer labels.

Quint frowned as he opened the door. "Hey, baby, you need help?"

Kaitlyn nodded as she handed the majority of the

bags to him before reaching for a couple more bags and a Styrofoam to-go container. "Thanks."

"Been shopping?" he asked dryly before easily jogging up the stairs to her front door.

"Yesssss," she said with emphasis from behind him. "My parents turned my credit card back on today, and I treated myself to a little shopping excursion after work."

Quint made a face. "You mean *they* treated you," he pointed out.

Kaitlyn remained quiet.

Quint reached the top of the stairs and looked back at her. She had paused midway.

"What?" he asked.

"You say that like it's a problem, Quint," she said. "They see I'm working hard and congratulated me, but you're making me feel some kind of way."

Quint shrugged. "Kaitlyn, look, if you okay with your parents paying your bills again, then it has nothing to do with me."

Kaitlyn dropped her head as she continued up the stairs to stand before him with the straps of the shopping bags around her wrist and the container of food in her hand. "You're right. It doesn't."

He eyed her. "Whatever, Kaitlyn. Could you unlock the door?" he asked, irked and sounding it.

She literally stomped her foot. "What do you mean 'whatever'?" she snapped.

Quint looked annoyed. "Yo, why all the attitude?"

"Why all the judgment?" she shot back.

Quint bit his bottom lip and shook his head as he stared at her.

Kaitlyn brushed past him to unlock the door with her free hand and hold it open for him to carry in her bags. "Why are we arguing?" she asked as she flipped the switch to bask the living room with light before sitting the bags and food by the table under her oversized photo.

Quint set the bags on the sofa. "Look, I apologize, okay? It's none of my business and I'm out of it," he said, coming over to press a kiss to her temple before picking up the plate.

Kaitlyn held up her hands. "Okay, I don't get it. That's all."

Quint looked down at her. "I know," he said with the utmost seriousness.

And that's what concerned him.

He said nothing, and he had hoped for the best, but he had not missed little things that proved Kaitlyn was reverting back to some of her old ways, and her family was once again enabling it. He had not missed that last month the check to pay her rent had been drawn off her father's business checking account, not her own. She was beginning to miss a random day here and there of work. Last week she was looking through catalogs for new cars.

Quint noticed it all and said nothing, but he thought a lot about it because the woman he fell in love with was the funny, confident woman who faced adversity and overcame her shortcomings to kick ass and take names to be a better person.

It frustrated him that the same family that had done a great thing in making her take responsibility for herself couldn't see that they were slowly undoing their work.

He could see it, even if they couldn't, and it frustrated the hell out of him.

* * *

Kaitlyn stirred in her sleep and rolled over to find her bed empty. She lifted her head off the bed and looked around. Quint's spot was cool, so she knew he had been gone from her bed for a while.

Flinging back the covers, she climbed from the bed in her footed pajamas to leave the bedroom in the darkness.

Maybe he's watching TV, she thought.

But the living room was empty as well.

Kaitlyn turned and walked across the short length of the apartment. In the kitchen she opened the back door; and through the slats of the wrought-iron railing, she could see the light on in his shed. She made her way down the stairs and over to the workshop. Without knocking she eased the door open.

Still dressed in his pajama bottoms and a wife beater, Quint looked over his broad shoulder at her before turning back to the piece he was working on.

Kaitlyn frowned at the coolness she felt from him. His dismissal was colder than the January air whipping around her. She stepped inside the shed and closed the door behind her, glad for the space heater he had running.

"Couldn't sleep?" she asked.

"Yeah," he answered.

"You shoulda woke me up," she said, reaching up to touch his arm and lightly squeeze his bicep. "I woulda put you to sleep."

Quint shifted to the other side of the crib . . . and away from her touch. "I really want to concentrate on this," he said.

Kaitlyn stiffened her back; she felt completely dismissed.

"Cool," she managed to say; then she turned to

leave the shed, even as the hurt of his distant treatment literally caused a pang in her chest.

Once back in her apartment, she removed the footed pajamas and balled them up to toss in her dirty clothes hamper before climbing into her bed, naked. She lay there for a long time with her hand stretched out to palm the spot where Quint usually lay.

In the moments just before her eyes finally closed, as she drifted off to sleep, she knew he was not returning to her bed that night.

The next morning proved her right, and Kaitlyn thought about that as she sat at her desk, gazing out the window at downtown Charleston. She saw nothing of the views, though, because her thoughts were on Quinton. After they had words about her shopping spree—something she still didn't understand—they had eaten the food she brought from her mother and then lounged together as they watched TV. He even spent the night at her apartment, but they hadn't truly spoken to one another. That night they hadn't made love or even touched one another in their sleep.

"Kaitlyn, did the manager of the Charlotte store e-mail you her choices for the fashion show?"

She looked up at her boss standing behind her. The tall and handsome blond man was twisting his diamond band around his finger. She knew that meant he was annoyed. Pulling up to her desk, she accessed her company e-mail.

"No, not yet," she answered. "Do you want me to call and request it before close of business today?"

He winked at her and smiled; his veneers were as

bright as egg whites and a little too large for his mouth. "Thank you," he sang in a falsetto before turning and heading back into his office.

Kaitlyn quickly made the call, but her thoughts never strayed from Quint. She just didn't understand how he could be so annoyed by something her parents had done for her. She hated to think he was intimidated by her parents' wealth, because there was nothing she could do about that.

Usually, throughout the day, if he wasn't too busy, he would call her. Today she received no calls, and she refrained from calling him because of his cool treatment of her from the night before. Another first.

When Kaitlyn headed home for the night, she was intent on sitting Quint down to talk. She hated feeling disconnected from him, but she didn't appreciate feeling judged either.

Or put aside. Forgotten. Dismissed.

As she pulled her car into the complex, Kaitlyn spotted Quint talking to contractors outside Mrs. Hanson's old apartment. Her neighbor had understandably found it hard to live in the same complex as the woman who had been sleeping with her husband, so she had moved out last month. With his lover being married—and not looking for a new roommate, word on the street was Mr. Hanson was back home with his mother. Quint was busy getting the unit ready for a new tenant.

He looked down at her as she climbed from the car. Kaitlyn was surprised when he took a moment out of his life to lift his head in greeting. She arched her eyebrows at him and sucked her teeth before she went around the back of the complex to climb the stairs and enter her apartment through the rear.

"Humph. You give me your ass to kiss last night

and didn't bother to call all day, and now I get a homeboy head nod. Negro, *please,*" she muttered, slamming her purse and keys on her kitchen table as she kicked off her heels and sent them flying across the floor in two different directions.

Her front door opened and Kaitlyn looked down the hall as Quint walked in and closed the door behind himself. She eyed him as he came down the hall and bent down to press a kiss on her. She turned her head and his lips landed on her cheek.

"It's like that?" he asked, rising to his full height.

Kaitlyn leaned back to look up at him with her eyes wide. "It was like *that* last night," she reminded him, then brushed past him to walk into her bedroom.

Quint followed behind her. "I thought we could go and grab something to eat," he said. "I wanted to talk to you about something."

"Actually, I was going to meet some friends for dinner in Charleston," Kaitlyn said, paused in unzipping the high-waist leather skirt she wore. "Something wrong?"

"No, no," he assured her, coming over to stand behind her and undo the zipper for her.

Knock, knock.

They both looked up.

"Aw, hell, zip me back up?"

Quint did and then followed her out of the room. He went to the kitchen and Kaitlyn headed for the front door. She opened it and her face filled with surprise to find her parents standing there.

"Hey, I didn't know y'all were coming," she said, stepping back to let them enter as she hugged each one.

"We were just getting back from Charleston and we decided to stop by and see if you were home,"

Lisha said, moving around the apartment to look around at the photos Kaitlyn had displayed.

Kaitlyn wrapped her arm around her father. "Actually, I do have plans for dinner," she said.

Kael Strong looked around the apartment as well. "It's a little small," he said.

"It's a change from my last apartment," Kaitlyn agreed as she watched her parents share a look.

"If you wanted to move to a bigger place, we would be willing to help until you got on your feet," Kael said.

Kaitlyn's face filled with surprise before she squealed.

Her father winced and placed a finger in his ear.

A noise echoed from the kitchen. Her mother jumped to her feet in alarm.

Kaitlyn smiled. "That's Quinton," she said, turning to head to the other room. Confusion filled Kaitlyn's face to find it empty. The noise must have been the door closing as he left.

Without speaking to my parents, she thought.

"I thought you said Quint was in here," Lisha asked, entering the kitchen to look around at that room as well.

"I thought he was too," she lied.

"Now, listen," Lisha said, eyeing her. "We are not going back to the old days of flitting around the world on our dime. You keep your job and work on your career, and we'll help and be there for you. Understand?"

Kaitlyn nodded. "I appreciate the safety net, but I'm still flying on my own."

"We see the change, so we're willing to help you."

"Thanks, Mama," Kaitlyn said, reaching over to squeeze her mother's side.

* * *

It was cold. Bitter cold. Even in the South, January weather at night was brutal. However, Quint had bundled up in his sweat clothes, threw on a skully, and went for a long run. He took the back roads for the forty-minute run to Walterboro and didn't stop until he came up on his house. He breathed deeply as he felt the sweat dripping from his body under his clothes as he thought of his decision go forward about giving his tenants forty-five days' notice to move.

He made the call just that day. They were ending their annual lease and he decided not to renew it with them. He also gave his employer the same forty-five days' notice.

It was time to go home.

Quint nodded, feeling more assured of his decision before he turned and began the run back to Holtsville. Tonight he wanted to share his plans with Kaitlyn, but he had been busy all day getting the apartment ready to be shown. And then she had plans for the evening, so their talk was postponed.

Bzzzzzz . . .

Quint stopped running to reach into his pocket for his cell phone. The back roads were dark at night and he was glad for the glow from one of the homes' utility pole in their front yard as he answered the call from Lei.

"Daddy."

Quint frowned. "What's wrong, Lei?"

"Man, Daddy, Mama left me at my friend's house who lives down the street from us. Then she just called me, talking about she not coming home and asking if I can spend the night here. I don't have clothes and I don't have a key to the house."

Quint squeezed his phone so hard that he was sure it would snap in half in his hand. "I'm on my way. Let me talk to your friend's mother."

His heart was pounding hard and it had nothing to do with his run. He'd had it with Vita. Absolutely had it. Even as he thanked the neighbor for watching out for his daughter, and let her know he was on his way to get her, he was walking fast and hating that he was far from his vehicle.

Kaitlyn.

Kaitlyn might still be in Charleston.

He stopped running again and called her phone.

"Hello."

The sound of music and loud voices was so loud in the background that he barely heard her.

"Are you still in Charleston?" he asked.

"Hold on."

He fought for patience because his issues with Vita and Lei were not her fault.

"Yeah, I'm back."

The noise was gone.

"Are you still in Charleston?" he asked.

"Yes. What's wrong?"

"I hate to bother you, but I went for a run and I don't have my car, and Vita left Lei at somebody's house—"

"Give me the address. I'll go get her," Kaitlyn said without hesitation.

Kaitlyn had ridden with him to pick Lei up. "It's 12 Sycamore Lane, a few houses down from Vita's house," he said, feeling some sense of relief. "I just can't believe she would pull this kind of stunt."

"I'm leaving Anola's now. I should be there to get her in less than twenty minutes—if that."

"Thank you."

After they ended the call, Quint allowed himself a few moments of feeling weak, out of control, and out of sorts. Lei was his child and he heard the anxiety and hurt in her voice. And that had slashed him, just as deep as a sharp knife.

He dialed Lei back.

"Daddy, Kaitlyn just called me—"

"Lei, why didn't you call me earlier?" he asked as he walked down the road.

The line remained quiet.

"Lei," he said sternly.

"She usually comes home or at least lets me in the house first."

Quint stopped once again as he pulled the phone from his face to look at it. "Your mother been leaving you in the house alone? All night?" he asked in a hard tone.

"Yes, sir."

The reluctance in her voice angered him. A child should never feel required to cover for a parent. *Never.*

"She got a new boyfriend," Lei admitted into the silence.

Quint punched the air to release some of the emotions flooding him and causing his body to tense up.

"We'll talk when you get here. Love you, okay," he assured her, needing to get off the phone before he talked crap about her mother to her.

As much as Vita proved time and time again that her selfishness was endless, he never talked down about her to their child. It would only hurt Lei to point out to her that she was not number one on her mother's list of priorities.

Quint finished his run and was glad to reach the complex. Kaitlyn called to assure him that she had picked up Lei, as promised, but Quint wouldn't feel right until he laid his eyes on his daughter.

What should he do now?

Make Lei move back in with him? Or not? He wanted the choice to be hers, but as a parent he couldn't sit back and let Vita's level of competency as a mother be dictated by whether she had a new stiff one in her life.

Quint stepped up onto the front fender to lift his body up to sit on the hood of the truck. It didn't buckle under his weight, and he wouldn't have cared if it did. Just as the cold wasn't affecting him when his anger had him well heated.

He didn't know how much time had passed before Kaitlyn's car finally parked next to him. Lei hopped out and came around his vehicle to stand by him. "Kaitlyn stopped and got me some Mickey D's," she said, looking up at him with a little guilt in her pretty eyes.

Quint smiled down at her as he reached to stroke her head. "Go eat your food. I'm coming in," he said.

"Thanks, Miss Kaitlyn," she said over her shoulder before she used her key to unlock the apartment and enter.

Quint turned his head to eye Kaitlyn slowly walking over to him. She wore a sequined dress that fit her curves like a second skin. She looked beautiful and sexy; but in that moment he saw the old Kaitlyn and he wondered if he had changed his prejudgment of her too soon.

Kaitlyn came over to stand between Quint's legs and pressed her hands to his thighs.

"You good?" she asked, looking up at him and pretending unspoken words didn't still linger between them.

Quint nodded as he looked down at her. "Just disappointed in Vita. I have a feeling I haven't heard the worst yet."

"Have you talked to her?" Kaitlyn asked, playing with her oversized clutch bag.

He shook his head. "She's not answering her phone."

Kaitlyn had a lot she felt she could say, but she refrained. She never wanted Quint to feel as if she were trying to guide his actions to suit her fancy. He had enough stress on him; the last thing he needed was her in his ears with her nickel.

"You had fun at your dinner party?" he asked.

She looked back up at him as she nodded. "My friends Tandy and Anola threw me a surprise dinner party. If I knew it was going to be more than just the three of us, I would have invited you. We had fun."

"Probably not my type of crowd," he said, reaching out to pluck something from her hair.

"You don't know that," she said, feeling her guard rise.

"If these are the people who influenced the type of person you were when you first came here, then I'm pretty sure."

Kaitlyn leaned back and held up her hands. "Whoa. All that judgment from Mr. Perfect is a little much," she said in a tight voice.

"'Mr. Perfect,' huh?" Quint asked.

Kaitlyn nodded. "Also Mr. Judgmental. Take your pick," she said over her shoulder as she turned from him.

"Says Miss Materialistic, Miss Daddy's Girl, and

Miss Afraid to Grow the Hell Up," Quint shot back, still sitting on the hood.

Kaitlyn turned back. "Do you have a problem with my family?" she asked, recalling her earlier thoughts of possible insecurity on his part.

"I have a problem with them taking the woman I love and turning her back into the spoiled little rich girl I couldn't stand," he admitted.

Kaitlyn looked up at him with disbelief carved in every inch of her face. "Because my family is able to help me, I shouldn't accept it to prove to you that I'm grown?"

"No, you shouldn't accept it because you're smart and brave enough and *woman* enough to get it all on your own," Quint stressed. "*If* you wanted to, but the hard road ain't for everybody."

And that hurt. He complimented her and then swiped it all away by insinuating she was weak.

"Are you jealous of my family's wealth?" she asked, more out of hurt than anything.

Quint slid down off the hood as he released a heavy breath. "For you even to think that lets me know you are every bit of the spoiled brat that I thought you were," he said, standing next to her and shaking his head in disbelief.

"Get the hell out of my face, Quinton," she whispered up to him as her eyes glistened with tears fed by anger and hurt.

"I'll do you one better and get the hell out of your life."

Kaitlyn's jaw literally dropped as she turned to watch him walk away from her and into his apartment without another word.

CHAPTER 16

"Wow. You look . . . *interesting.*"

Kaitlyn turned in her chair and looked up at her boss, Lyle Turner, who was frowning at her as he entered the office. She knew she probably looked a sight because she felt like there were bags under her eyes and grit on her lids. Nothing good ever came from crying all night—especially physically.

"Allergies," she lied.

"Really," he said in obvious disbelief, coming around her desk to stand behind her.

Kaitlyn turned back to her computer to pretend she wasn't straight out giving him her back. "I put the list of upcoming local designers on your desk. I think you will like the young lady from Atlanta the best," she said, trying to remain professional even as she felt like her world was shattered.

Kaitlyn couldn't believe that Quint had actually dumped her.

Like, really, Quint? Really?

Her pain quickly flipped to anger.

Who the hell is he to judge me?

And that was the emotional roller coaster she rode all night. In between listening to Mary J. and Whitney Houston songs, she tore up Pepsi floats and glasses of wine.

Tears and then anger. Back to tears and then more anger. It took everything she had not to go downstairs and knock on the door to knee him in the nuts . . . before kissing the hell out of him.

She hated that she sat there all night waiting for him to call or to come up and say he didn't mean it. To take it back. To say he was sorry.

But he didn't.

"Fuck him," she muttered, glancing over at the five-by-seven photo of Quint and herself that she kept on her desk. She slapped it down.

She wasn't chasing a man—*any* man. And especially not one who sat in judgment of her as if she had to be exactly who he thought she should be for their relationship to work.

Quint had been in his office since before the sun rose. He sat behind his desk and tossed a tennis ball up into the air as he wrangled with his thoughts. His concerns. His problems.

His relationship with Kaitlyn.

All night long he lay in bed and tried to let sleep top his thoughts. He failed.

Some of his worries were alleviated by Lei volunteering to move back in with him. Still, would Vita fight him for custody, when relinquishing their daughter meant giving up the child support he voluntarily paid her to help with Lei's care? Or would she give up and enjoy her new relationship?

Did he make a mistake in resigning from his job, starting a new business, and taking on his mortgage again? Should he forge ahead now that Lei was back with him? Or play it safe?

And then there was Kaitlyn. In the months during their relationship, he had seen so much growth in her from the partying, self-involved "it" girl she had been.

But now, she seemed to be wavering at the first opportunity not to stand on her own two feet, to fall right back into being a label fiend and a shopping addict. She seemed poised to go back to losing some of the independence she claimed.

Quint really had to consider if he wanted to be with a woman who allowed her family such involvement in her life. He liked the Strongs, but what possible sense did it make for them to spoil her, then punish her for living the life they created for her, and then reward her for being independent-by-force by spoiling her some more?

Kaitlyn was a relationship girl, and he had been happy with her over the months. He had discovered and accepted that he loved her. He had even imagined himself with her for the long term, but he refused to saddle himself with a woman who would forever be comfortable playing the role of the baby of the family.

He cared for her, but he would have had more respect for her if she had stiffened her back and turned down any help from the family. He did not want to marry a frivolous woman. He had been down that road before. He wasn't taking the trip again.

The door to his office opened and Quint looked up as Lei stepped inside. She was dressed in clothing she'd left behind at his house.

"You finally up?" he asked.

She nodded as she closed the door behind her. "Mama called and woke me up."

Quint checked the time on his cell phone. It was well after nine in the morning and Vita was *just* calling.

"Why didn't you wake me up?" Lei asked, dropping down upon one of the chairs in front of the desk.

Quint tapped his fingers against the top of the desk. "After what happened last night, I thought you and I needed to talk about just what's going on at your mother's house with you."

Lei looked over at him and nodded in understanding. "I told Mama I wanted to move back home with you," she admitted.

"And?" Quint asked as he leaned back in his chair and fiddled with his cell phone on the desk.

"And she said no."

Quint looked up to the ceiling before he looked over at her. "You know I love you, and I would walk to the ends of the earth for you. That's my job as your father," he began. "This situation with your mom can get a little complicated, so I don't think the moving back and forth between the two of us is a good idea."

Lei looked pensive.

Quint sat up and pressed his elbows on the desk. "Think about it and be sure that you're sure. And if you say that you are, then I will talk to your mom and make it happen. Of course you can visit her whenever you want."

Lei looked down to the floor. "I'm sure. I love Mommy, but . . ."

Her words trailed off, and Quint felt a chill to his core as a tear fell from his daughter's face. He jumped to his feet and came around the desk to pull her to her feet and hug her close.

"Your mother loves you," he assured her, not wanting her to feel pain from Vita's actions. "But I'll fix it. Okay? I'll fix it."

One week later

Kaitlyn knocked on Quint's front door and then fidgeted as she waited for him to open it. When he did, she pushed the box she was holding into his hand.

"Your things that you left at my apartment," she said, not even looking at him as she turned away.

She turned back in surprise when she felt his hand lightly grasp her waist. She eyed his hand and then lifted her head to eye him.

"Yes?" she asked coolly.

Quint looked down at her. "I just wanted to say that I'm sorry things didn't work out. I'm not mad. I still care about you, but we just see the world different," he said.

Kaitlyn hated that she still had such a strong reaction to him. And it all was so familiar. The vibe. Her pounding heart. Racing pulse. Energy. Chemistry. She missed him.

"Is that it?" she asked, wanting to get the hell away from him just as strongly as she wanted to kiss him.

Quint looked exasperated. "I'm trying to apologize, Kaitlyn."

"For what?" she asked, fighting hard to keep it cool.

It had been a week—a dang-on week—since they

even spoke hi or bye to one another. His apology was late. Real late.

"Whatever, Kaitlyn," he said.

"See if all your judgment keeps your bed warm," she snapped.

Quint turned with the box still in his hands. "So sex is all you think is important to me," he said, his voice hard.

She felt all her emotions rev up and forced herself to stay composed, while her insides shattered at the change in them.

"It's the only damn thing you never complained about," Kaitlyn retorted.

Quint looked down at her with those intense eyes of his. "You really seem to be enjoying the single life."

Kaitlyn had been hanging out with Tandy and Anola more. He noticed. Why did the thought of that excite her?

"You thought I was going to sit home and cry about you ending things? *Never*," she stressed. "Life goes on. Don't be mad."

"Grow up, Kaitlyn," Quint muttered.

She watched his back as he turned on her. "And you have to learn how to love unconditionally!" she shouted.

Again he turned back and eyed her.

"Because if I ever was the woman you loved—and you said last week—then you don't love with limits," Kaitlyn told him. "I didn't."

"Oh, so you did hear me?" Quint asked.

"Oh, so you do remember saying it?" Kaitlyn shot back.

Quint looked at her in disbelief. "Does every damn thing have to be a tug of war with you, Kaitlyn?"

A sharp come-back rose to her lips but Kaitlyn swallowed that back. "I just admitted that I love you," she said softly as if the moment was small when in fact it wasn't. It wasn't at all.

Quint's eyes searched hers even as he said, "Sometimes love ain't enough."

Kaitlyn laughed bitterly. "Real love is *always* enough, but don't worry. You don't have to put up with oh-so-horrible Kaitlyn anymore. I'm out of here. Tell Lei to call me sometime, if that's okay with you—"

"Kaitlyn."

"Good-bye, *Quin-ton.*"

Kaitlyn rushed into her car before the tears fell. She pulled out with a slight squeal of her tires as she got the hell away from the complex and her complex relationship with Quinton Wells.

Two weeks later

Quint sat across from the conference table and eyed Vita as she read over the documents that would legally revise their custody agreement. She looked up at him before she flipped her hair over her shoulder and twisted her own rhinestone-covered pen between her fingers.

Never once did Quint shift in his chair or flinch from her somewhat hostile stare. He sat there, looking professional in a pin-striped suit, being all about the business of taking care of his child, once and for all. The papers stated that he would receive full custody and she was allotted liberal visitation on weekends and some holidays. It was a complete reversal of roles from the arrangements that were agreed upon via their divorce.

Quint never wanted it to come to this, but he couldn't allow Vita to doctor her level of competency as a parent based on whether or not she was in a relationship. It wasn't fair to Lei for her mother to swoop in and out of her life on a whim.

Vita continued to flip leisurely through the papers as both of their attorneys looked on, in what had to be feigned patience.

"Vita, we both know you're going to sign the papers, so why this performance?" he asked, his voice cool as he deliberately patted the breast pocket of his suit jacket.

Her lips thinned into a straight line and her eyes glittered like wet glass as she finally placed the pen to the papers and signed them before sliding them over to her attorney.

Quint felt relief wash over him. Even though he offered her the hard-earned $5,000 from his savings to allow Lei to stay with him, things were never a done deal with a complicated woman like Vita.

Never.

One week later

Kaitlyn looked down at her phone on the floor as she stroked her chin while lying on the couch in her parents' den. Her hand literally itched to call Quinton and ask him why he threw their relationship away so easily. Why would he, and how could he?

"I have a problem with them taking the woman I love and turning her back into the spoiled little rich girl I couldn't stand."

A huge revelation and a backhanded insult all at once. Only Quint.

Had. Does. Had. Does.

She didn't know about his feelings but she was very clear about her own. She loved him. She told him that. He rejected her feelings.

Sometimes love ain't enough.

As if him picking the worst possible moment to reveal his feelings hadn't been bad enough.

She reached down and picked her phone up from the floor, using her thumb to scroll through her contacts until she came to his name. She flopped over onto her back on the couch as she looked at the shirtless photo of him that she saved in his contact info. She hadn't had the nerve to delete it yet.

Just like he wasn't deleted from her heart.

Being with Quint made her think of kids and love and forever. Maybe not in their immediate future, but definitely as part of their future together. Tears filled her eyes, but she blinked them away.

She hadn't seen him since the night she dropped off the box of things he left at her house. That had led to another round of insults between them, and she had decided in that moment to get away. To not fight for him or fight with him.

She moved back in with her parents that very night, until she could find a new place. Kaitlyn hadn't been back at the complex since then. Her mother and sisters-in-law packed her things up and called a moving company to deliver everything to the ranch. Kaitlyn had called work to decline going in and spent the day crying for everything she had and felt with Quinton, as well as for everything they could have had.

He ended it. He said the words and wrote the check.

Kaitlyn refused to give in and call him. With a heavy breath she let the phone slide back to the floor before she draped her forearm over her closed eyes.

"You okay, kid?"

She looked up as her father walked into the den and smiled at her before he lifted her feet and sat on the sofa beneath them.

"I'm good," Kaitlyn answered.

"How's the house hunting going?" Kael asked as he tapped her for the remote—*his* remote.

Kaitlyn shrugged as she handed it to him. "I haven't really been looking," she admitted.

"Oh. Okay," Kael said slowly as he flipped through the channels.

Kaitlyn shifted onto her side. "I might go with my friends to Vegas next week," she said as she frowned at the television. "Daddy, I know you not about to watch bull riding. Like, really? *Really,* Daddy?"

Kael easily picked up his remote just as Kaitlyn reached out for it. He set it on the wooden end table on the other side of him.

"Really," he assured her.

Kaitlyn arched her eyebrows and rolled off the chair to her feet, scooping up her phone. "I don't have a TV in my room," she reminded him. "All of my stuff is still in one of the sheds outside."

Kael immediately turned and swung his feet up onto the sofa as he settled in for comfort, with an obvious sigh of contentment. "Is that a weekend trip to Vegas?" he asked.

Kaitlyn paused on her way out the door and turned.

"No, the whole week. *We making memories,*" she stressed with a sassy snap of her fingers before continuing on her way to get dressed for a movie night with her friends.

Kael frowned deeply as he stumbled to sit up and watch his daughter leave the room. Since her return home Kaitlyn had been basically hit-or-miss with going to work. She had taken to hanging out with her friends again. She admitted she wasn't looking that hard for a house. She was shopping up a storm.

He let it slide so far, because he knew she was hurting over her breakup with Quint—something she had yet to explain. But how much more would he tolerate before he put his foot down again? And how much longer would he and his wife have to share their home and give up their privacy?

Kael frowned deeply. He couldn't remember the last time he could chase Lisha or walk around the house butt naked, if he wanted. And just last night, Kaitlyn came busting through the door just as he reached his hand over to lift the hem of Lisha's dress as they watched a movie.

Kaitlyn was ruining his retirement.

"Houston, we have a problem," Kael muttered.

One week later

Quint knocked on Lei's door.

"Come in."

He opened the door to find Lei lying on the middle of her bed with her legs extended up as she rotated her feet in the gold flats Kaitlyn had given her. He set the flat boxes he carried by her dresser.

"I thought you were packing," Quint said, smiling down at her and still amazed by the overall change from before Kaitlyn had come into their lives.

Lei's ponytail was gone, and she wore her thick, chin-length hair in a bob, which Kaitlyn had taught her how to shampoo and wrap in between her trips to the salon for her perms and trims. She wore the jewelry she received for her birthday and Christmas—small gold hoops, a puffed gold heart on a twisted chain, a charm bracelet, and a heart-shaped ring. She looked like a little lady.

Lei glanced over at him. "I texted Kaitlyn last night," she said.

An image of her face immediately flooded his mind. "Oh yeah? How is she?" he asked, licking his lips.

"Sad and pretending not to be . . . just like you," she said with another twirl of her ankle as she continued to eye him.

Quint said nothing.

"Well, anyway"—Lei stressed her conversation with a shake of her head, which was mature beyond her thirteen years—"she said she missed me, and if it was okay with you, she still wanted to keep in touch . . . with me."

"We'll see," Quint said, turning to head out of the room.

And there was his reluctance to introduce a woman to his child, because he didn't want Lei to feel the loss of another woman in her life. Just because he shut Kaitlyn out of his life, though, didn't mean he had to do the same for Lei. He stopped and turned around.

"It's okay with me," Quint told her.

Lei smiled and scooped up her cell phone. "Thanks,

Daddy," she said, sitting up on the bed to cross her legs as her thumbs flew over the keyboard.

Quint left the room and walked into his bedroom to finish packing his things for their move back to their home next week. His replacement as the apartment complex manager was scheduled to move in a week after that, and Quint wanted to be out and to have the apartment cleaned for her. She was an older woman, who appeared to be a little rough around the edges, and seemed not to be in the mood for *any* bull.

All he could do was wish them well.

Quint sat on the bed and opened the drawer to one of his nightstands. He reached in and pulled out the photo frame cushioned on top of a pile of scarves. The picture was of himself and Kaitlyn smiling as they cuddled on the couch for one of their movie nights. Lei had taken the picture and surprised them each with a framed copy for Christmas.

I wonder if she still has hers.

Quint looked from the box at his feet to the wastepaper basket near the bathroom door.

Why am I holding on to the picture when I let go of the real thing?

He rose to his feet and stood over the wastepaper basket with the photo in his hands.

We look good together.

Quint lowered his arm, but he couldn't let the picture go. He couldn't do it. Turning away, he released a heavy breath as he dropped the photo and frame in the box on the floor. He reached in the drawer again and pulled out the silk scarves. Picking them up, he let his curiosity win and pressed the soft material to his face. The subtle and sexy scent of Kaitlyn's perfume still clung to it.

They used the scarves the very last time they made love. . . .

Quinton scooped Kaitlyn's nude silken body up from the middle of his bed and into his arms to stand her on her feet at the foot of his four-poster bed.

Kaitlyn smiled as she let her eyes roam from his bald head, down the length of his sculpted body, with a leisurely stop at his condom-covered hard dick. She licked her lips and bit them softly as she reached to wrap both of her hands around his hot thickness. She gently massaged his dick in different directions with each of her hands as she pulled upward on it.

Quinton looked down at her hands and his dick between them. "That feels good," he told her, his voice thick with pleasure.

Kaitlyn leaned forward to bite his chin hotly before she licked it. "It'll feel better inside me," she whispered against his chocolate skin.

Quinton turned, with his dick still in her hands, to grab one of the scarves from the pile atop the dresser. He saw the curiosity in her eyes before he raised his hands and tied the scarf around her eyes and head like a band.

Kaitlyn smiled. "Okay, this some new shit," she said in a soft voice, which was filled with excitement and a little trepidation.

Quinton kissed her lips fully. "Let go of my dick," he whispered against her lips.

Kaitlyn did. She held both of her hands up in the air.

"Perfect."

Quinton grabbed the scarves, one by one, and tied her wrists to the posts of the bed until she was spread-eagle as she stood before him. He studied her body as he massaged the length of himself. She was gorgeous as she stood there with pride and sexiness and vulnerability.

He grabbed her hips and took one plump breast into his mouth to suckle deeply as he twirled his tongue around her hard nipple.

She shivered and moaned, flinging her head back.

He shifted to her other nipple as he eased his hand around her to squeeze her fleshy ass before gliding down the crease to play in the slick folds of her pussy. He eased his other hand down the front of her body to palm her pussy before he used his agile thumb to press deeply against her swollen clit; and his other hand, meanwhile, continued its onslaught.

"Ahh!" she cried out.

Quint buried his face against her cleavage as he stroked his finger inside her, enjoying the feel of her ridges. "Shit," he swore, feeling the slight drizzle of his own release as his dick hardened.

"Now, Quint," she begged.

"I'ma give you this dick," he promised, easing his fingers from her body to lift her legs onto his muscled thighs as he bent his legs and lifted onto his toes to glide his dick up inside her. Inch by delicious inch his thickness spread her and pressed against her walls.

They both cried out roughly.

"Damn, you tight," he swore, letting his head fall forward as he struggled for control as his entire body tensed and the muscles in his buttocks and shoulders flexed.

Slowly—finally—he began to rock his hips as he gripped her buttocks and brought their groins together. And then apart. And then together.

Each slide of his dick rubbed against her clit and

Kaitlyn felt goose bumps race over her as every pulse in her body raced crazily. The silk stretched against her wrists as she fought the natural urge to touch him, to feel him.

To be deprived of such an essential sense as sight—while her other senses were overloaded by his touch, his kisses, his words, and the stroke of his dick—Kaitlyn felt like she truly walked the edge of the line between pleasure and insanity.

She felt her climax coming on strongly as a fine sheen of sweat coated her body.

"I'm coming," she gasped hotly as she felt her pussy walls spasm against his tool.

Quinton bit onto her neck as his own release filled her as he fought the urge to cry out a soprano note and stop his upward thrusts as his climax made the thick tip of his dick extra sensitive.

Unable to hold him as he continued to stroke her to one explosive nut after another, she let her body go slack against her ties and his body and surrendered to the ride.

"Kaitlyn. Kaitlyn?"

She shook herself from her thoughts of the last time Quint had sexed her. She looked up to see Tandy and Anola staring at her over the rims of their shades as they all lounged poolside at the Mirage Hotel in Vegas.

"Huh?"

"Why your nipples all hard?" Tandy asked, tossing a towel over Kaitlyn's bikini-clad body.

Anola raised her margarita in toast. "I don't know what the hell you was just thinking about, but damn ain't no fun if your friends can't get some."

Her friends laughed as Tandy toasted that as well.

Kaitlyn just brushed the towel off her body and rose in her white strapless bikini to dive into the pool effortlessly. The coolness of the pool took the fire burning inside her down a bit, but the pressure of the water against her body felt too much like Quint's hands.

She couldn't escape him. Forget him. Drink him away. Party him away. Flirt him away.

Nothing.

She came up from beneath the water for air, but she dove back beneath the depths to hide her tears, which she couldn't keep from falling.

Kaitlyn loved and missed Quinton Wells. There was nothing she could do about it.

CHAPTER 17

One month later

Kaitlyn could hardly believe the many peaks and valleys of her life since her return from the Vegas trip with Anola and Tandy. What happened in Vegas definitely didn't stay in Vegas. And in the end she knew that was a good thing.

The trip and all the fun and frivolity it contained had begun to wear on Kaitlyn before they reached the midpoint of the trip. Waking up to a pounding headache and alcohol film on her tongue, with vague memories of dollar bills and gyrating naked strippers slathered in oil, wasn't the fun it used to be for her.

In Paris she had *lived* and enjoyed it.

In Vegas, however, Kaitlyn wondered if she could *survive* it.

When she got back to her parents', she had slept for almost two days straight to recover. She finally felt her head was on straight enough that she called her boss and discovered she had been fired for missing too many days of work—and not having enough focus on the days she did appear.

That was a reality check like no other.

After lying to her parents about her boss going out of town and giving her additional time off, she isolated herself in her room and reflected on a lot of things. She learned that being still made a person focus on things. Focus. Evaluate. Reevaluate. Make changes.

And she did *all* of that, and more.

Kaitlyn took a sip of the glass of wine she held as she flipped through the look-books of several designers. As she listened to the late Whitney Houston's *The Greatest Hits,* she had to admit it felt good to be back in her own space and back doing something far less pointless than just shopping.

The most grown-up thing Kaitlyn ever did in her life was swallow her pride and go back to Lyle to request her job back. She just thanked God he adored the Azzedine Alaia dress she wore, with a matching cardigan. The sheer off-white and metallic gold striped dress had a full skirt that ended just above her knees. He especially loved the thin gold band she wore around her waist as a belt.

"I want to be mad at you . . . but I can't," he had admitted, coming around his desk to pull her up onto her six-inch heels to air-kiss each of her cheeks. "To your desk."

And Kaitlyn had been back to work ever since. Even arriving early and working on some weekends to scout new designers for his boutiques.

She sang along to "You Give Good Love" as she looked around at the cottage she had moved into just last week. Kaeden's wife, Jade, had once lived there and suggested it to Kaitlyn when she mentioned finding her own place. Luckily, it sat empty and Kaitlyn scooped it up. And she hadn't missed the extra kick in her father's step around the house when she announced she was moving.

Kaitlyn didn't feel offended. The last week back in her own place and space had reminded her how good it felt to be on her own. It had been a minute since she enjoyed the freedom of walking around the house naked. And this was her first Friday evening at home and nowhere near a club, dinner party, or event of any kind.

She loved Tandy and Anola, but Kaitlyn had also decided to pull back from their friendship a bit. They just didn't want the same things in and out of life anymore. And she was okay with that.

Bzzzzzzzzz . . .

She set her wineglass down and picked up her cell phone. A text.

"Lei," Kaitlyn said, smiling as she used her thumb to open it. The little sweetie had made sure to stay in contact with Kaitlyn; and weeks ago Kaitlyn had even taken her and Kadina to the movies.

"'Doesn't my daddy look good?'" Kaitlyn read aloud, her heart already pounding fast as she looked at the picture of Quint in a tuxedo.

"Sexy ass," Kaitlyn muttered as she zoomed in on the picture.

Kaitlyn hadn't seen Quint in two months, and nothing about him had changed. Still bald. Still handsome. Still sexy as hell.

She set the phone back down on the table and looked down at his face. Nothing about her feelings had changed either. Her heart and pulse were still racing and pounding. Her stomach was fluttering with butterflies. Her memories were flooded with the good times—in and out of bed.

Picking up the phone, she texted Lei back: YES HE LOOKS VERY GOOD.

Kaitlyn ran her fingers through her hair, causing it to stand on end as she sat back in the chair and tapped her fingers against the tabletop. In time the pain and anger over their sudden breakup had dulled in her, but she couldn't lie and say that she didn't think of him often—especially since she stayed in contact with Lei.

Although she never questioned Lei about her father, Lei always found a way to let her know that Quint was not seeing anyone else. It was clear that little Lei was rooting for a reconciliation. That made Kaitlyn adore her all the more, and miss even more the times that the three of them had shared together.

Bzzzzzzzzz . . .

Kaitlyn eyed the phone before she picked it up again and opened the text she already knew was from Lei: Dadd jst tryiN his tux 4 a wedin 2moz. Not a d8. N no d8 4 wedin. ;-)

She frowned as she tried to decipher the teen's text lingo. Most times she got it quick.

Daddy just trying on his tux for a wedding . . . tomorrow. Not a . . . date. And no date for wedding, Kaitlyn finished.

Kaitlyn didn't answer Lei. What was she supposed to say? Thanks for the update on your daddy's personal life? Nothing. Never.

The sound of Whitney singing "Where Do Broken Hearts Go?" played throughout the cottage.

She sang along to the song, a little off-key but heartfelt.

Truth?

Her heart was broken.

She stood up from the table and grabbed her car keys before she left the house as Whitney sang: "And if somebody loves you . . . Won't they always love you?"

Apparently not, Whitney, Kaitlyn thought, closing and locking the door before she climbed into her car and drove to her parents'.

Kaitlyn was still softly singing the chorus into the quiet interior of the vehicle as she drove down the long road leading to their stately brick home. She made her way up the stairs and started to use her key to unlock the door, but she knocked, instead, with a little smile and shake of her head.

The door opened and she looked up at her mother standing there in a pretty rust cotton dress with a full skirt and long sleeves.

"What's wrong?" Lisha Strong asked, reaching for Kaitlyn's wrist to pull her inside.

"You going out?" Kaitlyn asked, surprised by the emotions she felt brimming on the edge.

Lisha hugged her close to her side.

And then Kaitlyn's tears fell.

"What's wrong?" Kael asked in alarm from somewhere behind them.

"I knew this was coming," Lisha said, steering Kaitlyn into the kitchen. "I'm pretty sure this is about Quint."

Kaitlyn nodded as she was eased down onto a stool and a big slice of apple pie à la mode was eventually slid in front of her. She looked up at the sound of the front door slamming suddenly.

"Where's Daddy going?" she asked as she wiped the tracks of her tears with her slender fingers.

"To see a man about a dog," Lisha said, very nononsense as she sat down on the stool next to her.

Kaitlyn frowned. In the South that was always an adult's answer to a child asking where an adult was going. The translation was *None of your business.*

Point made.

"You ready to talk about it?" Lisha asked.

Kaitlyn shrugged and felt the sadness come back in a rush. "Honestly, Mama, I loved him. I still love him and he ended things. He broke my heart, Mama. He just walked away from everything we had, like it was nothing."

Lisha made a sad face as she reached for Kaitlyn's hand and squeezed it. "Why?"

Kaitlyn looked up. "Huh?"

"Did he say why?"

Kaitlyn shifted in her seat as she felt swamped in the awkward moment. She shifted her eyes away from her mother.

"He thought . . . He didn't like . . . He said that he didn't like that I was going back to being the spoiled little rich girl. He . . ."

Lisha made a face that caused Kaitlyn to pucker her forehead.

"What?" Kaitlyn asked, leaning back a bit as her almond-shaped eyes widened. "What is that look about?"

Lisha held up both her hands. "You had us on the edge of our seats for a minute too, Kat."

Kaitlyn frowned.

"I'm not saying that Quint was right to end things, and I know nothing about how he ended them . . . but your father and I were regretting our decision to help you so much again, because you did go a bit backward. Right?" Lisha said slowly, clearly not wanting to offend her daughter, who was in pain . . . but needed to hear the truth.

Kaitlyn rose to her feet and paced a bit before she stopped. "Okay, I tripped a little bit, but what does that have to do with *him*?" she asked with attitude. "It felt like he was jealous—"

Lisha frowned. "Really?" she asked.

Kaitlyn's mouth moved, but nothing came out. Their disagreement about the exact same subject came back to her very clearly:

"I have a problem with them taking the woman I love and turning her back into the spoiled little rich girl I couldn't stand."

"Because my family is able to help me, I shouldn't accept it to prove to you that I'm grown?"

"No, you shouldn't accept it because you're smart and brave enough and woman *enough to get it all on your own. If you wanted to, but the hard road ain't for everybody."*

"Are you jealous of my family's wealth?"

"For you even to think that lets me know you are every bit of the spoiled brat that I thought you were."

Kaitlyn looked pensive as she pushed the painful memory away.

"Why else would he care if y'all paid my bills?" she asked.

"The same reason we all did," Lisha began simply. "He cares about and wants the best for you. You know we all thought you needed an adjustment to your thinking and to some of your ways, and that's why we put the restrictions on you in the first place."

Kaitlyn dropped back down onto her stool. "Still, he left. He decided. He didn't think I was worth it, and I can't front. It hurts. I cannot believe he hasn't called or tried to apologize or nothing. It's been a couple of months and I just am sick of thinking about him and missing him and being mad at him and—"

Lisha rose to pull her daughter into her arms as she sat. "Time heals all wounds, baby. I promise."

Kaitlyn leaned into her embrace and sought the strength and comfort she offered.

"But Mama's gonna give you advice about compromise that you *both* could use."

Kaitlyn wiped the tears from her eyes as she got schooled on life by her mother.

Quint hung the tuxedo in one of the two walk-in closets. He wanted to make sure everything fit before the wedding he was in the next day. Flexing his broad shoulders, he left his master suite and jogged down the wrought-iron spiral staircase to the lower level of the house. He headed around the base of the staircase to the sunken den, where Lei was setting up their usual Friday movie night. She was in the identical footed pajamas Kaitlyn used to wear on the colder nights.

"What's the movie?" Quint asked, easing down into the recliner and kicking his bare feet up. "Your pick."

"Bridesmaids," Lei said; there was a playful twinkle in her eye as she picked up the remote.

Quinton frowned.

"Someone once told me that what I wanted was important, and for me to never forget that," she reminded him as she plopped down into the recliner on the opposite side of the table beside him.

What could he say when his daughter gave his own words of wisdom back to him?

"Just remember that when you're old enough for a boyfriend."

"And when exactly is that?" Lei asked.

"When you're old enough to sign your name on a rental or mortgage agreement," Quinton answered easily without hesitation.

Lei tossed a popcorn kernel at him.

Quint caught it with one hand and then tossed it into his open mouth.

"You could take Kaitlyn to Mr. Kyle's wedding tomorrow."

Quint ignored the question and pretended to focus on the opening scene of the comedy. He didn't want to think of or be reminded of Kaitlyn Strong. And usually he failed.

It took the littlest thing for her to come to mind. Like how she had become a part of their Friday movie nights and always made sure to bring home takeout from Charleston restaurants to top their usual pizza fare. With the hint of a smile on his lips, he glanced over at the two boxes of Domino's Pizza on the low-slung and wide coffee table.

Kaitlyn didn't care for pizza. Or scary movies. Or gross humor.

She loved crispy crab cakes. And romantic comedies. And action flicks.

He smiled at the memory of her burying her head against his shoulder during his pick of a scary movie. He liked that she turned to him for comfort. He liked that she relied on him. Believed in him. Supported him.

He just wished that she could believe in and support herself. In the weeks following their breakup, Quinton had continued to love her. He came to realize that perhaps he did judge her as harshly as she had said, but he had been disappointed in her.

He had wanted more for her.

It stung to think she hadn't wanted it for herself.

And it pained him to remember the look on her face when she told him: "Real love is *always* enough."

Quint knew his love was real; because after all the time they had apart, there was no other woman he could imagine to replace her. There was no one to fill her shoes; no one to make him forget her.

I messed up, he silently admitted to himself as he shifted to a comfortable position in his chair and held his chin in his hands.

"Daddy, you want a slice?" Lei asked.

Quint looked up from where he was staring at the floor to find his daughter looking at him over her shoulder as she knelt on the floor by the coffee table.

"Nah, I'm good," he said.

Lei sat back on her haunches and eyed him for a long moment until she rose to her feet and came over to hug him.

"What's that for?"

She shrugged as she moved back to her spot on the floor. "You looked like you needed one," she said.

Quint continued to study her. "You been doing that a lot lately."

"You needed it a lot lately," Lei said very matter-of-factly as she plopped back down onto the recliner with a slice of pizza on a paper plate in her hand.

"You talked to your mom?" Quinton asked, deliberately changing the subject.

Lei nodded. "She and Larry are in Jamaica," she said, with an eye roll.

Quint eyed her. "You don't like Larry?" he asked.

"He's okay . . . I guess. He don't talk directly to me, like he's slow or thinks I'm slow," she said, peeling a pepperoni from her pizza to pop into her mouth.

Quint closed his eyes and shook his head. "He's probably not used to kids."

Lei shrugged. "All I know is Kaitlyn and me—"

"Kaitlyn and I," he corrected.

"There is no Kaitlyn and you, Daddy."

Quint opened his mouth and then closed it, not

bothering to explain that he was trying to correct her grammar. Lei was a straight-A student and he doubted she didn't understand what he meant.

"So Mommy has a boo who thinks I'm invisible, and then you erase your boo from my life," she said dryly, pulling a comical face. "Y'all really got it together for a future stepkid."

Quint couldn't believe he was being compared to Vita. Impossible. He had to literally bite down on his bottom lip to keep from saying, "Don't compare me to your mother."

Instead, he said, "I always make decisions with you in mind, Lei."

She turned in her recliner and faced him.

"Can I say something to you?" she asked politely.

That set Quint back a bit.

"I love you, Daddy," she began, reaching over to pat his hand in an assuring way.

Quint looked hesitant.

"It's okay to admit when you are wrong," Lei said gently.

What the hell?

"When was I wrong?" he balked.

"No one is perfect, Daddy," Lei said, with another pat.

A flashback of Kaitlyn's words was brought forward by his daughter's little life lesson to him: *"Whoa. All that judgment from Mr. Perfect is a little much."*

Quint scowled. "When was I wrong?" he asked again.

"Kaitlyn."

Quint reached for the bottle of water sitting on the end table between them. He took a healthy swig.

"Can I say something?" he asked her.

Lei nodded as she took a bite of pizza.

"You are killing me with the Kaitlyn hints, little lady."

"Oh, so you have noticed," she countered.

The doorbell sounded.

"Pretty hard to miss," Quint assured her dryly as he rose to his feet.

Her chuckles followed him out of the room.

Kaitlyn. Kaitlyn. Kaitlyn.

Missing her wasn't enough. Now he had his thirteen-year-old daughter giving him advice, filling him in on her business, showing him random pictures she took of Kaitlyn from their days living in the apartment complex. She was in his dreams and waking thoughts.

Kaitlyn. Kaitlyn. Kaitlyn.

Quint opened his front door and his eyes widened.

Kaitlyn's daddy?

"Step outside, son," Kael said. He was dressed in a crisp black button-up shirt and charcoal slacks.

Quint did as Kael asked, pulling the door closed behind him.

"How you been, sir?" he asked.

"Good, and you?" Kael asked.

"I been all right."

Kael grunted.

Quint waited patiently, because he was sure this was not a fruitless trip on the man's part.

"My daughter won't talk about what happened and didn't happen between the two of you, but I hope that you never disrespected her or hurt her," Kael said, casting a direct gaze into Quint's eyes.

Quint nodded. "I'm a father of a daughter so I can understand the desire to protect her but—and I mean no disrespect, sir—my daughter is thirteen."

"And she will always need you," Kael said as he pushed his hands into the pockets of his slacks.

"And I will always be there . . . with limits." Quint looked up to the darkened skies and then back at the elder man.

Kael just continued to watch him.

"Even your being here now makes me think I was right to have concerns that—and again no disrespect—she will forever be daddy's girl and never my woman, sir."

Kael chuckled. "You got it all figured out, but I'll check back in with you when the little boys start sniffing around and see if you still have all this bravado, son."

Quint smiled. "Sounds like a plan," he said, feeling like he earned a bit of the man's respect. "I want what's best for Kaitlyn."

"You don't think you're what's best for her?" Kael asked as he tilted his head back to assess the younger man. "Or that she's what's best for you?"

Quint fell silent.

"I'd like to hear the answer to that."

He looked up and Kaitlyn was climbing from her car, parked behind her father's black four-door Lexus. He hadn't even seen her pull up. His eyes feasted on her like he was hungry. The love he had for her caused his chest to feel like it had doubled in size.

"Boy, you are one fool," Kael muttered as he studied the obvious emotions on Quint's face. "You want to be right or you want to be happy, son?"

"Daddy, can you excuse us," Kaitlyn said, still standing by her car. "This is between Quint and me."

Kael gave Quint one last, meaningful stare before he jogged down the brick staircase. He kissed Kat on the cheek and climbed behind the wheel of her car. "You blocking me, so bring mine to me tomorrow," he said before starting to reverse down the drive.

"You and Mama enjoy your dinner," Kaitlyn called to him, even as her eyes stayed locked across the distance on Quinton as he stood on the porch.

"You sure?"

"Yes, sir."

Kaitlyn was a bundle of nerves and so completely unsure of the moment. She ran her fingers through her hair and took a deep breath that she hoped steadied her.

"You can come closer. I don't bite," Quint said.

Kaitlyn shook her head. "I'm here meeting you halfway," she began, struggling to find the words and afraid she would be rebuffed.

Quint's eyes squinted as he watched her, and he shifted on his feet.

"You were right. I slipped. I backslid. I lost my focus on myself and on every hard-earned step I took to be independent and grown," she said, licking her lips. "But you were wrong to assume that the woman you love was gone completely. You were wrong not to believe in me. And you were wrong not to give me more of a chance to prove that I could never be anything but the woman you love—flaws and all."

Quint came down a few steps.

Kaitlyn held up her hand and shook her head. "See, I got my shit back together and even better than before. But I know I could have just as well done it *with you* than *without you*," she told him passionately as she blinked back tears.

He came down another step.

"See, I made the first step to come here and meet you halfway in this process, but let's be clear," Kaitlyn said. "I made a mistake. I didn't cheat. I didn't hit you. I didn't *not* respect you. I didn't end it. You did."

She stopped long enough to swallow over an emotional lump in her throat. "You will have to come *to me* and apologize *to me* for breaking my heart," she said as a tear fell down her cheek. "*You* broke it, and this is the one and only opportunity I am giving you to fix it."

Quint came down the stairs and rushed to her. He took her hands in his and kissed them before he lowered himself down to one knee.

"You're right. I gave up too soon. I let my anger and frustration with Vita affect how I viewed you and your intentions. That was wrong," he admitted as he looked up to her.

Kaitlyn nodded in agreement as she licked her lips.

"I've been regretting it, but my pride wouldn't let me come to you and say I made a mistake." Quint's eyes were filled with emotions.

"Your pride? I swallowed my pride to be here, Quint. Never again," she swore.

Quint rose to his full height and released her hands to cup her face.

"Kaitlyn, I apologize for judging you and not giving you a chance," he said, leaning down to kiss her as his thumbs stroked away the tracks of her tears.

"And?" Kaitlyn asked, leaning back from him.

"*And* next time we'll talk it out instead of fight it out," he said, leaning toward her again.

"*And?*" Kaitlyn stressed, leaning back more until her back arched.

"*And* I want you back in my life and Lei's life.

Now can I have a kiss?" he asked, flashing a charming smile and deep dimples.

Kaitlyn shook her head no as she looked up at him. "And?" she asked softly, yet again.

"And I love the hell out of you, Kaitlyn Strong, and I promise to make it up to you."

"Thank you," she said, straightening her body to pucker her lips for the kiss they both wanted.

"And?" Quint teased lightly as he leaned back from her.

Kaitlyn brought her hands up to stroke his square chin and bury her index finger in one of his deep dimples. "And I love you, Quinton Wells," she whispered up to him fiercely.

Quint nodded in satisfaction as he brought his hands around to grasp the back of her head lightly before he lowered his head and pressed his mouth to hers with a moan filled with his hunger. Kaitlyn closed her eyes and enjoyed the feel of his tongue exploring her mouth.

Everything—*absolutely everything*—about their wild and explosive chemistry hadn't faded a bit. Although they missed each other, and loved each other, the time apart had only intensified it . . . until they both felt a lightness in their chests that was nothing but love.

Love and forgiveness.

"Y'all good now?" Lei asked as soon as they walked into the house. She was standing at the window.

"Enjoy the show?" Quint asked, standing behind Kaitlyn to wrap his arms around her body.

Lei nodded eagerly and smiled. "I turned the movie

off a long time ago. Y'all reunion was much cuter," she said.

They both looked alarmed.

Lei held up her hands. "Don't worry! I couldn't hear anything, but I got a kick outta seeing Daddy on his knees. That was *too* cute," she said with a sigh.

"I thought so too," Kaitlyn agreed, winking.

"Don't worry—I videotaped it with my phone."

"Good girl," Kaitlyn told her, moving from Quinton's embrace to hug Lei to her side as they strolled into the den. "Can I see it?"

Quinton smiled and shook his head as he watched his daughter and his woman together. It felt right for her to be there. With him. With them.

Thank God, she had more courage to fight for their love than he did.

Kaitlyn looked over her shoulder and smiled at him. Thank God.

Kaitlyn looked over her shoulder at Quint. She found his eyes on her and she smiled. She felt truly happy that they were both willing to meet each other halfway. To compromise. To not be afraid. To fight for love—as they should have done weeks ago.

Only time would tell if they truly would gain the happily-ever-after ending; but as they settled in the den and laughed together with ease, she didn't for one second regret her decision to follow her mother's advice.

Not one single second.

EPILOGUE

One year later

Kaitlyn sighed in pleasure as Quint shifted the soft curls of her shoulder-length hair from her neck. Trying something new she had her hair lightened to a warm amber brown with blondish highlights. Quint preferred the black but was getting used to the new color. Now the length was another issue.

"I love that you grew your hair back, but it gets in the way sometimes," Quint told her as he pressed a warm and titillating kiss to her nape as she lay nude beside him in the bed.

Kaitlyn eased over onto her back and reached up to rub his smooth bald head. "I love that you *haven't* grown yours back," she teased as she looked up at him.

"You know what else I would love?" Quint asked her, his voice serious as his hands traveled over her body. Kaitlyn arched an eyebrow as she turned over onto her side to take his limp but still impressive tool into her hands to stroke it to renewed life.

"What's that?"

"I would love to sleep with you in my arms every night and wake up to this beautiful face every morning," he said before placing soft kisses against her forehead and cheeks.

Kaitlyn shivered from the tender show of affection as she closed her eyes and enjoyed the tiny blessings from the man she loved.

"You know I don't want to live together before marriage, and it's not the best example for Lei," she said softly; her breath fanned out against his strong chin.

The kisses stopped.

Did I hurt his feelings?

Kaitlyn opened her eyes, and she gasped at the engagement ring Quint held in front of her face. She gasped dramatically as her eyes lifted from the ring to his eyes.

"Whoa," she said softly.

Quint sat up in bed and held the two-carat solitaire between his index finger and thumb. "I love you and even more than that I know that you love me. We have supported and inspired the best in each other, with your new boutique and my business doing so well. I want that kind of support and love and respect for the rest of my life."

Kaitlyn sat up in bed, cupping the sheet to her breasts, as she trembled with emotion. She said nothing at all as her heartbeat echoed inside her as she simply listened to his words, knowing they were heartfelt.

Quint moved to climb from the bed.

"Where are you going?" she asked, reaching out to wrap her hand around his wrist.

"I was getting down on one knee," he said.

Kaitlyn shook her head as she gazed at him.

"What's important is seeing what's in your heart and not seeing you on your knee," she told him, massaging his forearm and loving the goose bumps she felt under her touch. "Plus you did the knee before, remember?"

Quint took her left hand in his and slid the ring around the tip of her finger.

"Kaitlyn Strong, will you marry me?" he asked simply, but there was so much emotion in his voice.

"Yes, yes, I will marry you," she promised him in a whisper as he slid the ring onto her finger.

It fit perfectly.

He eased her down onto the plush pillows and kissed her as he pressed her hand to his heart to feel the hard and fast pounding against her palm.

"I was nervous," he admitted with a chuckle against her mouth.

Kaitlyn looked up at him, letting her eyes absorb every nuance of his face. "As if I would say no."

"I wasn't sure your daddy wasn't going to shoot me down," he said dryly.

Kaitlyn's face filled with surprise. "My daddy knows?"

"Your whole family knows."

"Lei too?" she asked, showing a toothy grin.

"She and Kadina helped pick the ring."

Kaitlyn held it up to gaze at it on her hand.

"I taught them well. They did *good*!" she stressed in pleasure.

Quint reached across her for her cordless phone. It beeped as he punched the buttons to dial and then put it on speakerphone.

Kaitlyn pressed her hand to Quinton's handsome face as someone answered the line.

"She said yes!" Quint said.

Kaitlyn jumped a bit as a loud roar and applause came through the phone line.

"Congratulations. Now hurry up and get down here to celebrate!"

Quinton chuckled and held the phone to her mouth.

"We're on the way, Daddy," she told him.

"Hey, Kat, you happy?" he asked, the seriousness of his tone heard clear through the line, even with all the noise in the background.

Kaitlyn looked at Quinton. "Very," she said with pure honesty.

"I just want you to know I'm proud of you," Kael said.

She dropped her head as she got choked up. "Thanks, Daddy."

Quint ended the call and lay down to pull her body on top of his. "Here's to happily ever after."

Kaitlyn tasted his lips and nodded her head in agreement. "Happily ever after . . . and a really good ring. Ow!"

They laughed together before they reluctantly rose to go and join their party and their awaiting family.

Turn the page for a look at
THE HOT SPOT
by Niobia Bryant

On sale now!

PROLOGUE

"Hey. This is Ned, Zaria, Meena, and Neema. We're not in. You know what to do. Kisses."

Beep.

"Zaria, this is Hope. And this is Chanci, girl. Girl, you and Ned give that thang a break and call us back. Or we'll try your cell. If we don't reach you, we'll see y'all later today. Bye!!!"

Beep.

"Hey, Mama. It's Meena and Neema. We called your cell but it's going straight to voice mail. Call us. We really need a care package. This campus food suuuuuuuucks."

Beep. Beep. Beep.

Using one clear-coated acrylic nail, Zaria Ali hit the button to delete all of the messages. Her childhood best friends, Chanci and Hope, were coming into South Carolina for their annual trip home and had indeed reached her on her cell earlier that day. Her twin daughters finally caught her on her cell to lovingly plead for all the home-baked goodies they wanted shipped overnight.

Zaria sighed heavily. The call she was expecting wasn't on the machine and that hurt. It really hurt.

Not even the thought of her best friends coming for her birthday weekend could make her smile. Chanci was flying in from North Carolina and Hope from Maryland. They had been childhood friends growing up in Summerville, South Carolina. Their lives had taken them in separate directions once they got married and got caught up in their careers. It was Zaria who reached out to them to reconnect after so many years, and the time had faded into nothing as they just fell right in sync with one another. That bond they had formed as children had withstood the years and the hundreds of miles between them.

And she looked forward to their sisterhood, their vibrancy, and the fun they would bring into her life and her world. *Lord knows I need to be cheered up.*

Zaria's eyes shifted around her home. They rested on a hundred different things that would forever hold a memory for her. But it didn't feel like a home anymore. She had thought it was a place meant for happily-ever-after. She was wrong. Painfully so.

No, not tonight. No memories. No regrets.

Her girls would be there, and maybe she'd tell them how Zaria—housewife extraordinaire who made it her business to put her husband before herself—had been made a fool of.

Zaria felt sadness weigh down on her shoulders a bit, but she shook it off. She shook him off. Matter of fact, she was shaking all men off for good. The risk of feeling this kind of hurt again wasn't worth it.

Chanci and Hope would easily take her mind off . . . things. And even if—no, *when*—they gushed about the men and the love in their lives, Zaria would refuse to think of the coulda, woulda, or shoulda with *him*.

No matter how much I miss him.

She'd been his wife since she was eighteen. She grew up in her marriage. She sacrificed so much. Her youth. Her happiness.

As she wiped the tears from her eyes, she wished that she had never gotten married at all. Never believed in love and the happily-ever-after. Never lost herself in the desire to be "the perfect wife."

"From now on, I'm going to enjoy life and never let a man knock at the door of my heart," she promised herself, her voice sounding strange to her own ears in the quiet of the house.

She'd spent the last two weeks singing the lonely-bed-and-brokenhearted blues. Barely been able to get out of bed. Crying until her head hurt and her eyes were sore. Calling his phone and pleading with him to change his mind. Making a complete fool of herself as she fought not to lose her mind. She hadn't told a soul what she was suffering through. Not her friends. Not her kids. No one.

Bzzzzz.

Pushing through the hurt and disappointment, Zaria smiled at the sound of the doorbell as she made her way to the front door. She heard their laughter even through the solid wood. Just knowing they were there to hold her if she faltered, to hug her if she cried, and to tickle her until she laughed made things feel better.

Zaria flung the door open wide, causing a slight draft to shimmy across her legs, bare under the dress she wore. She sadly smiled as Chanci and Hope danced past her into the living room, snapping their fingers and singing an off-key rendition of "Happy Birthday"—the Stevie version.

Shutting the door, Zaria crossed her arms over her

chest and listened to their cheerful serenade—a bad one, but a serenade nonetheless.

Chanci closed her beautiful green eyes as she flung her head back and hit a high note that would put a cat's wail to shame.

Hope froze midsentence and looked at Zaria, giving her the mother stare that was all too knowing. "Hold on, Aretha," she said dryly to Chanci, reaching out to lightly grasp her arm to stop her. "What's wrong, Zaria?"

Damn, she's good.

The rest of the song thankfully died from Chanci's lips as she opened her eyes and focused them on Zaria as well. Her face brightened and then became concerned. "Is something wrong?"

That's one thing about good friends. They knew each other—really knew each other—and there wasn't much that could be kept from them. Nothing much at all that could be hidden.

Not happiness. Not joy. Not sadness. Not heartbreak.

And why should it?

Zaria thought of him. All of him. And all of the emotions he brought into her world. The happiness. The joy. The sadness. The heartbreak.

One lone tear raced down her cheek and she swiped it away. Seconds later, their arms were around her, and all at once she felt weak with relief *and* strong from their friendship. In their little huddle, she admitted it. "Ned left me."

Chanci's and Hope's heads lifted. Zaria raised hers as well, and the two women shared a look before forcing their eyes back on her.

Zaria felt a piercing pain radiate across her chest.

"Awwwww," her friends said sympathetically.

Chanci and Hope shared another long look before leading Zaria to the kitchen and pressing her into one of the chairs surrounding the dining table in the breakfast nook.

"This calls for alcohol," Chanci said, her face determined, as if she were preparing for war.

Hope nodded in agreement. "Definitely."

As her friends moved about the kitchen, getting ready for one of their patented gabfests—which always included good food and drink—Zaria knew she would have to tell them about the tragic end to her marriage. She would set aside her embarrassment and bring them into the world of pain caused by the man she had loved and cherished for over twenty years of her life.

And for another woman. A younger woman.

Zaria released a breath shaky with her pain, her shock, and her disappointment. Still she felt some relief because she knew her girls would help her deal with it all.

Thank God for them.

CHAPTER 1

Two years later

The sound of the music in the club was a mix of a hard-core bass line overlapping a sultry reggae beat. The type of beat to bring out the need for a hard—or soft—body pressed up against someone else. The type of bass to make a heated body tic with each thump. The music made you forget your worries. A lousy day at work. An argument with a lover. The bill collector at the door or the phone ringing off the hook.

Any of it—all of it—was drummed out by the music.

And no one took more advantage of that than Zaria Ali.

She mouthed along with the song—one of her favorites—as she moved her hips like she didn't have a backbone. And even though her eyes were closed and her head was tilted back just a bit, she knew the eyes of men—and a few women—were watching her. Many were trying to build up the nerve to dance with her. A few had tried too bold an approach—a hand on her waist or below it—and were politely brushed aside.

As the live reggae band ended the song, Zaria grooved her way off the small dance floor in her leather booties, making her way to the bathroom as nature called like crazy. Thankfully it was clean and there wasn't a line as long as one of Beyoncé's performance weaves, which was surprising for a Thursday night. In her club adventures, she had seen things that made her afraid to even touch the doorknob and that even made her "perch" over a commode.

After leaving the stall, Zaria made her way to the row of sinks. She flipped her hair over her shoulder as she studied her image and washed her hands. "Not bad at all for forty-two," she said to her reflection, twisting her head this way and that to study herself under the bright lights.

Zaria raked her slender fingers through the twenty inches of her jet-black shiny hair that emphasized her light, creamy complexion and made people assume that she was of mixed heritage, but she wasn't. Her blunt bangs perfectly set off her high cheekbones, pouting mouth, and slanted eyes. She was tall—nearly five ten—but every bit of her size 10 frame was curves, and the skinny jeans she wore emphasized that.

"Humph, to hell with you, Ned," Zaria said, and then instantly hated that thoughts of her ex and her failed marriage still lingered on the edges of everything she did and thought . . . even about herself.

It's just that she couldn't forget all of the emotions she felt because of it. Surprised. Shocked. Lost. Confused. Hurt. Insecure. The list could go on and on.

I should have my shit together by now, right?

It had taken every last second of the last two years

to reclaim the confidence a cheating and neglectful husband snatched from her. To see the beauty in the mirror. Most she was born with, but other aspects she'd happily purchased: her hair—it was amazing what five hundred dollars and a hellified weave technician could do for a sistah; her full, lush eyelashes—she swore by MAC; and her two-inch nails—no need to explain.

When she was married to Ned, she had been but a pale version of the woman she saw now. His rules had dictated nothing less. No heavy make-up. No snug clothing. Her real hair in nothing snazzier than a bob. Nothing to draw the eyes of other men.

"If that fool could see me now," Zaria whispered as she twisted and turned a bit in the mirror to see herself from all angles. The twenty pounds she worked hard to drop revealed firm, plump, and high breasts; a relatively flat abdomen; and a perfectly round bottom—her best asset in combination with her curvy hips.

It was the kind of body that defied her age and she knew it. In the tradition of Vivica Fox, Halle Berry, and Salma Hayek, she was fortysomething and fabulous. Forty was the new thirty. She had the kind of body that some twenty-year-old women wished they had and even more twenty-year-old men wished they had in their bed.

Zaria used to think the dumbest thing she ever did was get married at eighteen years young and think it would last forever. But she topped that single foolish act when she cried like a baby when her high school sweetheart, her husband of twenty-two years and father to her twin daughters, left her two years ago for a twenty-year-old woman.

Viagra addict, she thought sarcastically of her ex.

When she married Ned Ali, he promised her the moon and stars. Too bad in the end he only delivered adultery and heartache. The last few years of their marriage had been pure hell.

Long, lonely nights.

Stilted conversations.

Bitter arguments.

Cold silence.

Robotic sex.

Zaria felt like she had wasted over twenty years of her life trying to be the perfect wife to a less-than-perfect husband. She'd even laid the blame for her unhappiness solely at her own door. *She* was doing something wrong. *She* wasn't sexy enough or supportive enough or anything enough.

In hindsight, she saw the truth of her life. She'd missed out on so much trying to grow up way too fast, far too soon. No dating. No parties. No clubbing. None of the things most teenagers and twentysomethings experienced and learned from. Not even a college education.

Zaria tried to ignore the pang of hurt in her chest. *Lord knows I messed up, and I have plenty of regrets, but no more. . . .*

During the last two years, she had made a concentrated effort to turn her life 180 degrees away from the past. It was entirely different from her happy homemaker days.

Zaria had a new career as a bartender that she loved. Freedom that she cherished. Friends whom she adored. She loved the control of her own life—which meant wearing what she wanted, seeing whom she wanted, and doing whatever she wanted *when* she damn well pleased.

Still, none of it was what she planned the day she

got married. Divorce hadn't been a part of the picture at all.

Releasing a heavy breath filled with regrets, she quickly touched up her makeup before heading back to the dance floor, shimmying her feet and hips to the lively sounds of the reggae band that seemed to call to her.

An hour later, Zaria was still in the middle of the crowded dance floor beneath the hot red lights. She danced alone with nothing but the bass-filled music and the body heat pulsating against her frame. She didn't miss the circle of men in T-shirts, button-ups, and jerseys that seemed to be transfixed by her movements. And *that* made her feel like she had the thing she lacked the most in her marriage. Control.

After her divorce, Zaria promised herself she would always be in charge. Life would follow her plan. Everything on her terms. Absolutely everything.

Zaria's eyes opened as she awakened slowly. She released a heavy breath and then frowned at the taste of her own morning breath—made all the more horrible by the liquor residue clinging to her tongue. *Way too much rum punch,* she thought as she slowly sat up in the middle of the bed and held the side of her slightly pounding head.

She winced and then blinked at the scraps of paper littering the top of her lavender silk coverlet. She reached out to drag them all closer, remembering she'd emptied her pockets of them as soon as she walked into her bedroom last night.

A dozen or so numbers pushed into her hand throughout the night. She had to laugh because none of those young hardbodies knew about the finesse of handing a lady his business card—that was, if they even had the kinds of professions that called for them. Oh no, instead, lying between her open legs on the bed were bits and pieces of paper, napkins, gum wrappers, the torn corner of a club flyer, and even a receipt. All with the names and numbers of men who wanted to get to know her better.

But nothing about the men stood out to her, and she knew she would never call them as she scooped up all the confetti and leaned over to drop them into the top drawer of her nightstand atop the rest of her "souvenirs." As if it wasn't full enough.

The drawer was her trophy, her misplaced self-esteem during the first year after her divorce. *Who gives a damn if Ned didn't want me? I have the names and numbers of plenty of men who do. Men to be called at my whim—well, if I had planned on calling them.*

Climbing from the bed, she stretched her limbs in her blue lace bikini and matching tank before using her knee to close the drawer. Her stomach grumbled loudly, but she stopped to brush her teeth and wash last night's makeup from her face before finally leaving her bedroom on bare feet to head downstairs to the kitchen.

She moved at a snail's pace about the kitchen until she had fixed and enjoyed a full cup of strong coffee, extra sweet with lots of cream. Her twins liked to tease that she liked a splash of coffee in her cup of milk.

Zaria leaned back against the counter, her eyes shifting to the round table in the center of the breakfast nook. She felt a little melancholy as she was filled with memories of her girls when they were just eight years old, with their heads buried in their books as they did their homework at that table every day after school. Now they were finishing up their sophomore year at Denmark Tech with their own apartment down the block from the campus.

She wished they could have come home, with her having a rare weekend off from work, but her girls were deep into studying for their finals. So, Zaria was alone in the big house. All weekend.

She bit her bottom lip and furrowed her brow.

Her house was clean. There were no chores to be done. No big meals to be cooked. No yard to be raked or tended.

So many things about Zaria's life had changed. Many, many things.

Many things *had* to change.

"Thank God," she muttered, quickly fixing herself another cup of coffee before she made her way back upstairs to her bedroom.

Her cell phone was vibrating like a sex toy, and she nearly tripped over a three-inch-heeled bootie lying on the floor, having to steady her cup to keep from spilling her coffee as she rushed across the room to grab the phone. "Hello," she said breathlessly.

"Ummm . . . Zaria?"

She smiled as she set her coffee cup on the nightstand. "Nigel." She sighed in pleasure, thinking of the tall and slender West Indian she met a few months ago at a Caribbean festival in Charleston. The College of Charleston grad student was handsome and smart and funny . . . and just shy of twenty-five.

He laughed. "I thought I dialed the wrong number," he said.

At the thought of spending the rest of her long weekend alone around her house, Zaria was glad for a little friendly diversion. "No, you got me."

"You're not busy?" he asked, surprised.

"Nope." She stood up and sucked in her stomach, turning her head to eye her side profile in the mirror.

"Must be my lucky day."

Zaria walked over to her closet. "Or mine," she said.

Beep.

"Then let's spend the day together," he offered.

Zaria reached for an oversized straw hat, plopping it onto her head. "A nice day at the beach sounds like a plan," she suggested, knowing her wish was his command.

It always was.

Beep.

Zaria frowned at the steady beep signaling another call coming in.

"When and where should I pick you up?" he asked.

She looked at her phone. It was her supervisor from the restaurant bar where she worked. "Hold on one sec," she said, putting Nigel on hold as she answered the other line.

"Zaria, I hate to do this. I know this is your weekend off—"

"You need me to work," she said, cutting to the chase and skipping the BS.

"We need you in an hour."

She shook her head as she took the hat off her head and set it back on the shelf . . . along with her plans for a fun day with a sexy young man willing to please.

The Hottest African American Fiction
from
Dafina Books

Sizzling Fiction from
Dafina Books